DEAD AWAKE

JACK MCSPORRAN

Also by Jack McSporran

Maggie Black Case Files

Book 1: *Vendetta*

Book 2: *The Witness*

Book 3: *The Defector*

Maggie Black Series

Book 1: *Kill Order*

Book 2: *Hit List*

Book 3: *Payback* (2020)

Book 4: *Origin* (2020)

Book 5: *Vengeance* (2020)

Secret Agent Housewife Series
with Eliza Gordon

Book 1: *Errands & Espionage* (2020)

Standalone Titles

Camp Blackwater (2020)

The Girl That Got Away (2020)

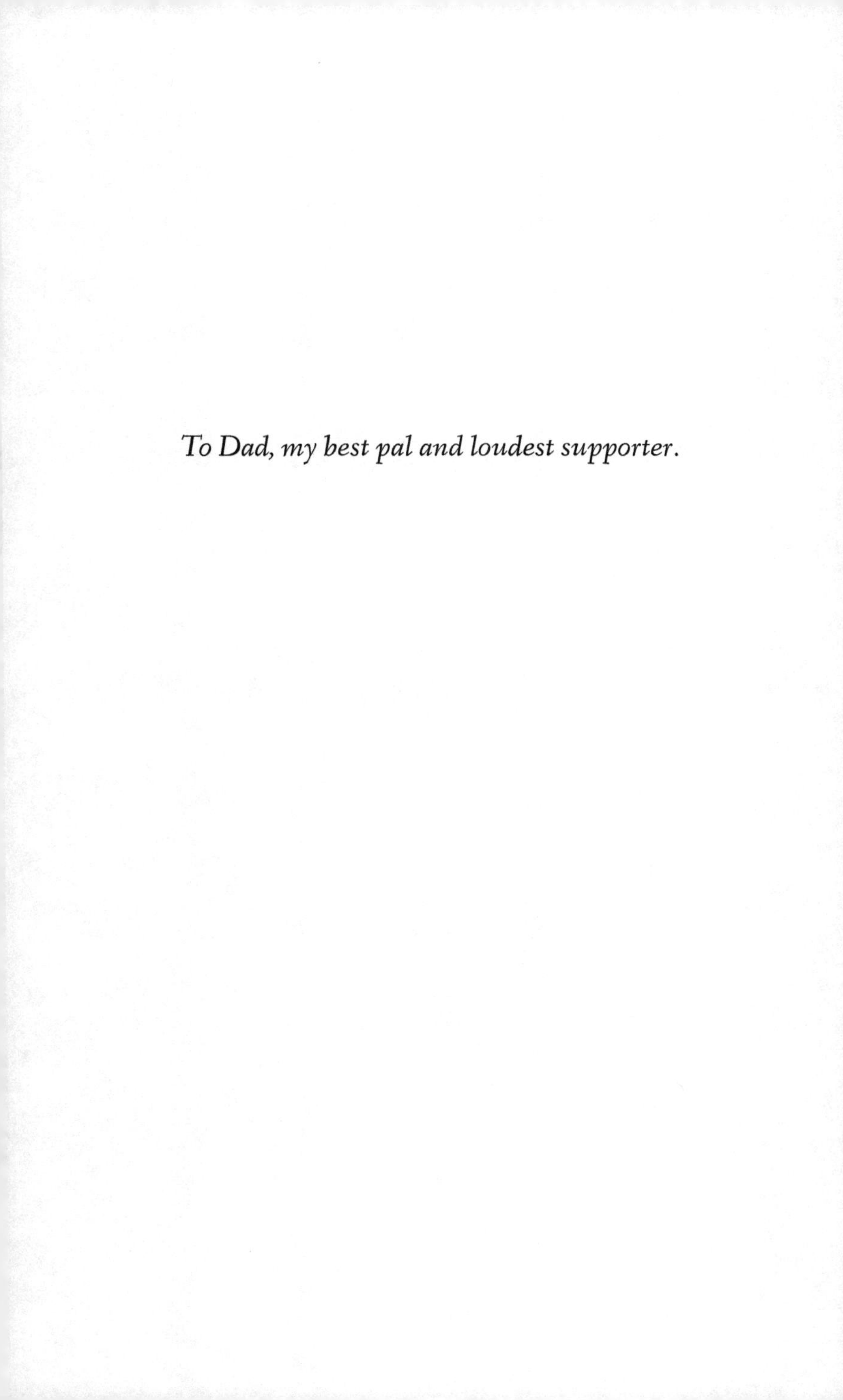

To Dad, my best pal and loudest supporter.

Chapter 1

Lenna Gallows peered down at the dead body and examined her work.

It wasn't her best, but she couldn't do anything inventive on the old woman. Simple and clean was the way to go when they were this age. Their thin, wrinkled skin didn't take well to what she normally did on someone younger.

The woman's mouth lay open, silent since her last and final breath. Lenna pried the lips back further with gloved hands and raised a curved needle with heavy-duty thread attached. She pierced it through the woman's gums, sewing the jaw closed with a neat loop stitch she had done so many times before tonight.

Selecting a lipstick from her kit, Lenna covered the lifeless blue lips with a deep ruby red, the color of blood that no longer coursed through the body's veins.

The door opened behind her. A man entered, dressed in his trademark black suit and tie, long, salt-

and-pepper hair tied back smartly from his face. "Honey, are you almost done? People will be arriving soon."

With a final inspection, Lenna put the lipstick back into the bag of cosmetics she kept exclusively for the dead and turned to face him. "Yep, just finished."

Lenna removed her plastic gloves, tossing them into a trash can in the corner.

"Will you help me out tonight?" her dad asked, closing the casket.

Lenna rolled her eyes. "Yes, Dad, because that's every sixteen-year-old girl's idea of a great Saturday night."

"So, yes?" He gave her a smile she found hard to say no to, his kind brown eyes showing the beginnings of crow's-feet at their edges. His happy-go-lucky disposition always seemed to surprise people. Everyone expected a mortician to be all doom and gloom.

"I have plans, but I guess I can change them."

He pulled her into him and kissed the top of her head. "What did I do to deserve a daughter like you?"

Lenna shrugged. "Just lucky, I guess."

Together they wheeled the casket out of the refrigeration room and down the hall of their basement to the industrial-size elevator at the opposite end.

The elevator hummed as they ascended. Hoisting the door, they wheeled out the casket and set it in place inside the front room used for wakes and funeral services, ready for the guests to arrive. For a big house, Lenna and her dad only used the second floor for living space, separating business from home life as much as possible, given the circumstances.

Her dad opened the lid and looked over their latest client. "I gotta say, kiddo, you're really getting good at this. She looks like she's sleeping."

Pride welled inside Lenna, and she forced herself not to grin.

"I kept it subtle with the makeup. Just enough to take away the ashen look."

Creating the illusion of life on a corpse could be difficult, and it took her a while to get used to the stage-quality makeup. It was a lot thicker than the stuff she used on herself, with heavy layers needed, what with the clients being dead and all.

The doorbell rang, and her dad answered, ushering in an old man with a grim, hollowed face. A woman in her thirties walked in behind him with a little girl by her side. Their resemblance to the dead woman was clear as day. The daughter had the same high cheekbones Lenna had dusted with blush; the little girl's nose was slender with a bump near the top, just like her grandmother's.

The girl's eyes shifted around the place as she played with a strand of unruly red hair. She looked up at her mom and grandfather, but they were too focused on their dead loved one at the front of the room.

Lenna slipped out, leaving her dad with the mourning family, and went upstairs to change.

She rummaged in her closet and brought out an old faithful: a black dress that fell to just above her knees.

It was simple but well tailored with short sleeves and a white collar. She'd found it at a thrift store and snatched it up for an epic deal of ten dollars.

Styled with black tights and a pair of killer heels, Lenna checked that her pastel-pink hair was still in the ringlets she'd curled earlier, and skipped back downstairs.

The little girl was on the bottom step.

"Hey." Lenna sat down next to her. "What are you doing back here?"

The girl stared at her patent leather shoes, a curtain of hair swept over her face. "I don't know."

"What's your name?"

"Hallie."

"That's a nice name. I'm Lenna."

Hallie was only five or six. Her lip pouted, and she didn't meet Lenna's eyes.

Lenna reached over and tucked her wave of amber hair behind her ear. "This is a rough time, huh?"

Hallie nodded. "Everybody's sad, and Grandma's gone."

Lenna bunched up to Hallie. Death was confusing for kids. She should know.

"I was around your age when my mom died. It sucks when people you love leave, but they're not really gone. You still have all your memories with them, and no one can take those away."

Hallie looked up at her.

"My mom and I would go for ice cream every Sunday. She always got strawberry, and I got anything with sprinkles. If it was nice out, we'd go to the park to eat it and watch the baby ducks play in the lake."

"Grandma baked cookies with me all the time," said Hallie. She covered her mouth and whispered, "She even let me eat the dough because I was her special helper."

"See?" said Lenna. "Even though you'll miss your grandma, you'll always have those times to think back on."

"I guess." Hallie's pouty lip disappeared.

Lenna stood and took Hallie's hand, leading her from the stairs to the kitchen. She took a jar from the counter, removed the lid, and bent down to Hallie.

"Now I don't know if these will be as good as the ones you made with your grandma, but double chocolate chip always cheers me up."

"Thank you." Hallie put her little hand in the jar and picked out the biggest cookie. She took a bite and her eyes lit up.

"Why don't you go back to your mom and give her a big hug?"

"Okay," said Hallie with a chocolate-covered smile.

Lenna watched her scamper off and returned the jar.

The back door opened as she was filling a jug with cream for the guests' coffee and her best friend Corey stepped into the kitchen.

"I have our whole night planned. It's all about the classics." He pulled out movies from his backpack, one at a time, a big grin on his face. "I've got *Halloween*,

The Shining, and the pièce de résistance, *Night of the Living Dead.*"

"Retro," she said. Corey loved horror movies, especially when they watched them at her house. "But we have a wake tonight, and I said I'd help out, so we'll have to watch them after everyone bails."

Corey sat down at the kitchen table. "Aw, man."

"I know, but it shouldn't be too long."

"Okay, I guess I'll just hang out in your room."

"Or, you can keep me company." She ruffled his messy black hair.

Corey froze and blinked through his thick, square-rimmed glasses. "Uh, I would, but I don't have anything else with me to wear."

He gestured to his hoodie and jeans, like they won him a free pass from the boring few hours that lay ahead. Like hell he had.

"That's okay," said Lenna. "You left your suit here from last time, so I got it dry cleaned. It's in my closet."

If she'd learned one thing from attending hundreds of funerals, it was to always have a spare outfit at the ready.

"Fine." Corey got up from his chair and dragged his feet upstairs.

Ten minutes later, he came back down sporting his smart suit and thin black tie. He still wore his Converse, but he pulled it off.

"How do I look?" He spun around, sarcasm on point.

Lenna picked up the jug of cream and a little

porcelain bowl of sugar, signaling for him to get the spoons and extra cups. "Come on, everyone's here already."

They milled through the mourners and placed the stuff next to the coffee urn and tea set. Her dad stood beside the widower, a full head taller than the old man, and spoke with those offering their condolences. The poor guy didn't look like he could talk much.

Aside from Hallie, Lenna and Corey were the youngest ones there. Wakes tended to be heavy on the old people when it was for someone who died in their senior years. The room was filled with clouds of cotton-candy hair and the sickly aroma of lavender perfume, which tickled the inside of Lenna's nose.

Corey stood next to her and looked around. "Should we play a game of Guess Who's Next?"

Lenna hid a snort under a cough and nudged Corey with an elbow. "Don't make me laugh." Something told her their dark sense of humor wouldn't go down well with these people.

"We're running low on coffee," said Lenna. "Be back in a sec."

Lenna scooped up the empty urn and walked back to the kitchen. The phone rang as she finished refilling the coffee; she rushed to answer it so as not to disturb the mourners.

"Gallows Funeral Home, how can I help you?"

"Hey, Lenna, it's Joe. Is your dad around?"

"Sure, hold on and I'll get him." Lenna put down the phone and went to find her dad. Whenever the hospital rang, it was usually a receptionist who called, not the pathologist himself.

"Dad," she said in a hushed tone, "Joe's on the phone."

He quickly excused himself from a group and made for the kitchen. Lenna followed him, busying herself with the coffee. Joe never called unless it was important, especially not this late on a Saturday.

"Hey, Joe, what can I do you for?"

Her dad's face dropped a couple of seconds later as he listened.

"Oh, I see." He ran a hand over his head. "We'll be ready for her when you need us. Just give me a call in the morning and let me know when she's coming."

Something was wrong. Something had happened.

"Okay, Joe. Take care."

"What?" asked Lenna as soon as he hung up. She didn't like the look on his face. The grim expression didn't belong there. "What is it?"

Corey walked up behind them. "Is everything okay?"

Lenna frowned, her stomach doing backflips. "Dad, what's wrong?"

Her dad took a deep breath. "Joe says we should be expecting someone tomorrow. They got a body in earlier today."

"And?" They were a mortuary; bodies came and went all the time. It was a revolving door of dead people.

His eyes were hesitant. He opened his mouth, and then closed it.

Lenna gripped the handles of the coffee urn. "You're freaking me out."

"Honey, it's Alicia."

The urn slipped through Lenna's fingers and clattered to the ground. Coffee splashed over the wood floor and pooled at her feet like spilled blood.

Alicia.

Something painful ripped through Lenna's chest.

Her legs grew weak, her thoughts colliding in a tangled mess.

Alicia was dead.

Arms wrapped around her, and Lenna screamed.

Chapter 2

When your house doubled as a funeral parlor, you literally woke up and smelled the roses. Or the lilies, or whatever flowers the families chose for their loved one's big send-off that day.

Lenna dragged herself out of bed and got dressed, her mind numb as she donned a black skirt and gray blouse with little spikes on the collar. She traipsed downstairs to the kitchen to discover her dad flipping pancakes.

"Morning, kiddo," he said, his voice soft in the way he spoke to families who had just lost someone important to them, like anything too loud might scare them off.

"Hey," Lenna mumbled, her voice rough from crying the night before.

He put a plate stacked with pancakes and blueberry syrup down on her usual spot at the table and pulled out her seat for her to sit. Lenna didn't complain at the extra fussing.

His face was a map of concern as he sat across from her. "How are you feeling?"

"Exhausted."

Lenna surveyed the fluffy pancakes and her stomach turned. She couldn't eat. Instead, she poured herself a black coffee. The liquid burned but it soothed her throat and warmed her cold insides.

"I'm sorry if I caused a scene last night. I hope the family wasn't upset."

Her dad reached out and put his hand over hers. "You don't need to apologize for your feelings. The news came as a shock, and the family was just concerned that you were okay."

A shock was an understatement. It wasn't every day you got a call telling you that your ex-best friend was dead. It hit her like a punch to the face.

"Do you want to talk about it?" asked her dad.

Water pooled in Lenna's eyes and distorted her vision. "I just can't believe she's dead."

Her dad brought out a pack of tissues from his suit pocket, a staple in their line of work, and passed one to her. Lenna dabbed under her eyes, careful not to smudge her mascara.

"It's so dumb. We aren't even"—Lenna stopped and corrected herself—"we weren't friends anymore."

"I know you guys weren't on speaking terms, but that doesn't change the fact you grew up together. You kids were inseparable most of your lives. It's okay to mourn her passing."

Lenna took a deep breath and steadied herself. "I hate how things ended between us. I guess I always thought we'd somehow start talking again and work things out, you know?"

That would never happen now. The realization made her lose it, her tears hot as they ran down her cheeks. Things would never go back to the way they were with them. Alicia was gone and she wasn't coming back.

Lenna's dad went to get up from his chair, but she motioned him back. She was fine. She wasn't the one lying dead in the hospital morgue.

Lenna cleared her throat. "What happened to her? How did she die?"

She'd been too distraught last night to ask. Part of her wasn't sure she wanted to know now. No answer her dad could give would make her feel better.

"A dog walker found her body in the park yesterday afternoon. The police don't know much, but they suspect she'd been there since the night before. The hospital's waiting on test results coming back from the lab, but Joe said it looks like a drug overdose."

"An overdose?" Alicia hadn't so much as looked at a drug when they were still friends. How was it possible for someone to change so much in such a short time?

Her dad shook his head. "I know, it's so sad. Her poor parents."

"Are you going to see them today?"

Her dad checked his watch. "The hospital is bringing Alicia here in thirty minutes and then I've got to leave for the service," he said, referring to the funeral of the old woman from last night. "I told the Santoses I'd be there right after, but I can leave it until later if you want me to come back and stay awhile."

"Go, I'll be fine." Lenna cupped her hands around the hot mug, head down. "I just wish there was something I could've done to help. Maybe if I'd reached out to her sooner, or wasn't so stubborn over our fight, she wouldn't have—"

"You can't think that way," her dad interrupted. "None of this is your fault. There wasn't anything you could've done to stop this."

Alicia getting in with the wrong crowd and doing drugs wasn't on her; Lenna knew that. If she'd known, maybe she could've done something, but she hadn't known, and none of that mattered now. Alicia was dead.

"All you can do," continued her dad, "is help lay Alicia to rest."

"I will," said Lenna.

Lenna lay on her bed and stared at the ceiling. The delivery people from the hospital had come and gone hours ago, her dad soon after.

She tapped her fingers on her chest, her mind doing overtime.

Her grandmother always told Lenna to follow in her dad's footsteps and take over the business when he retired. "I told him," she used to say, "become a mortician and you'll never be out of work."

She was right, of course. One of the only guarantees in life is that it will end. Death happened to everyone, and bodies needed to be dealt with.

What hadn't occurred to Lenna was that some of those bodies would be people she loved. Theirs was only one of two funeral homes in Denwood, so it stood to reason that people Lenna knew would wind up in the basement from time to time. Like old Mr. Taylor from the ice cream shop, and the woman whose name she couldn't remember who taught at her middle school.

She was too young when her mom died to be helping out, and some other funeral home cared for her grandparents. This was the first time someone she was close to in life had arrived at the house in their death.

Alicia was directly two floors down from her right now. Cold and unmoving.

Lenna got to her feet. She was driving herself nuts lying there alone with her thoughts, and there were other clients who needed tending. Staying busy would help.

The elevator was only used for transporting arrivals and taking out filled caskets, so she took the other entrance from the kitchen and descended the staircase into the bowels of the house.

Lenna put in her headphones and blasted her favorite playlist for company, walking past the embalming room and cremator furnaces to their storage room for the dead.

Goosebumps formed across her skin at the change in temperature, the refrigerated unit doing its job to keep the bodies on ice. Decomposition started as soon as someone died, but the cold helped slow the process.

Lenna eyed the stainless steel unit. It looked like a huge silver filing cabinet, only instead of sorting the contents with colorful alphabetical dividers, they used toe tags. It stood ominous at the back of the room, tall and imposing. Lenna hadn't checked how many corpses lay within it, but she knew of at least one.

Alicia.

Forcing her gaze away, she focused on the job at hand.

Two bodies lay on metal slabs in the room's middle, both of their funerals scheduled for tomorrow. Her dad had already dressed one, a man suited and booted in what looked like his church clothes.

Lenna gave him a once-over and straightened his tie. His eyes were beginning to sink, so she fished out a pair of eye caps from the drawers to her right. Back at the body, she pushed open the man's eyes and slid the glass caps over them. In addition to making the eyes appear normal, they also stopped them from opening, which would be a major disaster. Something about seeing dead, vacant eyes freaked people out.

She finished with him five minutes later, a light cosmetics job adding to the flush of his skin courtesy of a cocktail of formaldehyde and other embalming fluids injected into his arteries.

A chill ran its fingers down her neck all the way to her feet. Colder than usual. Lenna rubbed her hands together and blew into them for heat. Maybe she was getting sick.

Shrugging it off, she worked on client number two, a woman in her midforties. Lenna started on her hair, which had been washed with the rest of her body. Her locks were a chestnut brown under the florescent lights, a few shades lighter than Lenna's mom's, from what she could remember.

The family didn't specify how they wanted this client's hair done. Lenna considered the woman's sweetheart face and decided on elegant waves with a bit of volume. She pulled a curling iron from their supplies and plugged it in.

Her playlist stopped out as she waited for the iron to heat up, even though she had hours of songs on it. An eerie silence enveloped the room, palpable, like a presence. Lenna stole a glance toward the door behind her.

Nothing.

The chill returned, stronger this time. She bit down to stop her teeth from chattering, her muscles tense.

Lenna took a deep breath to try to calm herself, the sensation of being watched making her itch. A little cloud formed as she exhaled. When had it gotten so cold?

Crossing the room, she checked the temperature on the unit.

Normal.

Her body yelled at her, insisting that something wasn't normal. Her eyes lingered on the drawers, three rows of four.

Lenna gave herself a shake. This was ridiculous. She grew up around the dead. Stuff like this didn't scare her. She was more scared of Crocs and the people who wore them than she had ever been of dead bodies.

She was overreacting. Wigging out because Alicia was in there—that's all it was. No reason to lose her shit over it.

Nevertheless, her palms started to sweat. She rubbed them against her skirt, unable to stop the unnerving sense that she wasn't alone. This had never happened before.

Lenna inched closer to the drawers. Her hand reached out, almost of its own accord, toward the last drawer of the middle row. It drew her in like the tide of a hungry sea.

Ice ran across her nerves as she wrapped her

fingers around the handle.

She pulled her hand back at the sensation, but something inside told her to open the drawer. She couldn't explain it nor understand it, but the feeling was there.

Hesitant fingers moved back to the handle, her heart drumming against her ears. Before she could think better of it, Lenna yanked open the drawer in one forceful pull.

A pained whimper escaped her lips.

Alicia Santos's dead body lay before her, eyes closed, face paler than Lenna had ever seen it. Her skin had gone waxy, the beautiful coloring washed out.

A white sheet covered her from the chest down. The visible signs of where they cut her open during the autopsy began near her collarbone, black twine stitching together the Y-shaped incision that adorned her young, lifeless form.

Even in death, despite her sickly pallor and her tangle of long dark hair that had been left to dry after the postmortem, Alicia still looked beautiful. She appeared younger than her sixteen years, so vulnerable and out of place down here, in a place she should never have been exposed to until her body had worn out with old age.

The pull inside Lenna remained, more intense now that she stood next to the body. Alicia looked like a dark angel sleeping for eternity.

Gravity drew her closer.

Her hand drifted above Alicia's closed eyes and the

urge to open them came over her. She needed to see them, to see into her soul.

No.

Snapping out of it, Lenna tore her hand back from the dead girl's face. Panic filled her. What the hell was she doing?

A dark compulsion whispered to her, telling her to touch Alicia's corpse. It niggled at the inside of her mind, incessant, pushing her to do it.

No.

She needed to get out of there. Had to get away.

Lenna tried to put the drawer back into the unit where it belonged, away from her and out of sight. The white sheet covering Alicia's body got caught in the side and stopped the drawer from sliding back in no matter how hard Lenna pushed.

She tugged the fabric free, fraying the material in her haste, and reached for the handle.

But Alicia grabbed her first.

Chapter 3

Lenna's shriek echoed across the room as she stared down in horror at the hand latched onto her arm. She froze, too stunned to move.

Alicia held her in a death grip, her stiff fingers digging into Lenna's flesh. She tugged her arm, but it made no difference.

Fragmented thoughts smashed together, unable to make sense of what she saw. This couldn't be happening. This wasn't real. She was imagining things. Maybe she had fallen asleep. It could be a dream. A nightmare.

But nightmares didn't hurt, and her arm throbbed at the relentless hold of the corpse before her. Lenna's mind reeled, trying to rationalize it as she thrashed and twisted, desperate to get away from the body's hold on her.

Dead bodies moved all the time. It was part of the

process. Putrefaction. That could be it. Gasses from decay escaping the corpse.

Just a natural part of the process. Normal.

Except it wasn't. Dead bodies didn't have motor function. They couldn't reach up and grasp for things. Couldn't squeeze.

Lenna's legs turned to jelly. She tried to yell for help, but it got trapped midway, her throat tight and chest heaving.

A sharp intake of breath sounded from Alicia's blue lips, and her dead friend's eyes opened.

Lenna screamed.

Alicia screamed too.

They caught each other's gaze for a split second, and Alicia's hold loosened on Lenna's arm.

Lenna took her chance and squirmed free from Alicia's grasp.

Lenna spun on her heels and ran for the door, not daring to look back to see if Alicia followed. Heeled footsteps resounded in the room along with their screams. Reaching the door, Lenna swung it open, lunged out, and rammed it shut from the outside, putting her whole weight against it.

The handle had no lock. There had never been a need for one. Corpses didn't wake up and go wandering around the basement. Until Alicia.

Lenna pushed off against the door and willed herself to run.

Down the hall, she reached the stairs, taking two at a time until she got to the kitchen.

No one was in the house. Her dad was gone and she was all alone with a living corpse.

"Screw this."

Lenna seized her car keys and raced out, into their hearse, and sped off out of the driveway.

Lenna sat a few streets away from her house, tapping the steering wheel with trembling fingers. Rain rattled off her windshield.

She'd finally gone crazy. Watched so many horror movies that now she was starting to believe messed-up crap like that happened in real life.

Was this some weird coping mechanism? Did she want Alicia to be alive so much that her mind came up with some twisted delusion of her coming back?

The pain of Alicia's grip still pulsated over her arm like a lingering phantom.

Lenna unbuttoned her shirt cuff, afraid to look but needing to at the same time. Pulling the material back, her eyes widened as she saw a purple bruise, right where Alicia had touched her.

She squeezed her eyes, blinked a few times, and checked again. There it was—the unmistakable shape of a hand.

Lenna pinched the bridge of her nose, her body bone tired now as the adrenaline wore off.

Nothing she knew about the dead could explain what she'd seen. She had heard stories from her dad, industry myths really, about morticians who went to work one day and found their client had woken up from a crazy deep coma, pronounced dead in error due to an extremely low heartbeat.

That wasn't the case with Alicia.

No, she was dead. They'd completed an autopsy on her. She'd been cut open and examined. No way could she be alive.

If she wasn't alive, then what the hell had Lenna just seen? It must have been real. She had the bruise to prove it.

Lenna had spent countless hours in that room working on clients and not once had she felt what came over her back there. Not ever.

Something inside of her was drawn to Alicia, like a moth to a flame. It took her over, became all she could focus on. She knew before she opened that specific drawer that she would find Alicia there. She couldn't explain how she knew, but she did.

And the cold. It clung to her like cigarette smoke on fabric.

Lenna turned the heat up full blast in the hearse, but she was chilled to the bone.

Cell phone in hand, she rang the most called number in her contacts.

"Y'ello," answered Corey on the first ring.

"Are you home?" Even Lenna heard the quiver in her voice.

"Yeah, is everything okay?"

"I don't know. I'm coming to get you." She hung up and pulled onto the street.

Corey stood outside waiting by the time she got there.

He climbed in on the passenger side. "Len, what is it? What's going on?" He put his hand over her forehead. "You look like you've seen a ghost."

Lenna let out a sound resembling a laugh and a cry.

Corey wrapped his arms around her and hugged her tight. "God, you're freezing," he said into her hair. He pulled back and looked her over.

"I'm fine," she lied, fooling no one. She stared out the car window into the afternoon rather than look at Corey, who saw everything.

The trees danced with the wind, clutching to their last few remaining leaves like loved ones on the brink of death. The small-town street was carpeted with the ones that had fallen, in radiant shades of reds, yellows, and oranges. It was getting dark.

"Are you going to tell me what's going on?" said Corey after a while. "Is this about Alicia?"

She trusted Corey more than anyone, but she couldn't expect him to just nod his head and believe her. He was a total science nerd; he didn't believe in anything like this. Whatever *this* was. She didn't either, for that matter.

Lenna started the car and turned to her best friend. "It's better that you see for yourself."

Lenna led the way down to the basement using the handrail to keep steady. Corey followed right behind her, his steps easy because he hadn't seen what she had. Yet.

"Brace yourself," she warned him, stepping back from the door.

Corey opened it without hesitation and walked inside. Lenna averted her gaze, ready to run if they had to.

He popped his head through the entrance a moment later. "Uh, what am I supposed to be looking for here?"

"Alicia."

"Oh," he said, like something clicked into place. He came out of the storage room and gave her another hug. "It must be a shock having to see her like this. Maybe you should stay away from down here until the funeral."

Lenna broke from his embrace. "No, it's not that."

"Then what is it? Your own mortality? 'Cause I gotta tell ya, it sure put my life into perspective knowing that I could die at any time. I really need to find a boyfriend."

Ignoring him, Lenna dragged Corey into the room and pushed him toward the still-open drawer.

He turned back to her, his face a little startled. "Is that her?"

"Yes. Go look at her and tell me if you see anything."

"See anything?" replied Corey.

Lenna moved closer to the exit. "Just go and look at her."

Corey raised his hands in submission and went over to Alicia's side. Lenna kept on the balls of her feet. She wasn't the most athletic person in the world, but she'd run like a bat out of hell if Alicia moved again.

"What am I supposed to be looking for?" Corey asked.

"Is that really me?" said a voice behind Lenna.

She spun to find Alicia standing in the corner, eyes pinned to her body across the room.

Alicia moved into the light, her body stiff and ungraceful. "Am I dead?"

Lenna reeled back and bumped into a table, knocking down a bunch of tools resting on it. They clattered to the floor like thunder in her ears.

Something touched Lenna from behind and she flipped out, throwing her fists behind her. Had they all woken up?

"Hey, hey," said Corey.

Lenna yanked his shirt and bounded for the door, ignoring the dead cheerleader in the room. "Come on!" she screamed, putting all her weight into dragging a reluctant Corey away.

"Wait." Corey held onto the door frame.

"We need to get the hell out of here."

Corey used his superior strength and stopped her in her tracks. "What's the matter? What's going on?"

"Didn't you see her?" Lenna said, still trying to move them both toward the stairs.

"Yes, and she's dead and that sucks, but there's nothing we can do about it. That's not going to happen to us. Alicia took a whole bunch of drugs. We'd never do that."

Lenna raised a hand in front of his face, stopping him midsentence. "No, I mean, did you see her. Did you see her walking around?" She screamed the words; she couldn't help it.

"Walking?" Corey's brow burrowed in confusion. "Around?"

He let her go and headed back inside.

"No, don't go back in there," she hissed.

"There's nothing here," he called back, his voice placating.

He didn't believe her. He didn't see Alicia. Maybe she had gone mad after all.

Pretending she wasn't terrified, Lenna returned inside.

Corey stood in the middle of the room. "See, nothing to be worried about. You're just—"

Alicia came out from behind Corey at that moment and walked right past him. Well, not past him so much as through him.

"Wow!" shouted Corey, jumping like he had just been electrocuted. "What was that?"

Lenna screamed as Alicia continued to walk toward her.

"Will you stop screaming?" said Alicia, her voice much louder than Lenna's.

Hearing Alicia's familiar voice sent Lenna into complete silence.

"Thank you," said Alicia, exasperation clear in her voice.

"Did you feel that too?" Corey spun around, rubbing the tops of his arms. Little clouds of steam formed next to his mouth as he breathed into the cold.

"I told you," said Lenna.

Corey pointed to Alicia's corpse, laid out on the drawer. "But she's still there."

"Yeah, but she's also here," Lenna replied, gesturing to the living dead girl as she took another step back from her.

Corey shivered like someone had walked over his grave. "She's really here?"

"Will somebody please tell me what the hell is going on?" Alicia's blue lips moved like normal, talking like she was still breathing.

"Do you see her right now?" Corey asked, nearing Lenna and the exit. "What's she doing?"

Alicia snapped her head toward Corey, her dead face harsh. "Uh, hello. Girl, interrupted."

"Okay, guys," said Lenna, every part of her body shaking. "Please, one at a time."

Corey's eyes widened. "Is she talking to you? You can hear her?"

"Of course she can hear me, you idiot," snapped Alicia.

"Yes, but he can't hear you," said Lenna, more to herself than to Alicia.

Lenna's heart calmed down to a riot. The fact that Alicia wasn't charging at her or trying to eat their brains helped. She leaned against the wall and took a deep, shaky breath.

"Oh my god, Len. You're like that Haley Joel Whatshisface kid." Corey lowered his voice and whispered. "I see dead people."

Alicia aimed a thumb at Corey, her face scrunched up like a ball of aged paper. "Is this guy for real?"

"You really felt her?" Lenna asked Corey. "You felt her walk through you?"

"I felt something that wasn't normal, that's for sure." He looked from side to side. "Len, is this really happening?"

Lenna eyed Alicia. "I think it is."

"Promise this isn't some kind of joke." He shot a glance up to the corners of the ceiling. "I'm not on some crappy, hidden-camera TV show, am I?"

"I promise. You know I'd never do that to you."

"This is very sweet and all," said Alicia, waving her hand in the air, "but do you think you can bring your attention back to me for a second?"

Corey walked over to Lenna and took her hand. "Have you always been psychic?" he asked, whispering like they were at a funeral.

"No, I mean, I don't know." Was that what she was? She'd never seen a ghost before now, if that's even what Alicia was.

Alicia clicked her dead fingers at Lenna. "Do you have ADD or something? I'm right here."

Lenna leaned into Corey. "She's still talking to me."

"Maybe you should talk back," he said.

"Yes, maybe you should. You can start by telling me what the hell is going on." Alicia folded her arms over her chest, covered by the white blanket wrapped around her. She looked exactly like the Alicia on the slab, only animated.

"I don't know," Lenna stuttered. "You're at my house. You were brought here because you died."

"Alicia?" called Corey, like their classmate was deaf instead of dead. "If you can see a white light, maybe you should walk toward it."

Alicia huffed. "Uh, can you please send him back to whatever cave he crawled out of?"

"Shut up," said Lenna.

"Oh, sorry," said Corey.

"No, not you, her." She pointed to what was nothing but an empty space to him.

Corey held a hand to his head. "This is so weird."

"What should I ask her?"

Alicia groaned, a gurgling noise coming from her throat as she did. "I'm not a frickin' Ouija board, Lenna."

Lenna's chest tightened at hearing Alicia say her name. This was the first they'd spoken in so long, and this was real. Alicia was dead and there they were, talking.

"Ask her if she killed herself," said Corey.

Whatever Alicia had been about to say next died on her lips.

Lenna's ex-best friend paused and frowned. "Kill myself?"

Chapter 4

"You didn't kill yourself?" Lenna mirrored, for Corey's sake, and to make sure she had heard Alicia correctly.

"No, I think I'd remember if I killed myself, wouldn't you?" A film covered Alicia's eyes, making them appear clouded, like thick smoke trapped in two glass orbs. Lenna tried not to look at them.

"Okay," said Lenna. "I think I need to sit down."

She stumbled over to the nearest empty table and hoisted herself up onto it with shuddering arms. She struggled to take it all in. Lenna spoke to the dead all the time down there when she got bored, but they'd never replied before. She needed an aspirin.

Corey jumped up to sit next to her and Lenna leaned into him. He seemed to be taking it well. Then again, he didn't see Alicia in all her deathly glory.

A concoction of mixed emotions swirled inside Lenna. She and Alicia had so much past that it made the present complicated, especially since now only one of them had a future.

"I thought she overdosed, though," said Corey.

"Stop talking about me like I'm not here. And what is he talking about with the overdose shit?"

Alicia's tone was biting, razor sharp and angry like so many of their final interactions together, when their friendship shattered into tiny, unsalvageable pieces. Lenna witnessed the change in Alicia back when they were freshmen. It was painful to watch her friend morphing into someone she wasn't, someone Lenna didn't like. Two school years on and Lenna didn't recognize the girl. If the Alicia she knew, her Alicia, was in there, she couldn't see her.

Lenna kept her voice clinical, her walls fortifying between them. "The final reports aren't back yet, but they found drugs in your system. It looks like you died from an overdose."

"I don't do drugs," Alicia spat.

"Well, that's what you died from. What happened?" Lenna's dad said the police didn't know much. Now, Lenna found herself in the weird position of actually being able to hear it from the corpse's mouth.

"I—" Alicia's face went blank. "I don't know."

"You were found in the park. Why were you out there? Who were you with that night and what were you doing?" Lenna's questions were laced with a growing anger. How could Alicia be so stupid? How could she be so reckless?

"I don't know."

"How can you not know?"

"I said I don't know, okay? I can't remember, so get off my back," yelled Alicia, turning away from her. "You haven't changed at all."

And therein lay the problem. Lenna had changed, but her feelings about Alicia hadn't. She'd forced thoughts of her old friend to the back of her mind, brushed them off because it was easier to not deal with any of it. Alicia standing there in front of her had brought it all back. The hurt, the frustration, the anger.

The sadness.

Lenna's eyes filled with unshed tears. She pressed her palms against them and swiped them away before Alicia saw. "You changed enough for us both," she said.

"We could narrow it down," suggested Corey beside her, seeming to have kept up with the conversation he could only hear half of.

"What do you mean?" asked Lenna.

"We can narrow down how she died. There's only so many ways you can die, right? If Alicia's telling the truth and she didn't kill herself, then we can rule out suicide." Corey stuck out his thumb to count them.

He looked in the general direction of where Alicia stood. "Were you on any medication? Anything you could have had a bad reaction to, or took too much of?"

"Nothing," said Alicia.

"No," relayed Lenna.

Corey counted with a second finger. "If we're talking recreational, then maybe you just took too much of whatever high you were on and didn't realize?"

"I didn't take any drugs," repeated Alicia. For someone who couldn't remember anything about her death, she seemed adamant of that.

"You're sure you didn't?" asked Lenna.

Alicia sighed. "I'll admit, I like to have a drink when I'm at a party, and stuff like that does go on, but I never take any part in it. My body needs to be in top shape for dancing—cheering too. I wouldn't risk it. Dancing is my ticket into college and out of Denwood." Her face dropped. "Or at least it was."

Lenna's heart panged in her chest. Alicia wouldn't go to college. She wouldn't dance or wear her cheer uniform ever again.

Lenna closed her eyes, the clash of warring emotions draining her energy.

Memories of Alicia in elementary school circled in her mind, of her wearing her tutu for show-and-tell, and performing in the talent show. Lenna had even gone to a class with her but soon discovered she had two left feet. Alicia had always been a dancer, even then.

"She didn't use," said Lenna. "It wasn't an accident." The Alicia she knew would never have gone down that road, no matter how much she had changed since then. Lenna stopped and stared back at the dead girl. Then again, the girl Lenna once knew was nothing like this new Alicia. The one who switched up on her when they swore they'd always be friends. Forever.

"In that case ..." Corey took off his glasses and rubbed his forehead. "Oh boy."

Alicia stepped toward them. "What?"

"That leaves us with only one other option," said Corey, his face as serious as Lenna had ever seen it. He met Lenna's eyes and it hit her.

Corey nodded.

Lenna turned to Alicia, unsure of how to say it.

"Spit it out," ordered Alicia, looking from her to Corey.

The full force of what it meant pressed against Lenna, crushing her. "If you didn't take the drugs, then that means someone else must have given you them without you knowing."

Someone had done this to her.

Alicia stood deadly still. "No." She shook her head with vigor and her neck made an awful snapping noise.

Lenna got down from the table. "Alicia."

"No, this isn't happening." She paced, muttering to herself. "I haven't been murdered. Who would want to kill me? I haven't done anything to anyone."

Lenna was at a loss for words. Nothing she could say would make things better for Alicia. Nothing could change the real likelihood that someone had ended her life.

Guilt cut into Lenna like salt on an open wound. She shouldn't have been so hard on her, silently blaming Alicia for winding up dead. This wasn't her fault. She was a victim.

"No," said Alicia, unhinging before her. "I have to get out of here."

Lenna moved in front of her. "Alicia, wait."

Alicia pushed past her and strode for the door. The air caught in Lenna's lungs as the dead girl's skin touched her for the second time that day. She fell to her knees as a bitter frost bore into her shoulder and sent a stinging sensation through her whole body.

Corey was at her side before she got her breath back.

"I'm fine," she told him and got to her feet.

Alicia was at the threshold of the open door, trying to move forward but incapable, like she had tripped into some quicksand stopping her from moving another foot. She screamed in frustration, her cry desperate and defeated. Lenna watched, unable to do anything.

"What's happening?" asked Corey, paler than usual.

Alicia took a couple of steps back and charged at the space between the open door. She crashed into it with a hard smack, like an invisible wall stopped her from going any farther.

"She can't get past the door." Lenna looked back at the girl's corpse, lying in the drawer. "I think she's tied to her body or something."

Alicia screamed again, hitting the barrier with her fists as choked sobs escaped her lips. She slid to the floor, a broken china doll in a flimsy, handmade dress. Her whole body heaved, pained eyes unable to produce tears.

Lenna walked over to Alicia, careful not to touch her.

"Please, just go," she said, her voice barely a whisper.

Part of Lenna wanted to embrace her old friend, to take away all her pain. The other part of her was scared of Alicia. Scared of being able to see her and what her death meant.

"Let's give her some space," said Lenna.

Corey pushed the drawer with Alicia's body back into the refrigerated unit and followed Lenna in silence out of the room. The crying grew louder now that no one stood watching her.

Lenna rested a hand on the closed door separating them.

What good was being able to see Alicia's ghost if she couldn't do anything to help her? It didn't make sense. None of it did.

Chapter 5

The old clock on the wall ticked, the only sound in the whole room.

Lenna and Corey sat at the kitchen table.

"Are you okay?" Corey asked.

"I don't know," said Lenna. "You?"

Corey shrugged.

Lenna followed the grooves of the oak table with her finger. "I don't think it's a good idea to tell anyone else about this. Everyone will think we've lost it."

Going around saying you can talk to the ghost of your ex-best friend wasn't going to help the situation in any way, shape, or form. People would deem her mentally ill, or accuse her of lying and being desperate for attention. Besides, her dad would freak out, and it could really hurt Alicia's parents.

"Thanks for believing me," she said.

Corey smiled. "I've got your back. Always."

Lenna smirked. "Ditto, nerd."

She leaned back in her seat and dropped her arms, letting them hang. "I don't know what to do."

Today was the first time Lenna and Alicia had spoken since their big falling-out. Never in a million years did Lenna think their reunion would be under these circumstances. If you could even call it that. It wasn't all that long ago that she and Alicia were dancing around her bedroom, playing dress-up and building pillow forts, or sneaking downstairs at midnight for candy and daring each other to go look at the bodies downstairs. Now Alicia was one of them, and colder toward Lenna than ever.

Corey rested his chin on his arms. "Today's been rough, and I don't know about you, but I'm still trying to process it all. Sleep on it, and we can decide what the heck we're going to do tomorrow. Alicia's not going anywhere."

Lenna was bone tired, her eyelids heavy and thoughts clogged with questions she had no answers to.

A car engine sounded from outside. Her dad was home.

"Hey," he said, shrugging out of his coat and suit jacket. "How are you both holding up?"

"Fine," Lenna lied.

Her dad kissed her on the head as he passed and hung up his things in the closet. "You staying for dinner, Corey? How does pasta sound to everyone?"

Corey pushed out from his chair and stretched. "No thanks, Mr. Gallows, I better get home. Mom's making matzo balls."

"Say hi for me." Her dad went to the fridge and took out tomatoes, garlic, and his other favorite ingredients.

Corey mouthed a "call me" to Lenna, and left for his house a few blocks over.

Rolling up the sleeves of his crisp white shirt, her dad got to work, pulling out a chopping board and heating water in a pan.

Lenna stayed in her seat. She was a much better eater of food than she was maker. Whenever she offered to help him, he gently reminded her of the incident with the frozen meal, the microwave, and the fire department. She wasn't really up to it anyway.

"Sure you're okay?" checked her dad.

"Yeah," said Lenna, and changed the subject. "How did your day go?"

"Busy," he said, preparing the sauce. "We have another four clients coming in tomorrow on top of the two funerals."

Steam covered the windows as the water boiled and the pasta went in. Her dad dipped a spoon in the sauce and waved her over. "What do you think—more chili?"

Lenna leaned against the counter and tried it. "It's perfect," she said, barely tasting a thing, despite her dad's Jedi status in the kitchen. Her stomach grumbled up at her in complaint. She hadn't eaten anything all day and it was catching up to her.

"How were Mr. and Mrs. Santos?" Lenna asked,

busying herself by putting the things her dad was finished with in the dishwasher.

"They're doing as well as can be expected. We've scheduled Alicia's funeral for Sunday."

Alicia's funeral.

Bile rose in Lenna's throat. It wasn't right. Alicia was sixteen, and would be buried in the ground in a week's time.

"That's a bit long," Lenna said, trying to hold it together. Most of their clients were in and out after a few days, five tops.

"Mrs. Santos wants the family's priest to do the service. He's flying in from Puerto Rico as soon as he can."

The front doorbell rang.

"I'll get it," said her dad, turning the heat down on the stove. "Keep an eye on the sauce."

His footsteps traveled down the hall and the door clicked open.

"Hello, William Gallows, I presume?" said a woman's voice.

"Yes, how can I help you, officer?"

Officer? Lenna went out into the hall to see what was going on. A black woman stood at the door wearing a smart pantsuit and a stern face.

The woman flashed her credentials. "Detective Gibbs."

Lenna pricked at the superior way she regarded her dad. Who the hell did she think she was?

Her dad smiled at her, his well of patience much

deeper than Lenna's. "My apologies, Detective. Is everything all right?"

"May I come in?" she asked as she entered the house.

"Of course, please." He moved out of her way as she walked past, looking around the place. He closed the door. "Would you like some coffee? Tea?"

"No, thank you."

"Are you new in town?" her dad inquired. "I get to know most of the local police in my line of work."

"I just transferred. Promotion," she said, brusque, all business like the efficient bun that held back her hair.

"Oh," said her dad. "Congratulations."

"I'm just back from the medical examiner's office," she said, straight to the point. "His receptionist said that the body of a Miss Alicia Santos is now in your care, is that correct?"

"Yes," her dad confirmed. "She came in today."

"I'd like to see her, please."

"No," said Lenna before she could stop herself, wincing at how loud it had come out.

Both her dad and the detective turned to her. Detective Gibbs narrowed her eyes.

Lenna swore under her breath. "I mean, uh, she's not ready for viewing yet. We still need to prepare her."

"This isn't for a viewing." Detective Gibbs studied her like she might be slow. "And who are you?"

"This is my daughter, Lenna." Her dad walked

over and put an arm around her. His hand hit the spot on her shoulder Alicia had touched, and she had to bite the inside of her cheek, sure now that a bruise was there to match the one on her arm.

"I see," said Detective Gibbs. "And did you go to school with Ms. Santos?"

"Denwood High's the only high school in town." Lenna wiped her palms on her skirt, stopping herself from leaning on one foot to the other.

The woman took out a little notebook from her jacket pocket along with a pen, which she clicked ready. "You wouldn't happen to have spoken with her on Friday? Seen her around anywhere?"

"No, I haven't seen anything," said Lenna, a little too quickly.

Detective Gibbs was about to ask another question, but her dad got in before she could.

"Detective, I have to say, this is quite an unusual request," he said. "What need do you have to see the body?"

She raised her chin at him. "I'm in charge of the case."

Her dad crossed his arms. "Yes, but her body is in my care now, like you said. Any information you need about the body can be gathered from the autopsy report or the medical examiner himself."

"It's because of the autopsy report I'm here." The detective flipped back a page in her notebook. "It mentioned some markings on her hand that I seemed to have missed on site at the park."

Her dad didn't waver. "I'm sure photographs were taken."

"I'd rather see them in person." Her smile was tight.

"I'm afraid I can't allow that. The body has been released back to the family, and they left their daughter in my care. Any request you have to see the body will need to be approved by the girl's parents."

"I'm just trying to do my job." The detective unclicked her pen and put away the notebook. "I could get a warrant, you know."

Lenna clamped her jaw to stop from opening her mouth.

Her dad raised an eyebrow, calm as ever. "That seems unnecessary but, by all means, go and get one."

Detective Gibbs had no reply. Her eye twitched.

Her dad walked over and stood by the door, his meaning clear. "Is there anything else I can help you with?"

"No."

Without another word, Detective Gibbs left and got in her car.

"That was weird," said her dad.

Lenna watched Detective Gibbs drive down the street until her car turned out of view. "Very weird."

Chapter 6

Lenna tooted the horn. A few minutes later, a disheveled Corey stumbled out of his house, patting his messy hair down as he yawned.

"Couldn't sleep either?" she asked as he fell inside the car.

Corey pulled the hood of his black hoodie over his head and groaned. The words "I HATE MONDAYS" were printed across the chest. "Nope. How are you holding up?"

"Okay." How could she complain when she was alive? Alicia was the dead one.

"Did you go back down to see her?"

Lenna bit her lip. "I couldn't face it."

It was easier for Corey. He didn't have a history with Alicia. He'd met her, and felt the wrath of her insults, their freshman year of high school. He never got to meet the girl Lenna knew, the one who would never have cast her aside for popularity. The one who would have believed her over some guy.

They stayed silent for the rest of their short journey. Lenna pulled into a parking space and they got out with a couple minutes to spare before the bell.

A girl a few spaces down got out of her car and stomped toward them, face as sour as an out-of-season lemon.

Lenna raised an eyebrow as the stranger stopped in front of her and Corey, blocking their path. "Can I help you?"

"Don't you think coming here in that is just a bit insensitive?" The girl stabbed a finger at Lenna's hearse and waited for a response.

"What, my car?" asked Lenna.

"Who even drives a funeral car around? That's so damaged."

It was the spare hearse her dad kept for double funerals. It made no sense for him to fork out cash to buy her a car when they had a perfectly good one already. Besides, Lenna kinda liked it.

"Whatever." Linking her arm with Corey's, she turned her back on the girl and walked the other away.

"She was on edge," said Corey.

"Something tells me she won't be the only one." Everyone would know about Alicia by now. News traveled fast in Denwood.

If the students of Denwood High were bees, then Alicia was definitely their queen. Or at least she had been. Now, the whole hive buzzed around in a state of shock, some sad, others angry. An alarming number seemed disturbingly excited that there was a big drama flying around.

The noise in the hallway was deafening as they entered. Everyone stood in clusters of rapid chatter, the topic of conversation identical to the one next to it.

"It's pandemonium," said Corey.

The PA system rang through the entire school and everyone stopped talking to listen on with eager ears.

"Attention all students. Please make your way to the gymnasium immediately for an emergency assembly."

A stampede began before Principal Stein had even finished, students fighting their way past each other to get front-row seats on the bleachers. Lenna and Corey followed behind. After everyone had been herded in and seated, Principal Stein arrived with someone Lenna recognized.

"That's the detective who came to my house last night," Lenna whispered to Corey. Detective Gibbs wore another pantsuit, black this time, with a pair of flats designed for comfort over style. She studied the students with interest.

The microphone on the stand Principal Stein stood behind screeched as he addressed the school.

"Good morning, students and faculty. As I'm sure most of you are aware by now, we have some tragic news. Student Alicia Santos was found dead on Saturday."

He paused for dramatic effect, but this was news to no one.

"Alicia was a great advocate for Denwood High," he continued. "She led as captain of the cheerleading squad, despite only being a junior. She was loved by her classmates and made so many great friends over the years. Her shining personality and never-ending kindness will be greatly missed by everyone who knew her."

Someone snorted from the back, two rows up, and Lenna turned. Nichole Roach, editor of the school newspaper, sat shaking her head with a dark scowl.

Queen bees never made it to their throne without stinging at least a few people.

Principal Stein continued talking about Alicia like he was her best friend; like he could have pointed her out from a crowd of students this time last week. Like he was the one who had been friends with her since kindergarten, when Alicia punched Katie Fletcher in the nose for picking on Lenna and they'd become instant friends, inseparable from that day on, until things shattered between them years later.

"To help us all through this extremely difficult time, we have a staff of counselors available if you want to discuss what happened or how you're feeling." Principal Stein gestured to the group of adults standing near the gym door. "You are not alone in your grief. We are all hurting from this terrible loss."

Detective Gibbs said something into the principal's ear. He stood away from the microphone and gave her the floor, not quite able to hide his annoyance.

"Morning. My name is Detective Julia Gibbs, and I'm heading the investigation into Alicia Santos's death."

Gibbs's stone face was unreadable as she scanned over each student, row by row.

"We're looking for anyone who might have information on the events leading up to Alicia's death. If you had any contact with her, or saw her at all on Friday, I need to speak with you. Nothing is too small in this investigation. If you know anything, or know someone who might, please come and see me as soon as possible. I'll be interviewing people all day here on campus, and you can contact me at the police station after that."

"What happened to her?" called someone from the crowd.

"I heard she killed herself."

"I heard she OD'd."

Detective Gibbs waited until the outbursts stopped. "We're treating Alicia's death as suspicious and that is all we are revealing at this time. It is vital we gather information on her whereabouts on Friday so we can build a timeline of where Alicia was and who she was with. So far, we haven't been able to gather much intel, so your cooperation is critical."

Principal Stein cut her off.

"Okay, kids. You heard what the detective said, so if you have any information that could help, please be in touch. This will be a tough time for us all, but know that we are here for you and grieving alongside you."

People started crying around them. Lenna took Corey's hand and squeezed it.

Resting her head on his shoulder, she inhaled his familiar scent of sweet cologne and boy. "I love you, stupid face."

Corey leaned into her, his voice tight. "I love you too, booger brain."

Lenna sat in second-period English, unable to focus.

Alicia's seat was empty near the window, as far away from hers as possible.

They'd spent so much time in school avoiding each other in the hallways, pretending they weren't in some of the same classes, acting like the other was a ghost. Now one of them really was.

Someone had placed a flower on the desk. It lay there with its head drooped, sad and slowly dying.

Did Alicia die slowly, or had it been quick? Did she suffer? She was suffering now, all alone in the basement with no idea what happened to her.

Lenna got up from her chair. It was all too much.

The teacher called her name, but she didn't listen, didn't stop. She ran out of the classroom, tears falling free, and headed to the bathroom where she locked herself in a stall.

People went in and out of the bathroom, but no one

disturbed her. A while later, Lenna gathered herself together.

At least the police suspected something wasn't right. An investigation could lead them to think that *something* was *someone*. Someone had killed Alicia.

She was about to leave the stall when two voices made her stop.

"Everyone's calling it a suicide."

"Seems legit. I mean, I'd buy it."

Lenna leaned up against the door and peered through the little gap at the hinges. Ellie Parsons and her stepsister Zara stood in front of the mirrors dressed in their cheer uniforms, adding fresh layers of lip gloss.

"Really?" asked Zara, running a hand through her braids.

"Of course," said Ellie. "Look who she went out with. It's not a stretch to believe she was using too."

"Trey uses?"

"I hear our star quarterback has been pumping up on steroids," continued Ellie, looking at her stepsister in the mirror with sly eyes. "Among other things."

Lenna's nails dug into her palms at the mention of Trey's name. Did Alicia lie to her? Was she really taking drugs? Trey was a bad influence. Lenna never trusted him and was right not to. Not that Alicia wanted to hear any of what she had to say at the time. Had he gotten her into using?

Zara shook her head. "God, some people are so screwed up."

Ellie smacked her lips and checked her reflection.

"That reminds me, I need to call and get some Special K for the party Friday night."

"Cool." Zara held her cell phone and tapped away at the screen. "I can't believe Trey even went out with her."

Ellie shrugged. "Guys like easy girls."

"Speaking of which, did you see Kayla at the assembly?"

Ellie scoffed and put her lip gloss into her bag. "She couldn't even be bothered to put on some fake tears for a couple minutes over her supposed best friend."

"She was probably too busy trying to keep a smug grin off her face. She's a shoo-in for captain now," said Zara, who didn't seem happy about it.

"True. Now there's no one to stand in her way anymore. She must be so glad Alicia's dead."

Zara giggled. "You're such a bitch, Ellie."

"Just saying it as it is, girl," said the cheerleader, taking it as a compliment. "Come on, let's go and see one of those counselors so we can get sent home early. I'm so over today."

The pair walked out of Lenna's restricted viewpoint. When she heard them leave, she exited the stall and slammed her fist on the sink tap, watching the water spurt out of the faucet and travel down the drain.

Ellie and Zara were supposed to be Alicia's friends. They'd been on the cheer team together since freshman year and that was how they spoke of her? With friends like that, Alicia didn't need enemies.

Lenna washed her hands and dried them with some paper towels, Trey stuck in her mind. A toilet flushed and one of the stalls behind her opened.

Kayla walked over to the sinks.

Lenna stood at the trash can, still holding her paper towels and unsure of what to say or do. Alicia's new best friend must have heard every word her fellow cheerleaders said about her.

Kayla washed her hands, impassive and posture upright as she walked over to dry them.

Lenna moved out of her way and cleared her throat. "Hey, are you okay?"

Kayla ignored her. They'd never really spoken before. Kayla had been Lenna's replacement.

She tried again. "I'm sorry you had to hear what those assholes said."

Kayla dropped her paper towel and fixed her long, blond hair in the mirror. For someone who had just lost her best friend, she seemed in remarkable control of herself.

"It doesn't matter," she said, face set hard. "I own them now."

Chapter 7

Lenna sat in math class, waiting. Her workbook lay open on her desk, fingers tapping the desk as she watched the clock above the whiteboard.

The bell rang right on time and Lenna packed her things, out the door before anyone else. She turned the corner at the end of the hall and found Corey by her locker.

"Hey," she said, stuffing in the books she didn't need for the rest of the day. "Did you get it?"

Corey pulled out a copy of a class schedule. "Thanks to the lovely old lady in the front office, I can tell you that Trey should be in gym class right now."

People milled around them, winding their way toward their next class.

"Great," said Lenna, heading down the hall as it emptied.

"What about class?" called Corey.

"Nobody cares today."

"Fine." Corey hoisted his backpack and followed.

The gymnasium lay at the other end of campus, right next to the football field and the outdoor tracks. Using the back entrance of the school, they turned left and headed outside to the fields. Overcast smothered the sun in opaque swirls of gray, shrouding everything below in a depressed gloom.

They had to wait the entire period for the class to be over, hiding behind the gymnasium building. They didn't dare risk being seen by any teachers, all of whom would march them straight back to whatever class they were skipping. Lenna and Corey especially wanted to avoid Coach Marwick, who liked to dish out detention like free samples at the grocery store.

The hour dragged, but eventually the students returned to the locker rooms. Coach Marwick stayed outside and began setting up hurdles and arranging orange cones in the middle of the track for his next class, clearly eager to make the most of the first dry day they'd had in a week.

"Do you think this is a good idea?" asked Corey, struggling to keep up with Lenna as she snuck toward the locker rooms. "What if Ellie and Zara were talking out their asses?"

Lenna stopped and faced her friend. "What if they weren't? Trey's bad news and I can't sit around when he might know something."

Corey glanced back at the main building.

"Shouldn't we wait? I mean, if Trey knew something, he would've gone to the police, right?"

"Unless he has something to hide. Like maybe he was the one who got Alicia into drugs in the first place."

"Would Alicia lie about not using?"

Lenna didn't answer. Any level of trust and confidence she and Alicia shared had died long ago. Truth was she didn't know much about her old friend anymore. The Alicia she knew would never hang out with people like Ellie and Zara. Why be around people who clearly didn't like you? Neither of them gave a shit that she was dead.

They reached the locker room outbuilding and waited for Trey to come out. Lenna paced along the edge of the bleachers, biting her nail.

She checked the time on her cell. "This is taking too long."

"He'll be out soon," said Corey, leaning against the wall. "What are you even going to say to him anyway?"

"I don't know," said Lenna. "Go in and see if he's there."

Corey choked. "In there?"

"Yeah," she replied. "What's the problem?"

Corey's eyebrows rose. "You want me to go into a changing room with a bunch of seniors who may or may not be naked?"

Lenna couldn't help but laugh. "I'm sure there'll be nothing in there you haven't seen on those websites you like to visit."

"Very funny," he muttered, rubbing the back of his neck.

"Please," she said. "I have to speak with him."

Trey wasn't her number one fan after everything that had happened, but she had to confront him. Had to know where he was the night Alicia died and if he'd gotten her hooked on drugs like Ellie said.

"Oh, all right." Corey dragged himself inside.

He came back out a couple minutes later. "I can't find him."

"Did you look everywhere?"

Corey's cheeks were flushed bright red. "Not *everywhere.*"

"Screw it."

"Len," called Corey, following behind her as she walked in. "You can't come in here."

She closed the door behind them. "I'm already in."

"But you're a girl," Corey whispered, looking around the corner.

Lenna patted his back. "Yes, thanks for noticing."

"You know what I mean. If the coach catches you, you'll get in trouble."

Lenna waved her hand and budged past him. "I'll only be a minute."

Corey sighed. "We should not be doing this."

"Girl coming through," she yelled, announcing her presence. "Gentlemen, I suggest you cover up what you don't want seen."

Lenna winced at the assault of dirty socks and far

too much sprayed deodorant, surprised she could even see through the toxic mist.

A few guys whistled when she walked past them, but most gaped at her in shock, like they had never seen a female before. One guy snatched his bag and covered his bottom half as if he thought she had X-ray eyes that could see through boxer shorts.

Maybe her presence in this apparent sacred place would give her the upper hand with Trey. She wound up and down the rows separated by lockers and benches, unable to find the quarterback anywhere.

A hand came out and leaned against a set of lockers, stopping her and blocking her way past. Corey bumped into her back and gawked.

A guy a good head taller than Lenna stood in front of them with an amused curve to his lips. He wore no shirt, standing in only his shorts.

"Hi, I'm Elliot." He had a crooked grin that promised mischief with a blaring confidence that only came with being an athlete at Denwood High. Sports stood above all in the school's hierarchy, much to Lenna's chagrin.

"That's nice," Lenna said, turning around. She had zero interest in humoring some knucklehead's attentions.

Elliot spun around and blocked her again from the other side, separating her from Corey. "Where are you off to in such a hurry? I thought we were talking?"

"You were talking. I was leaving." Lenna made to walk away but Elliot grabbed her arm.

His hair was damp with sweat from gym class. "Hey, slow down. What's your name?"

"Elliot," called a new voice before Lenna could order him to let her go. "Leave her alone and hit the showers. You stink."

Another jock type stepped into view from behind Elliot and slapped him on the shoulder, his meaning clear. Elliot was taller and heavier built than the new guy, but whatever kind of alpha-male standoff was happening before her, the new guy won.

Elliot released Lenna and shrugged before heading off to the showers. "Whatever."

"Sorry about him," said the new guy. "He's got too much testosterone and too few brain cells."

"Or manners," said Corey, frowning as he watched Elliot saunter off.

"Thanks. Brayden, right?" Lenna asked, recognizing the new guy's face.

"Brendan," he corrected. "And you're Lenna. I've seen you around."

Denwood was a small town, so it wasn't a shock Brendan knew who she was. Nevertheless, she couldn't help the little flutter in her stomach at this boy knowing her name.

He was also a football player, from what Lenna could remember. Though he wore a simple white T-shirt, she recalled seeing him in a varsity jacket around the hallways.

"Yup, that's me. This is my friend, Corey."

"What's up, man?" Brendan said, nodding to

Corey, who sat down on the bench with a face somehow redder than before. "Can I help you guys with something?"

Brendan ran a slow hand over his damp dark hair, fresh from the showers. Though his frame was athletic, he didn't wear it the same as his bozo teammate Elliot. He held none of the same cockiness or arrogance, his face easy to spread into an infectious smile, accompanied by a pair of dimples at each corner.

"Actually, yes. We're looking for Trey."

"Oh." Brendan sobered and his smile dropped. "He didn't come in today. Me and a few of the guys tried to visit him yesterday, but he wasn't up for seeing anyone."

Lenna suppressed a deep sigh.

"Terrible news about Alicia," Brendan continued. "Trey was so down after they broke up. I can only imagine what my dude's going through now."

"He and Alicia weren't together?" Lenna asked. It was news to her, but then again, it wasn't like she followed the exploits of her ex-best friend's relationship, especially given how it played a huge part in their falling-out.

"No, but I guess he thought they'd get back together." Brendan offered an apologetic look, like he didn't want to speak ill of the dead. "They, uh, kinda did that a lot."

Lenna didn't need reminding of that. Back when she and Alicia were friends, it was hard to keep up with her and Trey's relationship. By the time Lenna realized they'd fallen out, the pair were back together again like nothing happened.

"What do you need him for?" Brendan asked, packing his gym clothes into his sports bag. Lenna caught the whiff of sweet cologne as he moved, which was a nice reprieve from the other scents of the boys' locker room.

"It's for the school newspaper," Lenna said. "We're doing a memorial piece for Alicia, and I wanted to speak with Trey to see if he had anything he'd like to say."

It wasn't the best lie in the world, but Brendan seemed to buy it.

"I don't think he'll come in the rest of the week," he said. "If he does, I can call you and let you know. If you want me to, that is," Brendan quickly added, his cheeks flushing a little, though not as beet red as Corey's face. Lenna couldn't help but find it adorable.

Coach Marwick's voice boomed through the room from the door. "All right, ladies, hurry up and get your asses out of here and to your next class. You're going to be late."

"Looks like you need to go," said Brendan, as Coach Marwick's voice grew louder and closer.

"Thanks for your help." Lenna grabbed Corey and sped for the exit before they were caught. She stole one last look at Brendan who waved her off before she and her best friend headed out the door.

Chapter 8

Lenna threw her keys on the kitchen counter and dumped her bag. The rest of school had dragged on longer than an overnight vigil.

A note was left by the phone, her dad letting her know he was away to make arrangements with a new client's family. She went straight down to the basement, keen to see Alicia before he got back.

"Oh my god, why the hell did you leave me down here for so long with all these dead people?" Alicia waved her hand over the embalmed bodies that lay waiting for their funerals the following day.

"You're dead too," Lenna said, shivering as the winter chill of death that surrounded Alicia's spectral form settled in.

"Yeah, but not *dead*, dead. How can you be around all these bodies all the time? I always knew you were weird, but this is on a whole other level."

"Says the talking ghost."

"What do you want?" said Alicia, her expression a master class on resting bitch face.

Lenna sat on a metal slab next to a freshly embalmed old man, moving his feet to give her space. "I came down to check on you."

Alicia sat across from her, a woman in her fifties by her side dressed in a yellow floral dress. "Why? We're not friends. Don't act like you care."

Lenna said nothing. Of course she cared. Just because they weren't on speaking terms anymore didn't mean Lenna didn't grieve the fact Alicia was dead. In many ways, Alicia knew her better than anyone. They'd been there for each other for so many big things in their lives.

Alicia was the one who showed Lenna how to deal with her period when it arrived, Lenna far too embarrassed to go to her dad about it. When Alicia broke her leg in fifth grade and thought she'd never dance again, Lenna was there to help her stumble around school on crutches until she was back on her feet and pirouetting like nothing had happened.

And when Lenna's mom died, Alicia had been the one to pick up the pieces. No matter what Alicia said to her now, or how much Lenna hated the girl her ex-best friend had become, she'd never forget or take away from the fact that Alicia was there for her when Lenna needed her most. The nights of crying in her arms. Or her first day back at school when Alicia warned and cussed out any kid who asked too many questions about Lenna's dead mom.

No matter what happened between them in the end, no matter how much they changed and grew apart, nothing could take away the years they'd spent together.

"Your dad was down earlier and never saw or heard me," Alicia said, breaking the awkward silence between them. "Why, of all people, do you end up being the only one who can see me?"

"Hey, I'm not thrilled about any of this either," Lenna bit back, their past and unresolved issues making the present situation all the worse. She didn't sign up for this. She didn't decide to wake up one day and see ghosts. Why couldn't she have discovered she could fly, or shoot lasers from her eyes instead?

"You're not the one trapped down here. What's going on out there?" Alicia demanded. "Do they know what happened to me?"

"The police have opened an investigation. They don't have much yet but were asking people to come forward if they saw you Friday."

"I've been wracking my brain all day and I can't frickin' think of a single thing I did that day. It's all blank. Why can't I remember?" Alicia slammed a fist on the table; it passed right through.

Lenna ran a hand through her hair. "Clearly something messed up is happening."

"Understatement of the century, Lenna. Someone killed me."

"About that," said Lenna. "I overheard Ellie and

Zara talking about you today. They seemed to think you were taking drugs."

Alicia sneered at the mention of their names. "They're ones to talk. Anyway, who cares what those idiots think?"

"They said Trey did too. Are you sure you didn't take anything that night? Were you and Trey on something?"

Trey was a bad influence, crafty too—and not in the scrapbooking, let's-sew-a-quilt type of way.

Alicia stuck her dead fingers out. "One, those bitches make up shit about everybody. Two, Trey and I broke up, so I wouldn't have been with him. And three, I told you, there is no way I would take anything. Period."

"How do you know if you can't remember that night?" Lenna challenged. Why was she always so quick to stick up for Trey?

"I just do, okay?"

"Does Trey take steroids?"

"Give it a rest. I told you, we broke up."

Lenna rolled her eyes. "Oh, for what, like an hour?" Alicia and Trey used to break up and make up at least twice a day when she and Lenna were still friends.

"No, for real this time. We broke up a month ago. But what does that have to do with anything?"

Alicia really was blind to him. Nothing had changed. "Uh, hello. Did you ever think that he could be the one who killed you?"

"Trey would never hurt me," said Alicia, though Lenna could have sworn she saw a flash of doubt there.

"Maybe he didn't mean to." It could've been accidental. The courts would call it manslaughter, but it made no difference to Alicia. She was still dead.

Alicia got up from her spot on the slab. "You're just saying this because you don't like him. You never did."

"You're damn right I don't like him," spat Lenna.

"You were always jealous of me for having him," said Alicia, voice rising. "I can't believe you would try and say he killed me. Lying back then was bad enough."

Lenna laughed. "Jealous? I don't think so. I felt sorry for you, and I never lied."

"You did."

"He was cheating on you, Alicia," said Lenna, shouting now. Old wounds she thought were healed split open and began to bleed. "I saw him with my own eyes, and yet you still stayed with him. You would rather call me a liar than see the truth."

Alicia tossed her hair back. "Whatever."

Lenna grasped the edge of the metal slab, knuckles bone white. "You always made excuses for him when he treated you like dirt. You made me look like a jealous bitch instead of admitting to yourself what was really going on. We were supposed to be best friends."

Alicia huffed. "Best friends? Yeah, right. You were too busy hanging around with that loser Corey to even notice me anymore."

"So, I wasn't allowed another friend? Is that it?

That's why you refused to believe me? That's why you cut me off and made fun of me behind my back?" Hurt and rejection cut into Lenna like their friendship had ended only yesterday.

"You were drifting away from me!" shouted Alicia. "Replacing me with Corey. What was I supposed to do? If I believed you, then I would've had no one left."

"You lied to yourself instead of facing the truth," said Lenna. "You tossed me out of your life for popularity, a bunch of fake friends, and a cheating boyfriend. I thought our friendship meant more to you than that."

Sure, they had changed, and their likes and interests drifted further apart as they graduated from middle school into high school—Lenna preferring fashion and alternative film to cheerleading and hanging at the mall with the "cool kids." But that didn't mean things had to turn so sour between them. They could've still been friends while they were off doing their own things with new people. They could still have been there for each other like they had always been.

Alicia's posture drooped. "It's not that simple."

"It is," said Lenna, swiping the air with her hand. "If you had dumped his ass back then, maybe you wouldn't be in this mess. I would never have left you alone."

"You already had," said Alicia, walking away.

Lenna followed her and spoke to her back. "No. If you felt that way, then you could've told me. We could've fixed it. But that's your problem. You never open up to people. You never let anyone in. Not really."

"Shut up," said Alicia, voice breaking. "If you were really my best friend, then you should've seen I needed you. I tried to kill myself and you weren't there."

Lenna froze.

"Yeah," said Alicia, spinning to face her again. "I was going through hell, and you didn't even see it. So don't you dare judge me for staying with the only person I had left."

Silence fell, tension thick in the air.

Lenna's arms fell to her side. How could she have been so blind? How could she have missed something so big in her friend's life?

"When did you ...," she mumbled, unable to say the words.

"A couple weeks after we had our big fight. Turns out I'm bipolar. I told everyone I went on vacation, but I'd swallowed a bunch of pills and ended up in the hospital. It destroyed my mom and dad. They blamed themselves, and I promised I would never do anything like that again. That's why I know I never got high, okay?"

Alicia went over to her drawer by the wall. She passed straight through, out of sight, and lay down with her dead body.

Lenna was numb.

She had no idea. Not once did she see it.

How could things have been so bad without her noticing? Sure, Alicia had changed, turned cold and mean toward her, toward everyone who wasn't part of the popular clique. Lenna saw all of that yet failed to see what was truly going on behind it. She'd been so hurt over their fracturing friendship, so angry, that she didn't stop to wonder *why*.

How could she have been so blind? How could she have missed something so important? Alicia had been there for Lenna after her mom, when she needed her most. Knowing what she knew now, Lenna couldn't say the same for herself.

"Hey, honey," came her dad's voice as he walked in. "What are you doing?"

Lenna cleared her throat and tried to pull herself together. "I came down to check the clients were all ready for tomorrow."

"I did them this afternoon," he said, putting a box down on the counter next to the deep-bottomed sink. "Figured you might not want to come here for a while. If you want, I can get someone in to help until after Alicia's funeral."

He still wore his coat and gloves, keys jingling in his pocket. She hadn't even heard him arrive home.

"It's fine," she said, arms wrapped around herself.

"The school called. Said you were upset and left math class."

Lenna closed her eyes. "Dad, I don't want to talk about it."

He shrugged out of his jacket and leaned against the counter. "It's important to talk about it. How are you feeling?"

Lenna looked over to Alicia's drawer. "Let's go upstairs."

"You're stalling," he said, waiting for her to answer.

Alicia didn't say anything, didn't come out from her drawer.

"I don't know what to feel," said Lenna, going over to her dad. What did it matter if Alicia heard her? She probably didn't care about anything she had to say. Lenna didn't blame her.

Her dad pulled her in for a hug. "I get it."

"You do?" she asked, slumping into him.

"You and Alicia weren't talking and now she's gone and everything is weird and complicated."

"It is." He didn't know the half of it.

Lenna sighed, her shoulders drooping.

"Things were so much easier when we were kids, you know? We didn't care about what we were wearing, or who was cool and who wasn't. There weren't any boys in the mix to complicate things, or dumb high school politics. It was just us. Simple."

Her dad nodded, understanding as always. He let out a little laugh. "I remember chasing you both around the house one day right before I had a service. You'd decided that the décor was too boring and thought a bit of color would help. Cue to me running after two little terrors in finger-paint-splattered dresses with pink and yellow handprints."

Lenna laughed despite her sorrow, recalling the glee of sprinting through the house and ducking through the rows of seats in the service room to avoid her dad's clutches.

"Or how about the time Mr. Santos and I had to go around town to get Alicia's mom's jewelry back after you both decided you'd have an impromptu yard sale and sell it all?"

"We were collecting money for the kitties at the rescue center," Lenna said, laughing again at her and Alicia's old antics. They thought they were being philanthropists instead of junior thieves. Alicia even said the mayor might give them medals for their efforts.

"I think Mrs. Santos wanted to leave you and her daughter at the rescue center that day." Her dad laughed. "You two definitely kept us on our toes, that's for sure."

"Yeah," Lenna replied, her laughter fading. "I don't even know when things began to change between us. It snuck up on us, and the next thing I knew, we were fighting."

"It's funny," he said, putting his jacket over her shoulders. "People talk all the time about how hard it is breaking up with their boyfriends or girlfriends, but they never talk about how difficult it is when you break up with your friends. It can be just as bad, heck, worse even. You and Alicia had been inseparable since kindergarten."

Lenna listened, stealing a look at the silver unit.

"It happens all the time. People change, they grow apart. You argue, say and do things you don't mean. Sometimes it ends bad. It's okay to still be angry with her and mourn her at the same time. The reason you girls were so mad was because you loved each other. It wouldn't have affected you the way it did otherwise. It would've been no big deal, right?"

Lenna nodded, clenching her jaw to stop her glistening eyes from spilling.

"Maybe you would've eventually patched things up, maybe not. You'll never know now, but you girls had history, and you can't rewrite that."

Lenna had gone through so much with Alicia. They'd been fixtures in each other's lives for as long as she could remember. Long, glorious summers filled with bike rides and water fights, countless sleepovers staying up way past their bedtime. They'd been joined at the hip since they were knee high. If only things had stayed that way.

"Come on," said her dad, walking to the door. "There's a gallon of ice cream in the freezer with our names on it."

"I'll be right up," said Lenna.

Her dad was right. She and Alicia did have history, and while she may not be able to change the past, she would do all she could now, in the present. She would do everything in her power to find the one who'd stolen Alicia's future. She'd find her killer and make sure they paid the price for what they'd done.

Lenna took one last look at Alicia's drawer and turned off the lights.

Chapter 9

Rain fell from the heavens, the sound drowning out the silence of night in a soundtrack to accompany Lenna's incessant thoughts.

The full moon took its monthly place at the top of the sky and illuminated her room with a white glow. The old oak tree by her window moved with the howling wind, its bald branches creating twisted shadows along her floor and up her wall.

There were so many questions she didn't have answers to. What happened to Alicia that night, and why could Lenna see her now? She'd never seen a ghost before. If that's what she was. Lenna ran a hand over the purple skin at her shoulder, peeking through the strap of her tank top, the matching mark on her forearm still sore. Ghosts weren't supposed to be able to touch you, and Alicia had walked right through Corey.

Was something wrong with her? Would she always see Alicia now? Would Alicia's ghost follow her around for the rest of her life?

Every question sprouted two more, like cutting the heads off a Hydra. Only this wasn't some Greek myth. It was reality.

Maybe if she managed to find out the truth about what happened to Alicia, Lenna could get some answers about herself too. She couldn't just close her eyes and pretend nothing was wrong. Whether Lenna liked it or not, she found herself in the center of something. Something dark.

The moon was too bright and Lenna rolled out of bed with a groan to close her curtains. Something caught her eye outside.

Someone was standing in her front yard, and he was looking right up at her.

Lenna stepped back, her heart banging against her chest. She glanced at her alarm clock, noting the time. No one had any good reason to be in her yard watching her, especially at one in the morning out in the pouring rain.

Lenna crept to the window again and peeked out. He hadn't moved since being discovered. She clung to her curtains. They locked eyes with each other, his gaze intense. Lenna had never seen him before. He was tall, dressed in a leather jacket and jeans, all black against pale skin.

He couldn't have been much older than she was. His hair was short, dark brown or black from what she could make out. It clung to his face in wet curls and waves.

His features seemed harsh in the skewed light, half of his face in shadow. The half she did see looked sharp, his deep-set eyes never once leaving her.

Lenna shuddered. Whatever he wanted, it sure as shit wasn't a date to prom. Her dad was just down the hall and she went to get him, but she stopped as the thought occurred to her.

What if the boy was a ghost too? Her dad wouldn't see him. Maybe Alicia wasn't the only dead person she could see.

Praying that wasn't the case, she glanced back out the window to get a better look at him. Alicia had tell-tale signs that she no longer walked with the living. Maybe he would too.

He was gone.

Lenna stayed by the window for a long time, waiting and watching for signs of the dark stranger. He didn't return, but the feeling she was being watched never left.

——————————

Chapter 10

——————————

Lenna cradled her second cup of coffee in her hands as she stood at the bay window of the reception room, looking out into the front yard.

She didn't get much sleep after catching the creepy stalker watching her. Images of walking dead people haunted her dreams.

She wore a long black sweater to cover her bruises along with some skinny jeans and her favorite pink Converse wedges. Her hair was in a simple braid, a testament to how tired she felt.

Stifling a yawn, she took out her cell and called Corey.

"What time do you call this?" he whined.

Lenna leaned her head against the windowpane, looking out at the dew-covered lawn. "Six a.m. Listen, tell your mom you're sick and come over when she leaves. I have an idea."

Corey scoffed. "Like that will work."

"Oh, right." Having a nurse for a mom meant Corey missed out on the wonders of playing sick for the day and watching crappy daytime TV. "Say you're too bummed about Alicia or something. Just come over as soon as you can."

"Aye, aye, captain."

Lenna hung up and finished her coffee as she waited for her dad. He had a funeral first thing and she planned to catch him before he went out so he didn't have time to fuss over her.

He came downstairs a while later, tying his tie. "You're up early."

"Couldn't sleep." She sat down and stared into her empty mug, solemn. It might have been overkill, but she needed this to work.

"I'm just having a hard time with everything," she said, not needing to lie. "I saw Alicia's empty desk in class yesterday and I can't stop thinking about how she'll never put on a beautiful dress and go to prom. She'll never graduate and leave for college."

"If you're not up to going in today, I can give the school a call. I'm sure it won't be the first call they've had like that this week."

Bingo.

"If that's okay with you," said Lenna.

"I'll give them a call before I head off. I'll be out most of the day, but if you need anything, you let me know, okay? Just call my cell." He kissed the top of her head. "Go try and get some sleep."

Lenna went to her room until she heard her dad leave. Corey arrived an hour later wiping sleep from his eyes. He pulled a chair out at the table but she pushed it back under before he could sit down. "Keep your jacket on," she told him, going into the cabinet and throwing him some granola bars.

"Why, where are we going?" he asked, ripping one open and taking a bite.

"To pay our respects."

***

Lenna pulled up to the sidewalk and put the hearse in park. The rain from last night had run dry, but the wind kept up, stubborn and determined to rid the trees of any remaining leaves.

"Whose house is this?" asked Corey.

Lenna took off her seat belt. "Alicia's."

Lenna hoped she'd made the right decision by coming here. Alicia's parents would be very fragile right now, but they might know something that could help.

Corey held his hand over the seat belt button. "Are you sure this is a good idea?"

She filled him in on her argument with Alicia.

"Wow, that's a lot," said Corey, wiping his glasses with his T-shirt.

Lenna worried at her lip. "Yeah."

Corey took her hand in his. "Len, what she did wasn't your fault. She had no right putting any of that on you, and don't forget how horrible she was to you back then. I was there for it all and it wasn't cute. She was the one who cut you out and pushed you away."

"I know all that," Lenna said, "and I love you for always sticking up for me, but I have to do this. She was going through a lot back then, and especially now. I think deep down she's still the nice girl I was friends with."

"Deep, deep, down," muttered Corey.

"I'm doing it for myself too. I don't know why I can see her, but there has to be a reason. Maybe if I dig into what happened to Alicia, I'll find answers about myself."

Corey considered her for a moment, then gave her a smile and said, "Okay, I'm in." He undid his seat belt and got out of the car. "Do you have a strategy before we go in?"

Lenna followed, locking the doors and wrapping her coat around her. "I was thinking we could just wing it."

"Of course you were."

Lenna's palms began to sweat. She hadn't seen Alicia's parents in so long. "Come on, it'll be fine. We go in as grieving friends, play it by ear, and see what they have to say. Hopefully they can shed some light on what Alicia did that day or where she went after school."

Corey fidgeted with his sleeves. "I'm not good at this stuff. What if I say something wrong and make things worse?"

"Hey," she said, "you're the smart one in this equation. I need you in this."

"Fine, let's get this over with."

Lenna punched him playfully. "That's the spirit."

At the bottom of the street, pushed on eagerly by the wind, they reached their destination. The house was like Alicia—beautiful and in your face. The walls were a rich yellow, crowned with a terra-cotta roof. It stood three floors high and had autumn-kissed ivy running up one side in lush shades of orange. It looked like it belonged in the Spanish countryside rather than plain old Denwood.

They walked up the path of the manicured front yard and came face-to-face with Detective Gibbs.

"Hi, Detective," said Corey, shifting around like he was guilty of something.

"Why aren't you two in school?" asked Gibbs in hello, checking her watch. "You're going to be late."

"We're here to see Alicia's mom and dad," said Lenna, eyeing the detective's gun. "What are you doing here?"

Gibbs's badge hung from her neck and glittered like she polished it at night. "That's official police business."

"Are you any further ahead with the case?" asked Corey.

"I'm following a couple of leads. Rest assured, we are doing everything we can to get to the bottom of what happened."

"What do you think happened?" asked Lenna.

They knew Alicia had been killed, but that didn't mean the police did. Lenna had hoped by now the police would have announced Alicia's case as an official murder investigation, but they seemed to be at least one step behind her and Cor

Gibbs opened her mouth to say something, then stopped. "I don't have time for this," she said, continuing down the path. "I better not see you both around town today playing hooky."

Lenna and Corey watched her go and then walked up the patio stairs. Lenna brushed a hand over the varnished mahogany door. Their most expensive coffin was made of the same type of wood.

She rang the doorbell and Alicia's mom, Camila, opened the door with a forced smile, misplaced with her sad eyes.

"Hi, Mrs. Santos."

Camila Santos was basically a forty-year-old version of Alicia, now with the hollowed cheeks of grief. She wore a black day dress, and her body curled in like she wanted to disappear and hide.

"Lenna." She embraced her tight, but stopped and froze. She clung onto a set of rosary beads around her neck and stepped back. "Is something wrong? Did your dad send you?"

Shit. So much for not upsetting them.

"No, not at all. Everything's fine. We're taking good care of Alicia. I just wanted to come over and pay my respects."

"Oh." Mrs. Santos let go of her rosary. "That's

sweet of you." She stepped to the side and waved them in. "Please, you'll both catch your death in that cold wind."

Mrs. Santos stopped at her choice of words. Her face crumpled, but she closed her eyes and took a deep breath, pulling herself back together with commendable determination. She led them into the living room.

"This is Corey Martin," said Lenna, making introductions. "He was friends with Alicia too."

"Hi, Corey," said Mrs. Santos, distracted and fidgeting where she stood. "Please sit down. Can I get either of you anything? A soda, some coffee maybe? I was just about to put on another pot. We've had a lot of people visiting as you can imagine."

"Two coffees would be great, thank you," answered Corey, polite as ever.

Lenna looked around, the house much the same as it had been the last time she'd visited before she and Alicia stopped being friends. Being there brought up so many memories.

Lenna's favorite hiding spot was still there. She'd sneak behind Mrs. Santos's piano, which sat in the corner of the room, and cover her mouth to stop from laughing whenever Alicia grew near.

Beyond was the kitchen where they used to bake cookies together, wolfing down batter every time Mrs. Santos turned her back until there was hardly any left to put in the oven. Lenna always liked spending time with Alicia and her mom, especially after her own mother passed.

Lenna gave herself a shake and focused on the present. She and Corey sat on a floral-patterned sofa just as Mr. Santos came into the room, passing his wife with a light touch to her arm. As soon as he saw them, his eyes narrowed.

"Who are you two?" Alicia may have gotten her looks from her mom, but the attitude and forthrightness were inherited from her father.

"You remember Lenna, Fred," said Mrs. Santos before heading into the kitchen.

"You Gallows's kid?" he asked Lenna.

"Yes," said Lenna, uncomfortable under his stare. She didn't really know Mr. Santos. He worked out of town a lot so she barely saw him whenever she used to come over.

He was a handsome man, with a head full of dark hair and a short, manicured beard. Muscles showed through the sleeves of his crumpled shirt like he spent more time at the gym than at home.

He studied them with bloodshot eyes and sat down in a chair near the mantelpiece that acted as the focal point of the room. A crucifix hung above it, looking down at a line of framed pictures of Alicia through the years. It began with a picture of her as a baby and carried on. Lenna recognized the most recent one at the end as that year's school picture, the background the same as the one Lenna's dad kept of her in his wallet.

Corey bobbed his head to the floor, careful not to be seen. A bunch of empty beer cans lay at Mr.

Santos's feet. Someone had started early. Either that or he hadn't been to bed yet.

"We're sorry for your loss, sir," said Corey, emulating Lenna's funeral voice. She placed a hand on his knee to stop his bouncing leg.

Mr. Santos leaned forward and focused on Corey. "Why haven't I seen you before?" He moved over to Lenna. "And I can't recall the last time Alicia spoke about you."

Corey began to stutter.

"We didn't hang out much outside of school anymore," Lenna said before Corey said something that wouldn't slide.

"Alicia had a lot of friends," added Corey.

That seemed to satisfy him a bit. Alicia had been one of the most popular kids at school. No way could he know all her friends. Mr. Santos bent down and picked up the last beer in the six-pack before him. He cracked open the can and took a long gulp.

Mrs. Santos came back, breaking the uncomfortable silence as she put down a tray of fresh coffee, the aroma filling Lenna's nose. Lenna thanked her and sipped the strong blend.

"Thanks for coming over," said Mrs. Santos, sitting down on the plush sofa next to them. "We've had a lot of Alicia's friends come by this week."

"I can imagine. Everybody loved her at school. I don't know how she managed to juggle all her friends on top of cheering and her dancing," said Corey, playing his part.

Mrs. Santos took a tissue from the box sitting on the glass coffee table and dabbed her eyes. "She's a very busy girl, my Alicia. Always rushing around."

Lenna reached out and put her hand over Mrs. Santos's. "It's been such a shock for everyone. Do you know where she went that night?"

"We don't know what she was doing that night." Mrs. Santos sniffed. "She told us that she was staying with her friend Kayla. We called over there when Alicia didn't come home the next morning, and the girl had no idea what we were talking about."

"Alicia wasn't there?" asked Lenna.

"Kayla hadn't spoken to her since school on Friday."

"Did anyone else see her?" Lenna pressed. Detective Gibbs would've told Alicia's parents if the police had heard from anyone.

"No one's come forward with anything useful. Someone must have seen her," Mr. Santos said, crushing his now-empty can and dropping it next to the others. His eyes scrutinized them.

"If only someone could give us information, anything at all. We just can't understand why our baby would say she was going to Kayla's when she wasn't." Mrs. Santos got up from her seat and picked up one of the pictures of Alicia from the mantelpiece, her beautiful smile radiant and full of life. "Someone must know what happened to her."

"Did the police find anything that might help

figure out where she went?" Corey asked, practical and logical as ever.

Mrs. Santos put the picture back in its place. "All they found was her cell phone, her purse, and a bit of ripped paper inside her jacket pocket."

"Did she make any calls that night?" asked Corey.

Looked like all those hours he spent watching cop shows were paying off. Lenna sat and listened.

"We don't know." Mrs. Santos's voice shook, on the verge of tears again. "The rain damaged the phone, so we can't look to check. Detective Gibbs said they're contacting the cell phone company to get the call records, but that could take a while."

So the police had nothing so far. Great. "Do you have the piece of paper you mentioned?" said Lenna.

"Why?" Mr. Santos asked. "It's just the edge of a flyer or something. Junk. It had probably been in her jacket for ages."

Lenna turned her attention to Alicia's dad. He was edgy. "We might recognize it if it's something to do with school," she explained, keeping her cool.

"The police have it, dear. The detective left a photo of it, though. Wait, and I'll go and get it." Mrs. Santos went back into the kitchen, talking as she went. "It's only a small bit, nothing's written on it."

As soon as she had gone out of earshot, Mr. Santos turned on them. "Why are you two really here? What are you up to?"

"Nothing, sir," stuttered Corey. "We're just paying our respects."

Mr. Santos scowled. "Paying your respects by quizzing us about our daughter?"

"We didn't mean to upset you," said Lenna, stepping in as the big man rose from his chair. "We're just trying to understand what happened to Alicia."

"I made a point of knowing who my girl associated herself with," he said to Lenna. "Last time she mentioned you, she didn't have anything nice to say."

"Mr. Santos, we—"

"No," he snapped. "I want you out of my house. Get out of my sight."

"Here you go." Mrs. Santos came in and handed them the evidence photo, oblivious to her husband's outburst. She stopped and took in the room, all of them up on their feet.

"Is everything all right?" She looked at her husband. "Fred?"

"Yes," said Corey. He took the photo and put it in his pocket. "Thank you."

"We'd better go," said Lenna, moving them toward the door.

"So soon?" asked Mrs. Santos.

"We're late for school," said Lenna, "but we wanted to come over."

"Oh, okay, dears." Mrs. Santos walked them to the door. She gave them each a hug, holding on a little too long. "Thank you so much for stopping by."

Chapter 11

"That was weird," said Corey, sitting next to Lenna in her hearse.

Lenna leaned back in her seat. "I guess he's just trying to deal. It can't be easy." They had been trying to help, but their sloppy attempt at recon only resulted in pissing off Mr. Santos.

Corey raised his eyebrows. "Or he could be worried we're snooping around and asking too many questions because he has something to hide."

"You've watched one too many horror movies," said Lenna.

Corey shifted in his seat to face her. "I'm serious. The guy gave off some bad vibes."

Lenna didn't buy it. "Bad vibes and killing your daughter are two very different things."

Corey held up his hands. "All I'm saying is that I don't think we should rule him out. Just because he's her dad doesn't mean he's automatically innocent. It wouldn't be the first time something like that happened."

Corey had a point. How many times had she seen stuff like that on the news? In most homicides, the victim knew their killer. Families killed their own. Lenna's dad had done a funeral for a family before she was born after the father killed his wife and three kids because he'd gone bankrupt and lost the house. He put a bullet in his brain when he was done.

"You're right." Lenna resigned herself to the possibility. "What's on that piece of paper?"

Corey dug it out of his pocket and examined the photo. "Like they said, nothing to really go on." He handed it to her. "Just the top of some kind of logo. It's been torn off so most of it's on the other half."

"Which we don't have," said Lenna, examining the photo. It was nothing but a blue background and a cut-off yellow circle. Whatever it had been for, they had no way of telling.

"We should speak with Kayla," said Lenna. "Maybe she was covering for Alicia if she told her parents that's where she was going." Mr. Santos was always strict with his daughter, maybe more than Lenna realized. Alicia could have been doing something or gone somewhere she wasn't allowed. If she planned on breaking his rules, then saying she'd be at Kayla's would be a good alibi.

"But then why hasn't Kayla told that to the police?" asked Corey. "If she knew something, wouldn't they know already?"

"She might still know something." Gibbs would've questioned Kayla by now, but just because Kayla had spoken to the police didn't mean she'd told them the truth. Best friends covered for each other, and maybe Kayla had taken that further by letting whatever she knew about Alicia go to the grave with her.

"She'll be in school," noted Corey. "So we can't do that right now."

Damn it. They couldn't take the day off being upset over Alicia and then turn up a few hours later questioning people. They'd need to wait to speak with Alicia's new best friend. Since Lenna didn't know Kayla's address, that would have to wait until tomorrow.

"What do the investigators do in those crime shows you watch?" asked Lenna. They still had most of the day left. There had to be something they could do to try to get some answers.

"The first thing they do is go to the scene of the crime."

The choice of words got to Lenna. Alicia's death was a crime, and someone needed to pay.

"Which in this case is the park." Lenna had always liked the park. Her mom used to take her there. It was filled with memories of collecting wildflowers and pushing each other on the swings, Lenna calling for her mom to push her higher and higher so she could reach the bright blue sky. Now the place she held so dear was the site of a murder.

"Or at least that's where they found the body,"

mused Corey. "She could have died somewhere else and been dumped there."

Dumped. Left like a piece of trash. Lenna's nails shaped crescent moons into her palms as she thought about the shrine of pictures on the mantelpiece and how Mrs. Santos cradled one close to her like a newborn baby. That shrine was all she had left of her daughter. Her baby had been taken from her.

She turned on the engine. "Okay, the crime scene it is."

D enwood's one and only park lay near the edge of town, adjacent to acres of forest that went on for miles. In the summer, people flocked there in the hundreds to make the most of the good weather, but Lenna and Corey only saw a handful of people in the late October morning, most of them dog walkers like the person who'd happened across Alicia's dead body.

Lenna didn't know where exactly in the park Alicia had been found, and any crime scene tape the police may have put up was gone.

The gates to the eastside entrance had a line of flowers tied to it and the surrounding fence, so they took that as a sign and drove in on that side.

"Man, I forgot how big this place was." Corey zipped up his jacket against the cold.

Mounds of leaves dotted the park, the only green

left coming from the grassy fields. Aside from a play-ground at the far end, there wasn't much there except a bunch of benches scattered around and the lake that sat near the forest edge.

The gravel crunched under their shoes as they wandered, keeping off the wet grass and walking on the pathways. "I still don't get why Alicia came out here by herself at night," said Lenna.

Corey stopped and spun around, taking in their whole view of the park from where they stood. "I definitely think Alicia was brought here. Maybe even after she died."

"I think so too." Alicia wasn't the type of girl who liked to hang out in a park at night, especially with the weather they'd had over the last couple weeks. They'd had a storm Friday night.

"What I don't get is how she was left. If I killed someone, I'd try to hide the body. I wouldn't leave it out for someone to find easily." Lenna pointed behind them to the edge of the park. "The forest seems like a much more logical place to hide a body. There'd be less chance of it being found, especially if they buried it. The lake's right there too. Weigh down the body so it doesn't float back up and you've got yourself an aquatic grave."

Corey raised an eyebrow at her.

"What?" she asked.

"Nothing, just remind me to never piss you off."

Lenna laughed but quickly grew serious again and linked arms with Corey. "You know what I mean, though. Why just leave Alicia out in the open like that?"

They walked on, benefitting from each other's body heat. "Maybe whoever did this wanted the body to be found," said Corey.

"Or," she added, "they had to leave in a hurry before they were able to dispose of her."

They hadn't gotten very far from where they'd parked when she felt it. "Wait," said Lenna, putting a hand out to stop her friend from going any farther.

"What?" Corey asked. "Do you see something?"

The cold sensation she'd experienced while being around Alicia crept upon her. The feeling was as unmistakable as the smell of a dead body; you only had to experience it once to never forget it.

She followed the sensation, the feeling growing stronger with each step. It traveled all over her body, the tips of her fingers like icicles.

Corey caught up to her, his breath making little clouds. "Lenna?"

"This way." Lenna veered off the gravel path onto the grass field and quickened her pace. They headed toward a patch in the field near some overgrowth and a crowd of bushes. The feeling drew her forward like a magnet. She stopped dead in her tracks right next to the bushes. The space around her felt removed from the rest of the park, different somehow. Hollow. Something had been taken. A life.

"This is where she died," she told Corey, even though she had no evidence to back up her certainty. A particular spot caught her attention. It lured her closer, her mind fixed on it. Standing before it, a turn of vertigo hit her, muddling her mind, thoughts swimming against a tide.

"There's something there, I can feel it." Lenna reached toward the open air with her hand, unable to help herself. Time seemed to slow as her fingers touched something and a searing pain like she'd never known attacked her from the inside out.

Lenna closed her eyes and screamed.

Chapter 12

The pain left her as quickly as it came. Lenna opened her eyes.

From what she could make out, she was still in the park. It was dark, everything cast in deep shadow. Corey was nowhere to be seen, but she wasn't alone.

All around her were forms and shapes, black as night as they moved within the shadows that covered everything, so dark she couldn't see beyond twenty yards. They hovered near, creating a circle around her like a pack of hungry wolves.

Lenna backed away, only to find more of them behind her.

They pushed at each other, fighting to get to the front of the horde. A fight broke out between two of them, semi-human in shape, as they pushed and scrambled to get closer to Lenna. The larger of the two seized the other by the arm and tore it off.

The appendage flew in the air, evaporating into nothing before it could hit the ground. The armless form let out an earth-shattering cry and fell back into the mass. Lenna looked for a gap in the crowd, somewhere she could run, but they had her surrounded.

Voices cried out to her, begging for help, for someone to save them. Whispers tickled her ears, some of them sinister and warped, their voices like scratches on a chalkboard.

They all spoke at once, becoming too much for her to handle.

A shape broke out from the gathering swarm, walking on all fours with arching shoulders. Predatory.

Before she could move, it sprung on its hind legs and pounced at her.

Lenna screamed and fell to the ground, raising her arms in defense. The shape crashed into her, but it didn't hurt. The thing burst into an explosion of shadow upon impact, dissipating like the arm of the other creature.

The others around her screeched and hissed as they backed away and disappeared into the darkness beyond.

The voices lingered. Their pleas ate into her soul, so desperate and insistent that she wanted to help them but didn't know how. Part of her wanted to reach out to those begging for her. To let them in.

No. Lenna pushed herself back to her feet and slapped her hands to her ears, trying to block out the screams.

The shrubbery next to her, the grass under her feet —everything in this place seemed devoid of color, like the very life had been drained out of the world.

White clouds came with every panicked breath but her body didn't feel the cold, didn't feel anything, like she was stuck in some creepy dream. A nightmare of her own making.

The hollowness in her chest remained, the sense of wrongness thick in the air.

Something lay on the grass before her, different from the shadowed creatures. Taking a slow step forward, the form came into view as flashes of lightning split the sky.

Lenna gasped as she realized what it was, or more correctly, who.

"Alicia," Lenna called, falling to her knees before her, Alicia's eyes glossy and unable to focus. "Alicia. Alicia, it's me. Come on, we need to get out of here."

Alicia's hair stuck to her forehead and beads of sweat clung to her skin. Lenna tried calling to her again, but she didn't react. She was out of it.

Lenna reached for Alicia to give her a shake, but her hands went right through and touched the grass underneath like Alicia was a hologram. A ghost.

Alicia needed help.

A beam of light came from Lenna's left. A set of twin spotlights fell over Alicia as she struggled to breathe.

"Help!" Lenna cried. Her voice echoed into nothingness, vanishing into the dark abyss like the forms of shadow. Alicia was ashen in the colorless void, her body twitching in places it shouldn't.

Someone, or something, came into view from where the light shone. Lenna's attention snapped to it, the voices still whispering in her head fading out into a niggling radio static.

A set of legs blocked her view of the light as someone stood in front of them. Lenna looked up to see the rough outline of a head, too dark to make out anything other than its human shape.

It looked down over Alicia's body, then back behind it. Lenna followed its gaze to the source of light. As her eyes adjusted to the stark contrast of their pitch-black surroundings, she saw the outline of something. A car idled just a few feet from them, its red paint boldly standing out among the darkness of the shadows all around it, like blood under moonlight.

The lights shining on them were headlights, running along the grass and over Alicia. Her chest heaved up and down now, her head moving from side to side in fevered panic.

"Do something!" screamed Lenna at the shrouded person staring down at them. "Why aren't you doing anything?"

Lenna moved nearer whoever it was and grabbed for one of their legs. Her clutch went right through, just like it had with Alicia. Her head pounded from the tortured cries in her mind, hair blowing to the side, along with the blades of grass in a wind she couldn't feel. The beginning of an overnight storm. A storm, she realized, that had already happened.

Rain crashed down, falling onto Alicia's struggling form. Lenna's heart ached at the sight of her, but she couldn't help. This had already happened. This was when Alicia died.

Lenna glared up at the person who still stood over them. This was them. Whoever had done this to Alicia was right before her, their face cloaked in thick shadow and impossible to make out.

Alicia cried out. Her lips quivered and saliva ran down her chin. She reached out with her hand to the person looking down at her, desperate for help.

Lenna watched the person turn and walk back toward the car. Not once did they look back.

Violent spasms shook Alicia, her whole body convulsing as foam escaped her lips.

"No," cried Lenna. She reached down and hovered her hand next to the dying girl's, unable to do anything as the inevitable happened.

Alicia clutched onto a ruby-colored rose, standing out from the dark hues of everything else like the car did. Gold foil was wrapped around the stem to prevent any pricks from its thorns. Alicia held it so tightly in her convulsions that the thorns tore through the foil and dug into her palm, releasing beads of blood that trickled down her fingers and into the soggy ground below.

The headlights moved as the car reversed, the driver leaving in a hurry. A deep, roaring anger swelled inside of Lenna as loud as the speeding engine. Alicia clawed at her chest with her free hand, screaming in pain, so loud that Lenna could hear it over the voices, penetrating her core in a way she would never forget.

The stalk of the rose snapped. The screaming stopped, and a look of shock painted Alicia's face as her limbs went limp.

The lights went out just as Alicia took her last, shallow breath.

L enna opened her eyes and took in a huge gulp of air, color all around her. Corey held her in his arms, shaking her and calling her name. She blinked against the light, like she'd been asleep for hours and woke up to the sun shining on her face.

"Len, please snap out of it."

The shadows were gone. She couldn't hear them anymore. Alicia's body wasn't there.

Lenna pinched the bridge of her nose, her mind groggy. A throbbing in her head announced the beginnings of a killer migraine. She peered up at Corey's stricken face.

"Hey."

Corey pulled her toward him and squeezed her in a tight, desperate embrace. "Jesus, Len. Don't you ever do that again, you hear me?"

"I'm fine," she said. She didn't think she'd ever be fine again.

"Like hell you're fine. What happened? You just fell and started screaming and rolling around. I thought you were having a seizure."

Her voice cracked when she told him. "I saw it."

"You're bleeding," said Corey, distracted. He pushed his arm up into the sleeve of his shirt and wiped gently at her nose. When he pulled back, she saw a smear of scarlet against the light blue fabric.

She put her fingers to her nose and felt the warm blood. Two circlets of red stained her fingertips. "It's just a nosebleed."

"Caused by whatever the hell just happened."

That didn't matter. Not after what she'd just witnessed. "But I saw it. I saw Alicia die."

Corey went quiet, eyes scared. "Who did it?" he asked.

Lenna groaned. "I don't know. Everything was covered in shadow. I never saw the person's face."

"Person—so just one killer?"

Lenna nodded, the simple action making her dizzy. "I couldn't tell. There was a car, a red one. There may have been more people inside."

"Male or female?" Corey asked, sitting her up straighter.

She tried to think back, careful to focus on anything that might give the person away, but she came up short. "Honestly, it could have been either. They were just a blur."

"Could you make out what they were wearing? Pants, a skirt? Anything that might hint at gender?"

She sighed. "Nothing. There was too much going on. I had no idea what was happening or where I was. There were a bunch of these, things, these shadow-like creatures surrounding me and talking inside my head. Alicia died right in front of me."

Lenna brushed the blades of grass around them. "She died right here."

"Did it take long for her to—?" Corey stumbled over the words. "Did she suffer?"

"I don't think she really knew what was happening, but she was so scared. She died terrified and confused and alone. She died right here with no one beside her. They just left her here. Drove off and left her."

Lenna tried to get up, her head protesting loudly, but Corey held her in place. "You need to just sit for a while."

"How could they do that to her?" She looked into her friend's deep blue eyes. "How could they leave her to die alone out here in the middle of the night?"

"We're not going to let them get away with it," Corey said, his voice unwavering, every bit the rock she needed him to be. "We'll find whoever did this, and they'll pay for it."

Her hands shook. Images of how Alicia died flashed in her head, forever etched in her mind now. Some things just couldn't be unseen.

"No wonder she can't remember anything about that night. She didn't know where she was or what was happening to her," Lenna thought out loud. "I could feel how scared she was. I watched her die. I watched her take her last breath. I saw it like I had been there."

Then she remembered something.

Lenna got up and staggered toward the exact spot where Alicia had died. She bent down and searched through the grass with her fingers. Corey called her name, trying to get her to stop, but she ignored him and scanned the area, manic in her search. It had to be there somewhere. The wind could've moved it.

Beside the tainted spot grew a bush that still clung stubbornly to its leaves, yellow as they were. She put her hand under the brush as chunky grains of frozen dirt found their way under her painted fingernails.

A sharp point stung her index finger and she yanked her hand out. She stared down at her clenched fist and saw blood trickle down from the thorns than punctured her skin. Blood the same color as the broken, gold-wrapped rose she held in her hand.

Chapter 13

Lenna stopped at the door outside their storage room for the dead.

Her nose had stopped bleeding, her head pulsing despite the two aspirin she'd popped. She dropped Corey off, making sure they were both home in time for their parents getting in from work. Her dad was away getting takeout, so she slipped downstairs before he returned.

Preparing herself for the intense cold, she entered.

Alicia sat on one of the metal slabs near the back, close to her drawer. Her death replayed in Lenna's mind, on repeat since she'd left the shadow place.

"What do you, and that ridiculous hair, want?" asked Alicia.

Lenna took a deep breath. Alicia knew, more than anyone, which buttons to push to get a rise from her, but they had no time for arguments and name-calling.

Lenna dragged in a chair from the other room and closed the door. "To talk."

"I have nothing to say to you. Just leave me alone." Alicia picked at her nails, which would no longer grow.

Lenna sat down, her bones aching. "Alicia, I didn't know you were hurting like that back then. All I knew was that you were hurting me. I'm sorry for my part, but I wasn't the only one in the wrong."

"It doesn't matter anymore," said Alicia, not meeting her eyes. "It's done, so stop pretending like you care."

"I do care." From what she could tell, Lenna was the only friend who did.

Alicia huffed.

Lenna rubbed her forehead. "Believe me or not, that's up to you, but I can see you for a reason. Nobody else has woken up dead in this place. Whatever's going on with me has something to do with you. It's linked somehow, I can feel it. We don't need to be friends, but we need to work together to find out what all this is. It's a win-win—I learn about why I'm the only one who can see you, and you find out who killed you."

Alicia didn't reply, but she wasn't telling her to leave either.

"I saw how you died," said Lenna.

Alicia's head snapped toward her. "What do you mean?"

"I saw it. Part of these apparent 'gifts' I have," said Lenna, making air quotes. Gifts. She sure as hell wished they came with a receipt. It wasn't a gift; it was a curse.

"How did I die? Did you see who did it?" Alicia's hand covered her mouth, her dead eyes wide.

"I saw someone, but they were hidden and I couldn't make them out." Lenna stuck to the facts. Maybe Alicia not remembering that night was a small blessing. "You seemed out of it, from the drugs. I'm not a doctor, but it looked like you had a fit or a heart attack. You just started shaking, and then you stopped."

Lenna held up the broken rose. "Do you recognize this?"

Alicia surveyed it, the head hanging down from where it had snapped on the thorny stalk. The petals were bashed and dying, curled in at the edges in a decaying brown. "No, should I?"

"You were holding it as you died." Lenna noted Alicia's left hand and saw the marks from where the thorns had dug into her palm, the ones Detective Gibbs mentioned when she came knocking at their door. "Did someone give it to you? Maybe earlier that day?"

"I guess," said Alicia. "I don't know."

Trey could have given it to her.

"Any ideas as to why you might have been in the park?" Lenna asked, keeping thoughts of Trey to herself.

"See, that's the thing I don't get. I never go to the park." Alicia got up from the slab she sat on, or hovered on, or whatever it was that ghosts did to stay on solid things they could otherwise pass through. She paced the room, her staggered steps like the walking dead.

"It looked like you got there by car." If Alicia got in the car willingly, she most likely knew who killed her. If she was even with it enough to realize she was in a car.

"Everybody drives," said Alicia. "It could've been anyone."

The park and how she got there was a dead end right now, so Lenna moved on. "We went to your house and spoke with your parents this morning."

Alicia froze, her face stricken. "Are they okay?"

"They're trying their best to cope. They still seemed in shock over it all."

Alicia played with the bottom of her hair. "What if they think I've killed myself?"

Mr. and Mrs. Santos hadn't mentioned that to her and Corey, but Lenna doubted it hadn't crossed their minds. Alicia had tried to take her life before. "They don't know what to think," said Lenna. "They can only go with what the police have told them, which so far isn't much."

Alicia's eyes were far off. "I can't have them thinking I did that."

"Okay, then let's make sure that doesn't happen."

Alicia gathered herself and sat down closer to Lenna. "What do you need to know?"

Lenna leaned forward. "Your mom said you told them you were staying at Kayla's house. They called her when you didn't turn up the next day, and Kayla said she hadn't seen you since school."

"That doesn't mean much," said Alicia, flippant. "Kayla and I cover for each other all the time. My dad likes to keep a close eye on me, so I need to play it smart when I'm going out."

"A close eye on you?" Lenna asked, dread circling in her gut.

"You know what he's like, hanging crosses and stuff all over the house. He's super into God, and apparently God doesn't approve of me going to parties and hanging out with people Dad doesn't like."

"So, your dad didn't like you going out with certain people." Lenna considered that. Mr. Santos certainly hadn't liked her when she and Corey visited. Before then, he never really spoke to Lenna when she was over. "That must mean he likes Kayla?"

"She's the only friend I have he actually doesn't seem to mind."

Lenna treaded lightly around Mr. Santos. Alicia wouldn't react well to him being a potential suspect, and Lenna needed her on board. "If you weren't with Kayla that night, then who could you have been with? And why would you use her as a cover but not tell her about it? Surely, part of the whole setup is to have Kayla say you're with her if your parents call looking for you?"

Alicia sat for a while, mulling over Lenna's questions. Lenna was about to ask another when Alicia spoke.

"Trey," she said, refusing to look at her.

"What about him?" Lenna asked carefully.

Alicia flipped her hair. "He'd been begging me to take him back ever since we broke up. I could have caved. It's not like I haven't taken him back before. Kayla hates Trey, so if I did go out with him that night, I doubt I told her. She would've given me shit for it."

Lenna clenched her jaw, thinking of the rose. "You two could've been on a date."

"This doesn't mean you're right," Alicia snapped.

"I know." They sat in silence again for a moment, the tension thick in the air.

"Why doesn't she like him?" Lenna asked. Add Kayla's dislike to Ellie's and Zara's, not to mention her own, and it seemed like popular opinion to not like Trey.

"Who knows?" said Alicia. "But she's never liked him. Whenever I'd go back to him, she wouldn't talk to me for days." Alicia laughed. "She always said I'd never learn, and that if I kept going back, I'd end up pregnant before prom, yadda, yadda."

"That seems a little harsh."

"Yeah, but like I said, she's never liked him." Alicia didn't seem to think much of it. Then again, she hadn't seen how Kayla acted in the girl's bathroom.

"I guess that means I should talk with Trey," said Lenna.

Kayla too.

Chapter 14

Lenna cried out as Alicia died in the rain.

Haunted faces circled all around. They screamed at her, desperate for help. Shadows lingered in the corners, watching. They whispered thoughts into her ears, thoughts of blood, and vengeance, and sweet, sweet, death.

One came up behind her and brought its hands around her throat.

Lenna screamed.

Her eyes darted open and she sat up, not knowing where she was.

"Hey, hey, it's me, it's me."

Lenna's heart clattered around in her chest, her breathing labored.

Her dad sat on her bed, his voice soothing. "It's just a nightmare. You were screaming in your sleep."

Lenna blinked a few times and rubbed her eyes,

still hearing remnant whispers somewhere in the distance of her mind.

Her dad rubbed her arm. "Are you okay?"

She nodded.

"Do you need some more time off school? I'm worried about you."

"No, no, I should get back." She needed to talk to Trey and Kayla. "I'm fine, just a little rattled."

"Maybe getting back to normal will help," said her dad. "Should we still do movie night tomorrow?"

"Of course," said Lenna. Their midweek ritual of pizza, popcorn, and movies filled with gratuitous violence always made her feel better. "I'll help you get the next day's clients ready when I get home and we can squeeze two movies in."

"Okay, honey." Her dad got up and stopped at the door. "Try to go back to sleep. I love you."

"Love you too."

Her dad left, and his light snores sounded from down the hall soon after. Lenna wiped the cold sweat from her forehead and looked at her alarm clock. Two thirty in the morning. Lenna covered her face with her pillow and groaned.

Another night of aggravated weather rumbled outside, the branches of the old oak tree scratching at her window. Rain dripped down the glass like never-ending tears, the very sky weeping over Lenna's loss of sleep. Or at least that's what she liked to think.

She lay on her side and pulled her sheets over her.

Her mind wandered and her thoughts turned to the night before. She flung her bedcovers back and went to the window, trepidation in each step.

A deep sigh of relief left her when she checked outside. All was as it should be. The neatly tended yard was empty save for the big sign for Gallows Funeral Home. Lenna reached up to close her curtains, but something moved in the dark.

Him.

The creep from the night before stepped out from behind the tree, hidden by the night and the thickness of the oak's trunk. He didn't run away or try to hide. He simply observed her, his face unreadable.

Lenna dropped her hands from the curtains. She'd had enough. She didn't have the time or patience for this shit. Dead or not, he was stalking her, and under no circumstances was she prepared to let that happen.

Lenna put on a black hoody and slipped her feet into a pair of steel-toe boots she'd found in a thrift shop. Taking the baseball bat she kept next to her bedroom door, she slipped downstairs as quietly as she could, careful not to wake her dad. If the guy turned out to be a ghost, she didn't want to have to explain that to her father.

She jumped down from the second last stair, knowing that the bottom one had a habit of creaking in complaint whenever anyone stood on it. Her annoyance flared into anger as she made her way through the hall and headed for the front door.

She'd never played baseball in her life, but she was pretty sure that she'd manage to hit her target without any practice. Assuming it wouldn't just travel through him.

Lenna refused to let this guy think he scared her. She didn't know what his intentions were, but she didn't plan on sitting around, waiting to find out. If she had to, she'd beat it out of him.

Looking out the windows at the door, she tried to find him to get an idea of where he stood before she charged out. She couldn't see him, but that didn't mean he wasn't there anymore. For all she knew, he'd been watching her longer than two days. The thought didn't sit well with her at all.

One hand on the bat's handle, she reached out for the door and counted down from three.

If he jumped out and tried to grab her, she was still close enough for her dad to hear her scream, and scream she would. The whole of Denwood would hear her cry out like a banshee if he came anywhere near her.

Three. Two. One.

Lenna turned the handle, swung open the door, and stomped outside with her bat raised high and ready to swing.

The rain fell on her, heavier than it had been last night. She turned around where she stood, keeping her eyes sharp for him, but there was no sign of him anywhere.

Certain he'd gone, Lenna made to go back inside, her clothes and hair sodden.

A note was stuck onto the door, left under the brass knocker. The paper had raindrops over it, the water blotching out the black ink of the scrawled message. Four letters filled the entire piece of paper.

STOP.

Chapter 15

Lenna scoured the hallways, looking for the new head cheerleader of Denwood High.

Things at school seemed to have gone back to normal, or at least as normal as things could get given the situation. The bell would soon ring for homeroom, and although Kayla would be there, Lenna didn't want to speak to her where prying ears could listen in.

She pushed past people in no hurry to get to their lockers, still half asleep and lost in that early-morning daze that normally afflicted Lenna too. Today, though, her whole body was wide awake and wired, unable to relax, despite three nights of barely any sleep. Lenna needed answers and she intended to get them today.

The note her stalker left gave at least one answer to the many questions that plagued her: he wasn't a ghost. Ghosts couldn't write a note on a piece of paper and leave it on your door. While she didn't need to worry about having to deal with another dead person only she could see, it did mean that whoever this guy was, he was alive and capable of much more than the dead were.

Lenna spotted Kayla among the crowd and called to her from across the hall, but her voice got lost in the hum of chatter. Lenna maneuvered through the mass of students, digging her elbows into anyone who refused to move out of her way.

Kayla was at her locker, putting in her combination. "Hey," said Lenna, trying her best to sound casual.

"What do you want?" asked Kayla, her face a little too impassive to be real.

Lenna leaned in, careful to keep her voice low. "Mind if we talk? In private?"

Kayla yanked some books from her overstuffed locker and put them in her tote bag. "About?" she asked, without looking at Lenna.

"Alicia."

Kayla's body stiffened as soon as she heard her best friend's name. She tucked her hair behind her ear and dug into her bag like she had misplaced something. "No."

"No, you don't mind, or no, you don't want to talk about her?" asked Lenna.

"Yes, I do mind and no, I don't want to talk."

Kayla's voice had a slight shake to it, about as animated as Lenna had seen the girl. Lenna pressed her, hoping for another crack in her rigid demeanor. "Please, it's really important."

"I'm not interested," replied Kayla.

"It's not about being interested. I just wanted to—"

The bell rang and everyone in the hallway made for homeroom, pushing and yelling in herds heading to each end of the school.

Kayla's locker door was covered with pictures and magazine clippings. She took one from the collage, distracted for a moment. She spoke when the bell stopped, the crowd growing thinner. "Whatever you want, I'm not giving it to you." She glanced down again at the picture in her hand and clenched her fist around it.

"It'll only take a minute." Lenna reached out for Kayla's arm, but she stepped back from her.

"I said no." Kayla slammed her locker shut so hard, the metal clanged upon impact. Releasing the crumpled photo from her fist, she tore it in half and let the two pieces fall to the floor before she turned and left, her footsteps echoing in the now-empty hallway.

One half of the picture lay on its front and showed Kayla smiling happily with her arm around someone, taken in one of those little booths found in every shopping mall. Lenna bent down and picked up the other half, which had fallen facedown. She turned it over and the grinning face of Alicia stared back up at her.

The final school bell rang, announcing the end of what had been a horrendously unproductive day for Lenna. Trey still hadn't come into school, and Kayla seemed to have vanished after their little run-in that morning.

"Things will be better tomorrow," said Corey, ever the optimist.

They walked to their lockers, Lenna dragging her feet. "They couldn't possibly get much worse." She wasn't cut out for this whole investigation thing. Her job had been to prepare the bodies of loved ones and make them look presentable for their funerals, not to discover why they ended up dead in the first place.

Corey bumped himself into her, giving her a smile. "Hey, you got hit on by a hot senior the other day. This week hasn't been a total loss."

"Yeah, he was a charmer," said Lenna.

"That Brendan guy seemed nice."

"I guess," she replied, distracted. The strap of her bag dug into her already tense muscles so she switched sides. "We really need to speak with Trey."

She stopped right in the middle of the crowd of pushing students, all eager to get home. A familiar face watched her from the other end of the hallway.

"It's him," she said.

"Who? Trey?" Corey looked around them. "Where?"

"No, not Trey. My personal stalker." He was unmistakable, seeming unfazed that she'd caught him watching her for the second time in less than twenty-four hours. Once her stalker seemed sure he had her attention, he made for the door.

"Come on." Grabbing Corey by the arm, Lenna weaved through the sea of students and headed straight for him. He may have gotten away from her last night, but he wasn't going to sneak off this time.

Corey followed, apologizing to the people they bashed into to get past. "Are you sure this is a good idea? Shouldn't we call the cops?"

"I want to know why he's watching me and what he meant by 'stop.'" She couldn't let him get away.

"Where is he?" asked Corey.

"There!" She pointed to the main entrance. "The tall guy heading for the door with the leather jacket."

"Move it, people," said Corey, navigating through the traffic. "This way, coming through."

Lenna pushed past people, ignoring their protests. They made it to the entrance and left the building in a run.

"Do you see him?" called Corey as they dashed down the stone steps.

Lenna scanned the crowd, trying to drown out the noises around them and concentrate. "No." Her heart sank. "He couldn't have gotten away that quick." They hadn't been that far behind him.

They ran until they reached the parking lot. Engines were already rumbling as the early birds lined up in a row to leave through the gate. Overcast covered the sky above them in an angry gray, blocking the sun.

"Is that him there?" said Corey, out of breath.

Lenna stopped running. "Where?"

Corey's chest heaved. "By your car."

Lenna snapped her head to where she had parked that morning and saw him, her mood instantly turning dark. "Yes."

He leaned against the hood of her hearse, in no hurry to leave. Corey wheezed, bent in half, hands on his knees.

"Take your inhaler," she instructed, worried he might have an asthma attack with all the running.

Corey rummaged in his backpack and pulled out the small device, pressing down to release and breathe in the medication.

Lenna looked back at her car to make sure the guy hadn't given them the slip, but he simply watched, his hands tucked in the front pockets of his dark jeans.

"Two puffs," she told Corey, knowing he hated needing to rely on inhalers. She had even taken to carrying a spare in her bag for the times he "forgot" to bring his own.

After another dose, Corey put his inhaler away. "Should I punch him?" he asked, his voice scratchy. "I feel like I should punch him."

"Let's hear what he has to say first, and then we'll both punch him." They walked toward her hearse, careful not to get too close. Stalkers didn't strike Lenna as the most together of people.

"Interesting wheels," he said in a husky voice as they stopped in front of him. His hair wasn't as dark in the light of day, and his eyes were steel blue. He wore a white T-shirt under his jacket, dark jeans with a rip at one knee, and untied boots.

Lenna glared at him. "Why the hell are you following me?"

"I can explain." His tone was calm, which only irritated her more.

"I think you better before I get my bat out of the trunk."

As they spoke, the lot emptied, the other cars in their row already gone.

The guy sniggered at her threat, his lips curving to one side. "Believe me, this is not my idea of a good time."

Corey stepped in front of Lenna with his back straight. "Why else were you standing in the rain and staring up at her bedroom like some creepy-ass serial killer?" The guy had a good few inches on him, but Corey didn't seem to care.

He looked over Corey and spoke to her. "I've been watching you."

"No shit, Sherlock," Lenna snapped, clenching her fists. "Why?"

He shrugged. "I was asked to."

Fear prickled insider her. "By whom?"

"It's best if I show you," he said.

Lenna gestured with an open hand. "Go ahead."

"I can't here."

"Of course you can't," said Corey, his words dripping with sarcasm.

The guy bobbed his head toward a beat-up Cadillac behind them; its red paint job had seen better days. "If you come with me, I can explain everything."

"Oh, okay," said Lenna, putting on a dumb voice. "Would you like me to tie myself up before I willingly get into your car?"

He looked down at his boots and scuffed the ground. "I didn't mean for you to see me. You weren't supposed to know."

Lenna laughed without humor. "Isn't that like Stalking 101? Don't let the girl you're creeping on know you're doing it?"

"If I wanted to stalk you, then we wouldn't even be having this conversation," he said, nonchalant.

"Okay," said Corey, dragging the word out, "because that's not weird."

The guy put a hand on top of his messy brown hair. "You're taking this the wrong way."

"And how am I supposed to take it?" asked Lenna. She glanced up at the sky, hoping the rain wouldn't start again.

He looked around them as stragglers walked to their cars, chatting with each other in no hurry. "We can't talk here. I'll answer any questions you have. Just come with me."

Lenna scowled, insulted at how stupid he must think she was. "Sure, I'll just put that down with the list of other things I won't be doing ever, like smoking crack and/or taking a shower with my plugged-in hair dryer."

"Are you finished?" he asked, as if he was the reasonable one in their argument.

"Oh, I'm just getting started," she said, her temper rising. His calm attitude could suck it.

"I know you can see the dead," he said bluntly.

Lenna studied him closely. Did he know? How was that possible? She called his bluff. "Well done. Your powerful skills of deduction have concluded that I, a girl who lives above a funeral home, see the dead. Excellent work. Maybe don't quit your day job just yet."

He studied her knowingly, not buying her bravado in the slightest. "Let me elaborate. I know you see the ghost of the girl who died last Friday."

Lenna's throat closed. How could he know that? Her palms began to sweat. The rain started to fall. "Is that what you want me to stop?" she asked, pulling her hood over her head. "Looking into her death?"

"It's not safe for you," the boy said.

"There's a killer on the loose. I wouldn't say it's safe for anyone." The rain got heavier but none of them moved.

"That's not what I mean." Drops of water dripped from his wavy hair, flattening the curls.

Corey frowned and waved at the stalker. "Hi, Vague, cryptic much?"

"Where do you want to take me?" A part of Lenna screamed inside not to go with this stranger, but she had to know what was going on, and if he knew anything ... She couldn't refuse him.

"You'll see."

"You mean, we'll see," corrected Corey, raising his voice above the rain as it hit the ground so hard, it bounced up again. "She's not going anywhere without me, especially with you."

The boy leaned against the hood with ease, like they were having a chat about the terrible weather. "Fine. It appears you know what she can do anyway."

Lenna couldn't figure him out. "How do you know about me?"

He turned his head to the side. "You think you're the only one?"

"I'm not?" Lenna hadn't given it much thought.

"I guess you'll never know if you don't come with me." He knew he had her. How could he not after pulling out the big guns like that?

"How do I know you're not lying to me?" she asked. The smell of wet asphalt filled her nose, her tights sodden from the rain.

"You don't," he replied.

"Well, seeing as you put forward such a strong case." Not that she would've believed him if he had said he was telling the truth, but still.

"I'm trying to help you."

"Who says I need any help?"

"Don't you?" He leaned forward, his hair stuck to his face the way it had been the first time she saw him. "I can give you answers to the questions you have. And the ones you don't."

Lenna folded.

"Fine." She raised her chin. "But I'm not going in your car. We'll follow you there. Now get off my hood."

"We're not going very far," he said, getting up. "I'm Damien, by the way." He put out his hand for her to shake.

Lenna ignored the gesture and walked around to the driver's side of her hearse, opening her door. "I'm Lenna, and this is Corey. But I guess you already knew that."

Damien shot her a grin as he walked off to his own car. "Yep."

Chapter 16

Lenna turned her wipers to full speed, the rain thundering down now and rattling off the windshield as they followed Damien in his Cadillac.

"I don't need to tell you this is a bad idea, do I?" said Corey with his hands over the heater. Condensation covered the windows, the radio muted for a change while they drove.

"Nope."

"Good, because this is a really bad idea."

Lenna gripped the steering wheel. "You don't think he's the killer, do you?"

"Considering we're following him to some unspecified place and haven't told anyone we're going, I sincerely hope not."

They drove for another five minutes or so, not even leaving Denwood. "At least we're still in town. I guess that's a good thing, right? We'll be safe here."

"Tell that to Alicia," said Corey.

Trees lined both sides of the forest, towering over them as they drove deeper down the country road. Damien took a right turn onto a dirt track leading into thick woods. Lenna knew Denwood pretty well, but she had never gone this far into the surrounding forest before. She slowed her speed, leaving a good gap between them. If things didn't turn out well, they might need the head start.

The road veered off in a tight bend and opened out to a patch of rough land with a rugged farm house in the middle. A large shed sat across from it, the wood brittle from age and lack of upkeep. Lenna drove past a tree stump with an axe wedged in it and parked her car behind Damien's.

She turned to Corey, her hand on the door handle. "Ready?"

"As we'll ever be," he said as he put his hood up and got out of the car.

The ground was muddy from the rain and Lenna's Doc Martens sunk into the dirt as soon as she got out.

"Where are we?" she called to Damien, eyeing the house with suspicion. Like the shed, it had seen better days. The paint was almost completely stripped off the exterior wood.

Damien ran from his car and up onto the hooded porch. He waved them over. "Come on. This is my house."

Lenna and Corey made their way over to him, in

no hurry despite the rain. Their shoes made thick, slopping noises with every step.

"If killer hillbillies run out of that house and kill me, I am so haunting your ass," muttered Corey.

"Relax," Lenna said, not sure if she meant it for Corey or herself.

Damien unlocked the front door and held it open for them.

"You first," said Lenna. No way was he going in behind them and blocking the way out.

Damien complied, his stride lazy.

"You live here?" asked Corey as they entered, looking around the hallway. There was no furniture or carpets. No pictures hanging up. Bits of wallpaper clung onto the damp walls here and there, curling at the corners. A thick layer of dust covered the floorboards, dotted with footprints like shoes walking over soft snow.

"We just moved." Damien's easy footsteps echoed across the room and bounced off the bare walls. "It's kind of a fixer-upper."

Corey leaned into her and whispered, "I'll say."

Lenna waved her hand in front of her nose, the stench of cigarette smoke thick in the air. "We?" she asked Damien. The floorboards creaked under their every move.

"Who's there?" called a frail, hoarse voice from down the hall.

"It's just me, Grams," replied Damien. He reached the end of the hall and opened the door to the right, holding up two fingers to ask them to wait outside for a sec. He hovered at the doorway.

"I heard voices," said his grandmother before bursting into a coughing fit.

"Yeah, I've brought some ..." He looked back at them and considered his words. "Uh, guests."

"Guests?" croaked the old woman. "We never have guests."

"You'll want to talk to these ones."

"I doubt it."

Damien beckoned them to follow as he entered the room. It had little in it except two old flower-patterned couches, a wooden coffee table, and a tiny TV by the corner. Sitting next to the window, looking out at the unkempt backyard and into the wild woods beyond, sat an old woman in an armchair.

She watched them both as they walked in, her brow burrowed between dark eyes. Gray hair came down to her neck and looked like she hadn't brushed it for a couple of weeks. It shot out in tangled tufts, making her appear both unhinged and a little startled at the same time.

"Who are these people?" she asked. "And why is her hair pink?"

In another context, Lenna might have found the woman's lack of brain-to-mouth filter amusing, but she was too on edge to find her anything other than freaky.

Damien crossed the room and planted himself on one of the couches, his arms sprawled over the back. "This is my grams, Irene Kelly."

"Hi, Ms. Kelly." Corey hung by the door like he was ready to bolt if—or when—the hillbillies came.

"Call me Irene," she barked, coughing into her fist. She held a lit cigarette in her other hand, the ash dropping onto the uncarpeted floor.

Damien nudged his head to Lenna. "Grams, this is *her*." He spoke louder than he had before, and Lenna spotted a hearing aid in the woman's ear.

"Yes, I know that," Irene said, irritated. "She shouldn't be here."

Damien rested a long leg over his knee. "She's already seen her. We were too late."

The old woman sighed, like a lifetime of worries rested on her small shoulders. She motioned to the couch across from Damien. "Sit down."

Lenna and Corey both did as she said, keeping as close to the door as they could.

"You have a lovely home," said Corey, breaking the awkward silence. An old clock ticked on the wall, its pendulum swinging back and forth.

"Lies," Irene snapped, her voice much deeper than it had been a second before. "I don't like liars."

Damien sniggered at their reaction.

Lenna spoke, the weirdness of it all too much for her, and regarded her stalker. "Now that we're here, do you think you could tell me why you've been following me?"

Irene glared at Damien, her voice back to the way it had been when she first spoke. "You let her see you? Stupid boy."

"She's been digging around, asking questions. I figured I'd try and scare her off, but she's already too close."

"Close to what?" Lenna asked, hating being spoken about like she wasn't in the room. She'd come for answers and she wasn't leaving until she got some.

Irene repositioned herself on the chair, wincing as she moved to face them better. "Don't play dumb, young lady. You know what, or rather, *whom*."

"Alicia," Lenna said.

"Oh, is that her name?" Irene didn't seem to care.

"Yes," Lenna replied, tapping her hand on her leg. "What happened to her?"

"How should I know?" the old woman asked, dusting ash off her sleeve.

Clearly nonchalance ran in the family. It didn't suit either of them. Lenna cocked her head, temper rising inside her like a boiling kettle. "Then why am I here?"

"What you're digging into is trouble." Irene took a draw from her cigarette. "And you're about to find yourself in a whole heap of it if you're not careful."

Smoke rose in tendrils, twisting and turning in the air, like the shadows in the dark place, morphing into different shapes as they moved.

"Is that a threat?" Corey moved to the edge of the couch, blocking Lenna's view slightly as he positioned himself in front of her, putting a protective hand over her arm.

Irene tapped ash onto the floor, her cigarette now a

little stump in her hands. "That's a promise," she said, blowing out smoke. "Believe me."

The woman clamped her jaw down and covered her mouth with her hand, like she was ready to throw up. She retched before her mouth flew open and bellowed, "Trouble!"

Lenna and Corey edged away from her as far as the couch would allow. The voice that left her lips was not her own. It belonged to a man. An angry one.

"Quiet," said Irene irritably, back to her normal voice, smacking the side of her own head.

Damien wore a bored look.

Lenna had seen enough. Sure, she wanted answers, but whatever was going on with Irene was way beyond anything she was prepared for. She stood and pulled Corey up with her. "We're out of here."

Irene cackled in her chair, looking incredibly scary for a senior citizen in a woolen cardigan. "Aren't you a feisty one?" she said, looking at her with a toothless smile. "Good, you'll need that."

Lenna hovered on the spot and turned back to the seemingly possessed woman. If she left now, she would be no closer to understanding anything. About her, or Alicia. "Okay, can we stop the doublespeak? Why am I here?"

Irene stubbed out her cigarette on the arm of her chair. "Tell me," she said patiently. "How long have you seen the dead? And I'm not talking about the stiffs in that funeral home of yours."

Lenna raised her chin at her. "How do you know?"

Irene opened her mouth to answer, but again the voice didn't belong to her. "Answer the question!" She shook her head like a fly buzzed around her and swatted at her crazy hair.

Lenna clutched Corey's hand tighter. "Since Sunday."

Irene gave herself a little shake and turned her attention back to them like nothing had happened. "We've caught you early, there's that, at least."

Lenna wanted to punch something and run away at the same time. "Caught me from what? What are you talking about?"

Irene sat back in her seat and clasped her hands together.

"We came here, to this little town of yours, because of you. I felt it." She inclined her head toward her grandson. "This one here isn't too pleased at me for uprooting him, but I had to warn you."

Lenna looked between Irene and Damien. "Warn me of what?" What could be so bad they had to move their lives, pack their bags, and come to Denwood?

"To stay away from that girl," said Irene, her tone grave.

"Why?" Alicia needed help, and it looked like Lenna was the only one who could give it to her. Alicia and the people who loved her deserved justice. "Did you know she was going to die? Why didn't you tell me? Or stop it?"

"If only that were the case," Irene said, sounding every bit as old and weary as she looked. "You never know what's going to happen, or when exactly, but over time, as the years slip by and you become irrevocably tied to death, you get a sense for when trouble is coming. I felt it a few weeks ago, like a dull pain in the back of my mind, niggling at me for attention like a spoiled toddler. I knew something was coming, and we followed it here, to Denwood."

"To you," Damien added.

"You came all this way from wherever you're from to stalk me?" Lenna demanded. Damien had scared her shitless, causing her to look over her shoulder every five seconds. It was bad enough to think there was a killer out there, never mind someone following her for who knew what.

"Massachusetts," Damien replied. "And I'm sorry if I scared you. Grams wanted to make sure she was right about you. That you could see the dead. When I learned Alicia had died and was in your house, Grams told me to watch you. To approach you only if I was sure you'd seen Alicia in her ... present state. I didn't know until it was too late that you were the one we'd come here for."

Irene cleared her throat with a loud coughing fit, breaking Lenna's attention from Damien and his storm-filled eyes. "We came here to warn you to stay away from the dead. Nothing good will come from communicating with that poor girl."

Lenna was about to protest, her mind doing over-time, but Irene seemed to hear her unspoken thoughts.

"If you don't turn away from the dead now, it could

be too late. This is one rabbit hole you don't want to go down."

"But I can't just ignore her," said Lenna. "She was my friend."

"You must," said Irene, like it was that simple. The old woman leaned forward and her gaze bore through Lenna like she could see into her soul. Her eyes widened, as if she saw something there she didn't like. "You've already seen it."

"What?" asked Lenna, her stomach twisting.

"The dark place, where the shadows lie." Irene's voice came out in a whisper, like even speaking about it was dangerous. "Waiting. Calling to you." She tapped the side of her temple with a finger. "Whispering inside your head. You've been there, I can tell. Did you see her die?"

"Yes," said Lenna, barely able to get the words out. She sat back down.

Irene nodded, almost sympathetic, her eyes knowing. "That, my dear, is Limbo."

"Limbo?" asked Corey, staring at the old woman, his face crumpled in confusion. "Like the dance?"

Damien snickered, and Irene looked at Corey like he was the crazy one.

"No, boy," she said, sobering. "Although you do need to watch your feet in that place. Dark things lurk around every corner."

"Okay," said Corey, his neck turning red. "I'll just shut up now."

Lenna thought of the things that circled around her

in the place Irene called Limbo. She'd felt their intentions among the endless cries for help, tasted their wanting, their craving for life.

"What is it?" she asked, needing to know, but not wanting to at the same time.

Irene looked out before her, not seeing them but lost in her own mind. "Who can say? There are many names for it, but they're referring to the same place. The void between life and death."

"Tell her about the girl," said the voice of a little girl from Irene's lips.

Irene swiped her hand in the air with impatience. "Hush, I'm getting to it."

Lenna sat up straight. "You mean Alicia? What about her?"

"That girl is destined to go there," said Irene.

A chill traveled through Lenna, having nothing to do with the poorly heated house. Wind slipped in through gaps in the walls, whispering and hissing from the cracks. "Why?"

"She has unfinished business."

Lenna wrung her hands, sweating under her shirt. "With what?"

"Who knows?" said the old woman. "It can be anything, really. But it's always significant. Something happened to that girl to make a part of her stay in this world. And let me tell you from experience, it wasn't anything good."

Images of Alicia lying helpless on the grass in the

park invaded Lenna's mind. "She doesn't remember what happened to her."

"They never do," said Irene. "As their ties to the living world break and unravel, so do their memories, starting from the most recent ones."

So it wasn't the drugs that had affected Alicia's memory. "Someone drugged her," confided Lenna, knowing something at last.

"Bingo!" cried a high-pitched voice. Irene threw her hand over her chapped lips like she could catch and put the words back into her mouth.

It was like she couldn't control her own body. Irene coughed again, and Damien handed her a handker-chief that she used to wipe her mouth, leaving a blood-stain on the cotton material.

"There you have it," Irene said, her voice strained. "Murder. A common enough reason as far as these things go."

"And that stopped her from crossing over or what-ever?" asked Corey.

"A soul can't move on to the other side if they still have tethers to the world of the living," explained Damien, his bored façade slipping the more they spoke.

"Lost forever!" shouted the man with the deep voice again, Irene's lips moving around like some badly dubbed movie.

"Be quiet," snapped Irene to herself. She looked up toward her forehead, her eyes going wonky. "I won't tell you again."

"What do you mean lost forever?" asked Lenna. She didn't like the sound of that, no matter which voice said it.

"Once you go into Limbo, you can't get out," warned Irene, rubbing her throat.

"I got out," said Lenna, recalling the feeling of vertigo that came with it.

"You're different," said Irene, like it was obvious.

"But Alicia," said Corey, with a kind of bleak fascination, "she'll be trapped there?"

"Not necessarily," interjected Damien, his eyes darting to Irene and then back at Lenna like he was confiding something he shouldn't.

Irene tossed her cigarette carton and it hit Damien across the head. "You hush, boy."

"What do you mean?" Lenna asked him, not sure she wanted to know. They had given her nothing but bad news so far.

Damien eyed his grandmother again. "Alicia's not there yet."

Irene smacked a fist against her armrest. "Now you listen to me, girl. You stay the hell away from anyone who isn't breathing. Nothing good will come from associating with the dead."

Lenna ignored her and focused on Damien. "Please," she said. "Tell me what you meant."

Damien ran a hand over his mouth, face unsure. He hesitated for a moment, then relented with a deep exhale. "If you resolve Alicia's unfinished business for her, then she can cross over."

Irene's mouth opened, the words practically spitting themselves out. "But you better be quick!"

"I said be quiet!" Irene pulled at her hair and her hand came away with a tangled lock caught between her bone-thin fingers.

Damien continued like it hadn't happened, his attention focused on Lenna. "But if her body, her physical tie to this world, is laid to rest before her unfinished business can be resolved, she'll be trapped in Limbo for eternity."

Lenna took a sharp intake of breath. "Trapped with those shadow creatures?"

Irene spoke with her head bowed, her hair covering her face. "They were human once. Strange what time does to the soul. And they've got nothing but time in that place."

Lenna's stomach stirred. "So those monsters, those things, they're people who didn't move on?"

"Yes," said Damien.

Lenna swiped her hand in front of her. "We can't let that happen to Alicia. I won't."

"Then you better find whoever killed her before they put her body in the ground," said Irene in another voice that wasn't her own, and sat up straight in her chair. "But I warn you, you'll pay the price."

Lenna froze. "A price?"

"Oh, there's always a price, dear." Irene gave a hollow laugh. "You can't just play around in Limbo and expect to come back out the same way you went in."

Lenna touched the bottom of her nose. "My nose bled when I came back."

Irene snorted, her voice back to matching her body. "That's nothing. Consider yourself lucky, and avoid that place until the day you die."

Lenna rubbed her hand over her head, pushing her hair away from her face. It was all getting too much. This time last week, her biggest worry had been finishing a history paper on time.

"Let's backtrack," said Lenna, pinching the bridge of her nose. Out of all the questions she needed to ask, one thing seemed paramount. "Why can I even go there in the first place if I'm not dead? Why can I see Alicia when no one else can?"

Irene gave her a sad smile, her wrinkled face almost gentle. "You've been touched by death, child."

Lenna went cold. "What do you mean?"

Irene tutted her tongue. "My, my, you sure are a fish out of water now, ain't ya?" She retched and yelled, "Fish out of water!"

"What's she talking about?" Lenna asked Damien through gritted teeth. "When did I become touched by death?"

Damien paused for a moment and bit his lip. "When you died."

Chapter 17

Lenna gaped at Damien. "I died?"

Time seemed to slow; every movement thick and sluggish like it had been made under water. His words had completely submerged her.

Damien sat forward. "You didn't know?"

"Len." Corey sounded far away even though he sat right next to her. "You need to breathe, okay?"

Her lungs burned like she was drowning, sinking to the bottom of the ocean the more she learned.

"I'm dead?" Her voice sounded muffled to her waterlogged ears.

Damien got up from his seat and kneeled in front of her. "No, you're very much alive."

"Then how?" She stopped herself and took a long, deep breath. "How could I have died?"

She imagined herself lying on a slab in their storage

room, someone else putting on her makeup for her as she lay still, watching them with dead eyes.

"I don't know what happened," said Damien, "but the only way to see the dead is to have died and then been brought back." He looked at her like she was a spooked animal, ready to buck her legs out in panic.

"I died for almost three minutes, before they brought me back," said Irene, watching them all from her chair. "The doctors said it was a miracle." The old woman scoffed. "Miracle, my ass."

Damien winced at her words like she had struck him. "Don't talk like that, Grams."

"Why not? I should have died that day. It was my time. Those doctors had no right bringing me back like that. It's all their fault."

Irene took out another cigarette from a second carton on the windowsill. The rain still fell, the sky rumbling in anger before a flash of lightning burst through the clouds.

How could Lenna not know about something so significant? She had no recollection of it. Nothing. When did it happen? How? Why didn't her dad tell her?

"So, I died," she said, hoping the more she said it, the more sense it would make. "And was brought back? That's why I can see Alicia?"

Irene struck a match and put it to her cigarette, its flame traveling down the small piece of wood as she inhaled deeply. "And any other stiff that comes by your funeral home with unfinished business."

"Yes," said Damien, answering her questions now that he'd scared the shit out of her. "When you die, your soul starts to move on. Even if it's only for a few seconds, you've still entered the transitional phase. Once death touches you, it never truly leaves. That's why you can see those who still linger after death."

Lenna played with a loose thread on her skirt, wrapping it tightly around her finger. Concern mapped across Damien's sharp angles, softening them. He had dark circles under his eyes, like he didn't sleep much.

Lenna leaned her elbows on her knees, her head dizzy. "But people are brought back all the time. Why doesn't everyone know this happens?"

"Not everyone with unfinished business can remain here after their body dies," said Damien. "It takes a strong will for their soul to stay."

Lenna thought of Alicia. Strong will sounded about right.

"What happens to the ones who can't stay?" she asked Damien, thinking of all the people who may not have the willpower to stick around after something horrible happened to them.

"They move on."

"But still," she said, trying to think about it logically. "I can't believe no one has ever stumbled across the ghost of a dead person before."

"Yeah," said Corey. "Wouldn't it be common knowledge by now, even if it's only the strong-willed ones who manage to remain?"

"Not everyone is around death all the time, like you are," said Damien. "Some with the ability to see ghosts never do because they're never around the places where the souls are likely to be."

That made sense, especially for those who had already avoided death and had been revived. Most people wouldn't want to be around reminders of what could've been. People avoided the dead, or anything else that reminded them of their own mortality.

The sky grumbled again, followed by another flash that covered the room like a strobe light. The clock continued to tick, like it counted down the hours until Alicia's funeral. To when she'd be trapped with the shadows in Limbo.

"Alicia can't go very far away from her body either," said Corey. Lenna could practically see the cogs moving in his head. "It's not like she could walk around town for someone like you to see her."

Damien returned to the couch now that Lenna had calmed down a bit. "They're tethered to their body. It's their physical selves that keep them here. As soon as that body has been laid to rest, they can't stay any longer."

"So, what you're basically telling me," said Lenna, trying to make sense of it all in her busy mind, "is that for someone to see a ghost who has managed to stay here, that person needs to have died and been brought back, and be around the ghost's dead body?"

Irene blew out a ball of smoke, like an old, dried-up dragon. "Yup, and those are some slim odds, if you ask me. There are more of us out there, though. Met a few of them in my time before you came along."

Those odds were increased for Lenna with her dad working in the death industry. She was surprised she hadn't seen any ghosts before now. Then again, most of their clients hadn't been murdered.

Lenna turned to Irene. "So, you're like me?"

The old woman laughed. "I don't know about that, but I can see the dead too, yes."

Lenna raised an eyebrow at the old lady's sass. "When did you know that you could see them?" Irene had been through it before—maybe she could help Lenna figure out what to do with this ability of hers.

Irene peered out the window as if it looked into her past. "I was a nurse," she said. "We couldn't afford to lose the income. I was revived after dying during childbirth and was back at work a month later."

They all sat in silence, the storm outside an eerie accompaniment to her story.

"A girl came in one night while I was working the late shift. Multiple stab wounds. The poor thing looked like a goddamn pin cushion. She didn't last long."

Irene took a draw of her cigarette. "Over the next few weeks, girls kept coming in, most of them DOA, all with the same wounds. It seemed like the city had a serial killer on its hands. Media shitstorm, you might imagine."

"I'll bet," said Corey.

"Anyway, one night the latest victim died in the ICU after putting up a good fight for two whole days.

She was a tough one, that girl. I walked in and found her ghost crying over her dead body.

"I felt it then. You know what I'm talking about." Irene said to Lenna. "The internal draw toward where the girl died. For her, it was right there on the hospital bed. I fell into Limbo right there and then. The staff thought I had fainted when I saw the girl had died. They put me on the empty bed next to her, and when I came back out of that hellhole, my life had changed forever."

"Did you see the killer?" Alicia's murderer was nothing but a phantom to Lenna when she was in Limbo.

Irene gave her a look, like she thought Lenna naïve. "No, you never do. Nothing in life is ever that easy, you can bet your bottom dollar on that. But I did get some things, clues."

Clues. The red car and the broken rose Alicia held in her hand as she took her last breath. It wasn't enough.

Irene retched, another one of the voices trying to get out, but she pursed her lips and swallowed hard before she spoke again.

"I went to the police like an idiot. They listened to what I had to say and laughed right in my face. They weren't laughing when I was able to tell them the murder weapon."

Lenna twisted the loose thread on her dress tighter around her finger, cutting off the blood flow as it dug into her skin.

"They involved me in the case after that," said Irene. "Under the radar, of course. They didn't want the media to find out that they were using a 'psychic' to help them track down the killer."

Corey leaned forward on the couch, glued to every word. "And did you? Track him down, I mean?"

"We did," said Irene, her eyes sad and haunted. "But not before he took another three girls. That sick son of a bitch did things to those girls you couldn't even imagine."

Lightning struck again, illuminating her face, every wrinkle and groove becoming more prominent, her hollow cheeks reminding Lenna of some of the clients who came into their house after a long stint in the hospital.

"After that, they kept on coming," Irene said, bitter. "It's like they can smell you, like a part of them knows to seek you out. They become drawn to you, like those souls in Limbo."

"This might happen again?" asked Lenna.

Irene leaned her chin on her fist and watched Lenna intently. "No 'might' about it. Unless you stay away from it altogether."

"Like you did?" asked Lenna.

"Oh, I never stayed away. Every night I lay in bed wishing they had let me die that day. I had been in labor for twenty hours with that one's good-for-nothing mother." She pointed to her grandson. "She took everything I had. Almost died herself, too, had the doctors not cut me open to get her out."

Damien got up and left the room, his jaw clenched and twitching. The door slammed shut behind him. Loud footsteps stomped up the stairs and another door slammed soon after. Irene acted like nothing happened.

"I worked in that hospital for five years and never did I feel like I had made a difference more than the day they caught the monster who killed all those girls." She shook her head. "I should've walked away then, but I didn't. The feeling's addicting, stronger than any drug you kids fool around with these days."

"If I do nothing," said Lenna, "then Alicia will go to Limbo."

"Yes. And do nothing you must." Irene raised her voice. "Do you want to end up like me? Because that's the only place this path will take you. That and a quick death, if you're lucky."

"Nothing!" followed the deep booming voice of the man who spoke out of Irene's lips, thunder crashing down outside along with it.

Lenna looked at Irene, at what she had become. It was like staring into a future laid out for Lenna the second she'd died, whenever that had been. The old woman coughed again, blood spattering onto her hand.

It was too much. She couldn't deal.

Lenna tugged at her finger, snapping the loose thread clean off her dress.

"Screw this. I'm out."

Chapter 18

Lenna sped down the country road, leaving her potential future behind her.

"I'm out," she said to Corey for the third time. "I can't do this."

The storm raged above them. It had gotten dark during their disturbing visit with Irene. Lenna's headlights illuminated the way out of the winding roads surrounded by a sentry of trees.

The rain battered the windshield, making it hard to see as they turned onto the main road.

"I just can't." Her head ached from the information overload, pounding behind her eyes.

She had died.

"Hey, calm down," said Corey, putting a hand on her leg.

A flash of light came up behind them, filling the hearse with an abrupt eerie glow. Corey looked out the back window. "What's this person's problem?"

Lenna checked her rearview mirror, but all she could make out was the blinding light coming from the car tailing them. The driver was far too close.

Lenna squinted to try to get a better look. "They have their high beams on." She beeped her horn, warning the asshat to slow down. The weather was bad enough without some idiot driver playing NASCAR.

"Just let them pass," said Corey, turning back around.

Lenna drove close to the side of the road, giving the impatient driver enough room to overtake her.

"They're not moving." She beeped the horn again and flashed her emergency lights to let them know she was letting them go ahead. Again, the car didn't speed up.

She focused on the road in front of her as a sharp turn approached, rounding it faster than she should have, worried about being rear-ended.

As the road straightened, the car didn't follow them. It must've stopped because there weren't any other turns or roads aside from the one they were on.

"Jackass" said Corey.

A guttural rumble came from behind them. At first Lenna thought it was a boom of thunder, but the noise continued for too long. The car screeched around the corner and headed toward them, the engine roaring like a lion on the hunt.

Lightning cracked the sky in half, giving Lenna a split-second look behind her.

"Shit," she said as the red car raced forward. She

looked back again, but all she could see were the blinding headlights, just like the ones she'd seen in Limbo.

"Lenna, watch out!" Corey yelled as the car tried to run into them. Lenna skid the hearse to the left, narrowly avoiding a collision. Her tires bumped up over the mound of uneven grass that followed along the road. The car shook and she held on tight to the wheel.

Their pursuer hit the brakes and slowed, revving the accelerator so the engine cried out. Lenna raced forward as fast as she could.

"They're trying to run us off the road," said Corey.

"Keep watching the car," Lenna told him as she followed another sharp wind in the road, the hearse's wheels dragging along the asphalt as she braked into the turn. "Try to get a look at the driver."

She rolled down her window to better hear the engine behind them. It taunted them with every rev, toying with them. The smell of burning rubber filled her nostrils as she put her foot down, trying to get as much distance between her car and her pursuer as she could.

The road moved into a long stretch, leading down for about two miles before they would see any sign of life at the edge of town. The wipers worked at top speed, barely able to keep her windshield free from the crashing rain that blocked her view.

The car's engine unleashed a mighty war cry and charged straight for them.

"Lenna, it's coming fast," warned Corey.

Her eyes darted to each side of the road, looking for a gap in the trees or a little dirt road, but there was nowhere to escape.

The hearse was doing maximum speed, but it wasn't enough. Funeral cars weren't built for speed, and it was easily outmatched by the car narrowing the gap toward them.

As it got closer, Lenna feigned right and then left, but the driver saw it coming and surged forward, straight into the back of the hearse.

The hearse jolted, sending her and Corey forward. Lenna hissed as her seat belt dug into her collarbone, stopping her from hitting the dashboard. She kept her foot on the gas and tried to straighten as best she could before the car crashed into them again.

The rain-slicked road made it hard for the wheels to find friction as her hearse carried forward while being pushed from behind. Panic screamed within her and refused to be silent.

Lenna turned the steering wheel in the opposite direction as the car tried to run them off the road, hitting the back bumper at an angle. She went to slam the brakes but the car was too close and going so fast, she didn't dare.

Ahead of them, lights from another car approached from the opposite direction.

Lenna beeped her horn with her fist, trying to warn them to turn around, but it was no use.

The red car must've seen it too, because it ran into

the back of them again and edged to the right, taking the hearse with it.

"I can't stop it!" Lenna tried to turn the wheel, but anytime she moved to one side, the red car followed, spinning her right back into the middle of the road and in line with the oncoming vehicle.

Lenna and Corey screamed as headlights flashed. The red car moved sharply to the right, sending the hearse skidding until it blocked the opposite lane. The red car sped past and off into the night.

The oncoming car beeped its horn, far too close for Lenna to reverse out of the way. Lenna closed her eyes and took Corey's hand.

Chapter 19

Lenna opened her eyes, surprised she hadn't died—again.

In front of them, an angry man in his forties gestured wildly from his car, profanity spewing from his lips. Corey took a puff of his inhaler, eyes so wide Lenna could see the whole round of his irises.

Her heart hammered in her chest, her hands and legs shaking. Lenna ignored the other car, reversed into her own lane, and drove forward, away from the driver who had managed to stop just inches from them.

She sped home.

It was too much. All of it. She couldn't take it anymore.

"Slow down, you're going too fast," said Corey as she raced down the road, trying to get as far away as she could.

"Lenna!" shouted Corey. "Stop the car right now."

Lenna pulled over to the side and hit the brakes, her breathing fast and shallow.

"Get out, I'm driving." Corey opened his door and ran around to her side without another word.

Lenna complied. She closed the passenger door behind her, dripping wet for the second time that day. "Someone just tried to kill us," she said, trying to process what had happened.

Corey's face was ashen. "Do you think it was the same person who killed Alicia?"

Her teeth chattered. "It has to be. Who else would want to kill us?"

Corey pulled back out onto the road and headed away from the forest. "It could've been a warning. Either way, someone wants you out of the picture. We must be getting close, too close, for the killer to attack us like that."

Lenna stared into the night. They could have died. She already had, if what Damien and Irene said was true. Things had gone from bad to deadly in one afternoon. Lenna wanted to help Alicia, but if ending up six feet under or like Irene was the price she'd have to pay, she didn't think she could.

"The police can deal with it," she said. "Detective Gibbs can go off and find whoever killed Alicia, but not us." Not her and especially not Corey. Shit just got real and it almost cost them their lives.

"Whoever that was must've been following us," said Corey, checking the rearview mirror every few seconds.

Lenna shuddered at his words, looking out as the trees gave way to clusters of houses and cul-de-sacs. "Maybe they'll leave us alone if we back off. If we stop looking into Alicia's death, they won't have any reason to try to kill us." The alternative was too terrifying to consider.

If they continued looking, they could both end up like Alicia. Her killer had gotten away with murder and it was clear they intended to keep it that way.

Even if it meant killing again.

***

Lenna got home and locked the door behind her. She'd told Corey to take the hearse and just pick her up for school tomorrow; she didn't want him walking home after what had happened.

She headed straight upstairs, giving the door to the basement a wide berth.

Lenna couldn't face Alicia right now. How was she going to tell her that she wasn't going to help anymore? It was like leaving her when she needed Lenna most all over again. Alicia wouldn't take it well, and Lenna couldn't blame her, but the risks were too much. It was down to the police now.

Upstairs, Lenna went to the living room, exhausted but too riled to sleep. Her dad was there, sitting on the sofa with the TV turned low.

Cold pizza lay in an open box on the coffee table

next to bowls of sweet butter popcorn and packets of strawberry Twizzlers. Movie night. It had totally slipped her mind, as had helping her dad with clients whose funerals were tomorrow.

"Dad, I'm sorry. I completely forgot." Lenna pressed her palms against her aching forehead.

Her dad turned off the TV. "You didn't answer my calls."

Lenna hadn't so much as looked at her cell since school. She fished it out of her bag and checked the screen. "My battery died."

It wasn't the only one. When had she died? Why couldn't she remember it? She should have some recollection of what happened. Why didn't her dad ever tell her? Why was she only learning about this now? And why did the news have to come from a complete and utter stranger?

"Where were you?" asked her dad.

Whispers called to her in the back of Lenna's mind. They all spoke over each other at once, their words lost in the rabble. They hissed and whined like an out-of-tune radio she had no control over.

"I got wrapped up in some after-school things," she lied, distracted by the voices.

Her dad got up from the sofa and began clearing up the food. "I called the school."

"Why?" said Lenna. What were they talking about again?

"You didn't come home, and you've not been yourself with everything going on, so I got worried. They said you weren't there."

Lenna closed her eyes. "Can we talk about this later? What's the big deal?" Why was he pestering her with questions when he should be explaining himself? Why did he keep the fact she'd died a secret?

"I'm not giving you trouble or anything, Len. You said you would be home to help out and never showed. I just wondered where you were, that's all." He studied her with parental worry.

"I was out," she said, dumping her bag in the corner.

"Where's out?"

"Just out, okay?" Lenna snapped. She left the living room, ignoring the confused look on her dad's face as she slammed the door. She went to the kitchen and raided the cupboards for aspirin, the voices scratching inside her head.

Drinking water from the tap, she swallowed two tablets. She leaned over the sink, splashed her face with cold water, and rubbed the back of her neck.

The whispers stopped, the chill of the water bringing her back to reality. She was just tired and in shock; that's all. Sleep called for her. She dried her face with a towel and put it on the table.

A file lay there and she picked it up, noticing the hospital's logo on the front. It was Alicia's death certificate. Joe, the medical examiner who did Alicia's autopsy, must have gotten the test results back.

Lenna flicked through the usual stuff at the beginning, past Alicia's name, date of birth, her address and contact details of her parents. The toxicology results were at the bottom of the next page.

Alicia had a cocktail of alcohol and gamma hydroxybutyric acid in her system, whatever that was. Her body shut down. She overdosed, just like Joe initially suspected.

Lenna read on and reached the medical history and additional comments section of the report, where anything that helped conclude the cause of death that may not be directly evident from the autopsy was noted.

Alicia's bipolar was discussed, together with her suicide attempt and her admission into a psychiatric unit where she received treatment.

Guilt cut deep, like a sharp, serrated blade, as Lenna read the printed words detailing Alicia's past. She had failed Alicia then, and she was failing her now too.

Taking all of Alicia's background and medical history into account, along with the results of the autopsy and further tests, the cause of death was concluded.

The death certificate fell through Lenna's hands and scattered across the cold, tiled floor.

Suicide.

Chapter 20

Lenna slammed the document down on the metal slab. "It's case closed as far as anyone's concerned."

It was seven thirty in the morning and Lenna sat in the basement going over what it all meant. Now that it was in black and white, there would be nothing to make anyone look into Alicia's death further.

Corey sat between two of their new clients who lay waiting on her dad getting back from that morning's service. Corey hadn't spoken once since they came down to tell Alicia the bad news. He typed away on his laptop, immersed in whatever he was doing.

"What do you mean?" asked Alicia, walking around the room like a caged animal sick to death of its confines.

"That's it. The police aren't going to investigate your case now that the ME deemed your death a suicide." Lenna tapped the floor with her black heels. It hadn't settled in yet.

Alicia stopped pacing. "But what about evidence the police have?"

"They must not have any. Any evidence they did have would have been mentioned and considered before your official cause of death was decided on. Nothing they have suggests foul play." Frustration bubbled inside Lenna. What had Detective Gibbs and her team been doing all this time? Eating frickin' doughnuts?

Alicia's killer must either be very smart, or very lucky. Perhaps both.

Corey clicked his fingers. "I knew it." He stared intently into his laptop, the screen's light illuminating his face in a shade of ghoulish blue like the dead people all around him.

"Knew what?" Lenna got up and leaned over him to get a look.

"Gamma hydroxybutyric acid," he said, the name rolling off his tongue like it was the easiest thing in the world to say. "I knew I'd heard it before. GHB for short."

"GHB," repeated Lenna, the name familiar. "Isn't that like a date-rape drug?"

"The very one," replied Corey, tapping a picture of a microscopic image on his screen. "Liquid ecstasy."

"But that's good, right?" said Alicia. "If they found the date-rape drug, then surely the police know I didn't take it willingly."

"What's she saying?" asked Corey.

Lenna repeated Alicia for Corey's sake, but she knew it didn't matter. Alicia's past cemented the wrong conclusion.

"That's the problem," said Corey, looking at the empty space where he guessed Alicia sat. "GHB is also used recreationally as a party drug."

Lenna sat back down. "The death certificate said there were no signs of rape, or a struggle, or anything else like that," she said. "From their limited point of view, there's nothing to suggest you didn't take the drugs yourself."

"With no signs of rape, no evidence, the alcohol in your system, and the incident from when you were in the hospital after deliberately overdosing, it's the logical conclusion." Corey closed his laptop. "They've got no reason to suspect murder."

Alicia hugged herself, looking small and scared. "So, what do we do now?"

They needed to end this once and for all. Last night had been too close, and in the harsh light of day, Lenna was forced to admit she couldn't walk away. It wasn't that simple, especially now that the police had stopped investigating. Lenna had to do this for Alicia, and for her and Corey.

Sure, it was dangerous, but there was no guarantee that Alicia's killer would stop coming after them. The only way to make sure they would be safe was to find out who did it and gather enough evidence to send their ass to jail. If they didn't, Alicia was headed straight for Limbo and an eternity among the shadows.

"We find who did this to you, and fast." Lenna filled Alicia in on everything they'd learned yesterday from Damien and Irene.

Walking away may have been the smart thing to do, and she didn't doubt the validity in Irene's warnings for one second, but the right thing wasn't always the smart thing, and sitting next to Alicia only solidified that. Lenna would walk away from it all, but only after Alicia's killer was brought to justice.

If he—or she—didn't kill her first.

"So, if we only have until my funeral—" Alicia started but didn't finish.

The weight of it all pressed down on Lenna. She could practically hear the clock ticking in her head, every second slipping through her fingers like the ashes of a corpse.

"Then we only have four days to find out who killed you."

Talk about a deadline.

Chapter 21

Lenna walked down the empty hallway with a new sense of resolve.

In her hand, she held the hall pass she nabbed by telling her history teacher she wanted to see one of the counselors the school had brought in. He gave it to her without question. Usually he gave you a pop quiz worth of questions for just asking to go to the bathroom.

History could wait for her to catch up. It wasn't like anything new was going to happen that she'd miss. She only had four days to find out who killed Alicia, so she had to work fast.

Lenna knocked and entered the senior chemistry class. Twenty pairs of eyes fell on her as soon as she walked in. Mr. Ross stopped whatever lecture he was giving and frowned at her.

"Hi, sorry to interrupt your class, sir. Principal Stein sent me to tell Trey Orson he needs to go to his office." She looked over the classroom for the quarter-back but couldn't see his face.

"He's not here," confirmed the teacher. He turned back to his class and continued his lecture.

Lenna's heart sank.

Someone caught her attention at the back of the class. Mr. Ross had his back to him, so he couldn't see Brendan waving at her. He shot her that easy smile of his, which sparked an idea.

"He also wants to see Brendan McAllister," she told Mr. Ross.

He folded his arms, his hands dusty with chalk and leaving marks on his wrinkled shirt. "What for?"

"He didn't say," said Lenna. "I'm just the messenger."

Mr. Ross gave an exaggerated sigh and turned to Brendan, who sat like the perfect pupil at his desk. "You heard the girl, McAllister. Get going."

Brendan got out of his seat, slung his bag over his shoulders, and left with Lenna, closing the door behind him. He eyed Lenna with suspicion, walking back-wards to face her as they walked down the hall. "I'm guessing Principal Stein doesn't want to see me."

Lenna smirked. "Obviously."

Brendan laughed, seeming far from annoyed to be dragged out of class for no reason. Mr. Ross was famous for being a snooze-fest, so Lenna figure she'd done Brendan a favor. She only hoped he'd reciprocate.

He wore his purple and yellow varsity jacket, the little devil logo for the Denwood Demons emblazoned on the back. "That's some aggressive journalism," he said.

Journalism? Oh, right. He must still think she wanted a comment from Trey for the made-up memorial piece for the school paper.

"I'm still looking for Trey, but I guess he's still not coming to school," she said, getting to business.

"You might find him at work."

Lenna stopped at the bottom of the stairs leading to the second floor where her next class was. "Where might that be?"

Brendan leaned against the handrail. "He works at the garden center off the freeway."

Yes. This was just what she needed. The garden center was fifteen minutes away, right outside of Denwood. Maybe things were finally looking up.

Lenna's heart sank as something came to her. "Won't he be off from work too?"

"I doubt it," said Brendan, playing with his backpack strap as he watched her. "He needs the money, you know?"

"Do you know if he's working today?" she asked.

"I don't."

Lenna leaned against the wall opposite Brendan, raising her eyes to the ceiling. Maybe things weren't looking up that much after all.

"If you want, I can find out what shifts he's doing and text them to you?" Brendan offered, cheeks flushing again like they'd done in the locker room when they first spoke.

She considered him, keeping her tone playful. "I think you just want my number."

He laughed and held up his hands, his white teeth gleaming at her. "I think you might be right, but I'm happy to help."

She cocked her head and pretended to consider it. She already knew she'd give Brendan her number. If he could get Trey's schedule, it was as good as his.

"Fine," she said, taking his cell and entering in her number. "I'll be expecting those shifts soon."

"Don't worry. I'll get them," he assured her. He touched her fingers as he took his cell back, in no hurry to break the contact. "Maybe then I could ask you out or something?"

Lenna pulled her hand away first. "You can ask," she said, in her best attempt at acting casual. Like she was used to flirting with boys who seemed to like her back.

Without another word, Lenna turned and went up the stairs, leaving him standing alone in the hallway. Boys, and whether they were actually flirting with her, would need to wait. She had bigger things to worry about than some guy.

Math had never been Lenna's strong point. To her, Pythagoras sounded like an infection that required a doctor's appointment. Besides, she couldn't see what the big deal was about triangles. Give her English class over math any day of the week. Heck, she'd even take a trip to the dentist instead of suffering through a whole period of equations and formulas.

At least now she knew where she could find Trey, and hopefully that would lead her one step closer toward solving a very different kind of problem. If only she knew who was in the equation. Unfortunately for her, there wasn't a formula for getting the answers she needed.

Everyone trickled into the classroom, all of them about as excited for the next hour as she was. She took a seat at the back.

Ms. Pearson walked in with her usual vacant expression and matronly pastel blue suit, ready to bore them to tears, but it was the person behind her that caught Lenna's attention.

Damien entered the room. Ms. Pearson spoke with him for a second and gestured to the empty seat next to Lenna.

"What are you doing here?" she asked as he walked up to her desk. He was dressed in head-to-toe black, in a stylish-but-not-trying-to-be kind of way. He smelled of rainy days and mint shower gel.

He pulled out the chair next to her and sat down. "Going to class."

"For what? To give me more bad news?" Ever since she'd first laid eyes on him, things had gone from bad to worse.

"Nope." Damien leaned back and pointed at the

chalkboard as Ms. Pearson started her class. "Just here to learn."

Lenna had assumed that Damien was older than she was. "Aren't you a senior?"

Damien shrugged. "Yeah, but I'm a flunk in math."

They sat in awkward silence for a while, listening to Ms. Pearson talk about something that went over Lenna's head. She felt very aware of the boy beside her, his presence making her uncomfortable. The normality of it all didn't fit with him.

He leaned toward her as Ms. Pearson put up something on the board that everyone else in the class started to write down. "Listen, I'm sorry about yesterday."

"Which part?" she whispered as the class fell silent.

"If I'd known you had no idea you died, I wouldn't have just said it like that," said Damien, mouth twitching like apologies weren't his thing.

"Quiet in the back, you two," called Ms. Pearson without turning around. She had the whole "eyes in the back of her head" all teachers had. It was like they all got a set when they graduated university.

Damien took no notice of the woman. "Anyway, I'm sorry. I guess it was kinda rough finding out about things the way you did."

"You think?" Lenna said.

Damien stayed quiet, running an index finger over the cartoon devil someone had etched into the wood of the desk.

"While we're at it," she said, "stop following me around."

"Lenna, I didn't know you'd be here," replied Damien.

"And stop calling me 'Lenna' like we're friends," she hissed. "You don't know me. You know nothing about me or my life, so stay the hell out of it."

"Have you decided what you're going to do about the girl?" Damien asked, unfazed by her outburst.

"Alicia. Her name is Alicia." Lenna tapped the desk with her pencil. "And I don't see why that's any of your business."

"I won't tell you both again," warned their teacher.

"Sorry, Ms. Pearson," said Lenna, kicking Damien's sprawled-out leg under the desk.

"I can help you," said Damien a minute later when the teacher's monotone voice had lulled the room back into semiconsciousness.

"I don't need your help." Lenna needed all the help she could get, but she didn't know if she could trust him.

"Stop being so stubborn. What you're getting into is dangerous."

"You don't think I know that?" she said, hearing the tremor in her voice, thinking of the red car. "You don't think I'd rather be sitting here worrying about next week's test? Besides, wasn't the whole reason for you and Irene coming here in the first place to warn me off from all this?"

"Yes, but I can tell you're not going to stop despite

our warnings. I thought seeing Grams would be enough to put you off, but if you insist on continuing to resolve Alicia's unfinished business, then the best I can do is join you. You're in over your head," said Damien, "and Alicia doesn't have much time left."

"I think you've done enough," said Lenna.

Ms. Pearson snapped her head toward them and shouted. "All right, that's it. Both of you go to the principal's office right now. I won't have you interrupting my class when there are people here who want to learn."

"But—" Lenna tried to protest.

"I said go." Ms. Pearson turned her attention back to the class as if she and Damien had already left.

Chapter 22

Great. This was just what she needed right now. Like a hole in the head.

"Thank you very much," Lenna snapped as she stomped toward the principal's office.

Damien walked beside her, his long legs making it easy for him to keep up. "Hey, I'm the one who should be thanking you. This is just how I wanted my first day at a new school to go."

Lenna slowed her pace. "You really weren't kidding about why you were in class?"

Damien laughed once, holding the straps of his backpack with both hands. "Grams may have dragged me here so she could try and warn you, but that doesn't mean I'm going to let it get in the way of me having some kind of life while I'm here."

Lenna hadn't really considered what it must be like for Damien. He up and left his life back in his hometown, left all his friends, and had to start a new school a few months into his senior year.

"Where are you from anyway?"

Damien shrugged. "Here and there. Grams moves us around a lot. Whenever she catches wind that another person with her abilities is about to discover what they can do, we pack up and head to warn them off."

"How does she know where we are?" Lenna shivered at the thought.

"Grams says she feels it in her bones, whatever that means. All I know, is that I'm uprooted from any semblance of a life I manage to make for myself and I'm forced to start over. We were in Boston for almost a year before *you*."

Lenna bristled. "Hey, I didn't ask you both to come here."

"No, but the fact you refuse to stay away from the dead means I'm stuck in Denwood until you see sense."

"Well you and your grandmother can go back to Boston. Once this is all over and I find Alicia's killer, I'm out. I don't want anything to do with Limbo or ghosts and their unfinished business."

"That suits me. This town is boring, and the people aren't exactly welcoming," he said, giving her a pointed stare. "How about we use that mutual interest to our advantage, huh? Let me help so we can catch whoever killed Alicia and end this."

Damien held out his hand.

"Fine," said Lenna, shaking his hand, hoping she hadn't just made a deal with the devil.

"Good," said Damien. "Now let's go and see what old Stein has to say."

Lenna carried on down the hall. "It'll beat the hell out of math."

They reached the waiting area outside Mr. Stein's office and found a bunch of people already there. They took two empty seats across from each other, everyone around them quiet.

"Hey, Lenna," said the girl next to her.

Nichole Roach, the editor of the school newspaper, sat next to her, visibly flustered.

"Hi," said Lenna. She had done some photos for the paper a while back, but she didn't really know the girl well.

"So, what are you here for?" asked Nichole, like they were a couple of inmates in a state penitentiary.

"Talking in class," replied Lenna, aiming her words at Damien. He shrugged. "You?"

"I wrote an article for the school paper," said Nichole with a flair of drama. "It didn't go down well."

"What did you write?" asked Lenna. As far as schools went, Denwood High was pretty liberal.

"The truth about Alicia Santos." Nichole handed her a paper out of her bag. "They didn't let it go to print."

Lenna read the headline. Nichole's piece wasn't an obituary so much as a smear campaign. She read the headline out loud so Damien could hear it.

"Alicia Santos: The Truth Behind Denwood's Sweetheart."

She skimmed the article, detailing Nichole's opinions on how much of an asshole Alicia had been and her frustrations with everyone for painting her to be some kind of golden child.

Lenna remembered Nichole's attitude in the gym on Monday morning when Principal Stein and Detective Gibbs told everyone about Alicia's death. It appeared Nichole's issues with Alicia ran deep.

"Wow," said Lenna, putting down the paper. She didn't want to read any more of it. "This is kinda intense."

"I'm only being honest," defended Nichole. "I'm glad she's dead."

A few people's heads turned as she said this, giving Nichole what she wanted: attention.

Lenna gave the paper back to Nichole. "No wonder they didn't let you run with that."

"People are going around acting like she was some kind of saint, but she was nothing but a bully." Angry tears ran down Nichole's face, her voice getting louder and louder. "She made my life hell."

"Apparently, the girl killed herself." Damien watched Nichole intently as he spoke. "Maybe she was going through her own stuff too."

"I'm surprised she didn't die of an STD," continued Nichole, taking the bait. "That girl gave it up to anyone who would have her."

Lenna exhaled. "Slut shaming? Really?" Like girls

didn't have enough of that shit to deal with from guys. Anyway, Nichole was talking crap. Alicia died a virgin. It said so in her autopsy report when they mentioned there being no signs of rape.

"Did you see Alicia on Friday?" asked Damien.

Nichole narrowed her eyes at his question, not quick to respond this time. Before Lenna could press her about it, the principal's door opened.

"Miss Roach," said Mr. Stein.

Nichole got up from her seat and sent Lenna and Damien one last glare before stomping into the principal's office and slamming the door.

So much for narrowing down the list.

<hr>

Principal Stein let them both off with a reprimand. After dealing with what Nichole had done, talking in class must have seemed like nothing.

With only twenty minutes left before the bell, Lenna and Damien headed to the front doors to beat the traffic.

"I guess we'll need to keep an eye on that Nichole girl, then?" said Damien.

"She's not the only one." Lenna filled him in on the growing list of suspects.

Lenna didn't even want to think about the number of disgruntled people like Nichole who had experienced Alicia's nasty tendencies. Alicia changed when she joined the cheer squad and became popular. Lenna might as well print out half the school's register if they were going to include all the students Alicia had screwed over on her way to the top.

Her cell rang, the screen showing an unknown number. "Hello?"

"Hey, Lenna," said a familiar voice.

"Hey." She put two fingers up to Damien, telling him she'd be just a minute, and walked a few feet away.

"I got those shifts you were looking for," Brendan said.

Damien leaned against the row of lockers and pretended he wasn't listening.

"Really?" said Lenna. "That was fast."

"Yeah, well, I knew you wanted them."

"Great, can you text them over?" This was just what they needed. They could start crossing off names on that list now that they could speak with their number one suspect.

"Sure," said Brendan. "I'll send them as soon as we hang up."

They both went quiet, neither rushing to end the call.

"So, uh, are you going to the party tomorrow night?"

"Party?"

"Yeah, one of my teammates' parents are out of town this weekend and he's making the most of it."

"I wasn't invited. Besides, parties aren't really my thing." Give Lenna a horror movie night any day over dodging drunk classmates and listening to their horrible taste in music.

"You could always come with me?" Brendan ventured. The hint of doubt in his voice brought back the butterflies in Lenna's stomach.

"You mean, like a date?" Lenna had no time for dating right now and cursed the timing. Football players weren't naturally her type, but Brendan seemed like a sweet guy and he'd gone out of his way to help her.

"I totally mean a date. Only if you want to, of course. No pressure."

Damien cleared his throat and waved at her to hurry up.

"Okay, it's a deal," Lenna said, before she thought better of it. Besides, depending on how things went with Trey, this could all be over by tonight.

"Sweet," Brendan said in victory, which made Lenna laugh. "I'll send over the house address with Trey's work schedule. See you then."

"Thanks for helping. I really appreciate it." Lenna hung up and went back to Damien. He raised an eyebrow in question.

"Just a lead I was following," she said, like it was no big deal. "I've managed to get Trey's work schedule. He works at the garden center next to the mall."

Her cell buzzed in her hand and she opened the text from Brendan. Someone seemed eager.

"When's the guy working?" asked Damien.

Lenna went straight to Friday, the night Alicia

died. Trey hadn't worked that night. She scanned the message and got to Thursday. She looked up from her cell. "Today. He's working in half an hour."

"Let's go, then." Damien kicked off the lockers and took out his car keys from his pocket. He stopped and asked, "Do you want to wait on your friend first?"

Corey would still be in class. Lenna didn't know what they were walking into, but if it was anything like last night, then it could get dangerous. If anything happened to Corey, she would never forgive herself. Something almost had.

"No, let's go," she said, walking out the front doors. "I don't want him involved."

Damien followed. "Oh, but you're fine with putting me in harm's way?"

"You're a big boy. I'm sure you'll be fine."

Chapter 23

Leaves and wet soil filled Lenna's lungs as they entered the garden center, much like the scent that surrounded Alicia when she'd died in the park.

"This place is huge," said Damien beside her as he took in the rows and rows of aisles filled with garden equipment.

All around them were flowers and saplings of all different shapes and sizes. It looked like someone had taken a green canvas and hurled Skittles all over it, every color of the rainbow found in a plant pot somewhere near. It was a good thing they hadn't waited for Corey. His allergies would've exploded in a place like this.

"Let's split up," said Lenna. "I'll take this side and you take the right. We'll cover more ground that way."

"What does the dude look like?" Damien asked.

"He's a big, muscled guy," said Lenna. "About six

foot three with dark brown hair. Just check his name tag if you're unsure."

Damien sauntered off into the first aisle on his side. Lenna watched him go and turned into the first row at her end.

A long line of sadistic gnomes beamed down at her as she walked past, their painted eyes sinister. Why anyone would want them hanging around their garden, she'd never know. They were almost as bad as porcelain dolls.

Lenna spotted someone wearing a green T-shirt with the center's logo on it and walked up to him.

"Excuse me," she said.

"Hey, can I help you with anything?" The guy appeared to be around college age, a scrawny redhead with zits spread across his forehead.

"Yes, actually," she looked at his name tag. "James, I'm looking for someone who works here—Trey Orson?"

James's face dropped at the mention of Trey. "He hasn't been in all week," he said.

"Why not?" she asked, catching him stealing looks at her chest. She refrained from smacking him across the side of the head. James wouldn't be too chatty after that.

"Sick, I guess. I don't really talk to him. He likes to keep to himself, you know?"

That meant no one here knew about Alicia's death, or at least James didn't.

"Tell me about it," said Lenna. "I've been looking for him everywhere."

"What for?" asked James with a little frown.

"I work on the Denwood High newspaper," she said, sticking to a lie that had worked before. "The principal wants a piece about the star quarterback of the Denwood Demons and, lucky me, I got stuck with the riveting job of writing it." She made sure to look irritated. "Like I've got nothing better to do than find out crap about some dumb jock."

"Bummer," James said, ignoring a woman who called for help to get something off the top shelf.

"I know, right?" continued Lenna. "I don't suppose you know much about him?"

James leaned his elbow on the shelf nearest him, like he owned the place. "Not really. Like I said, I don't talk to him much, but anytime I do, all he does is brag about his girl."

"His girl?" asked Lenna. She took a step closer to James.

"Yeah, that's all he ever really talks about," he said, his face reddening. "Kinda weird if you ask me."

It seemed James was yet another person who wasn't a fan of Trey. "Weird like how?" asked Lenna.

"Like he's obsessed with her or something. He always brings her up in conversation, even if it has nothing to do with what we're talking about."

"Can you remember her name?" asked Lenna, making sure Trey didn't have a new girlfriend they didn't yet know about.

"I can't remember." James clicked his fingers. "Alice or something like that."

"You mean Alicia?" pressed Lenna. Her heartbeat sped up.

"Yeah," said James. "Alicia, that's it."

"What about Alicia?" called a voice from behind her. Lenna turned and came face-to-face with Trey.

Trey stood so tall he cast a shadow over them both. His very presence made the hairs at the back of Lenna's neck stand on end. His hands were the size of catcher's mitts, and he looked like he hadn't slept in days.

"Hi, Trey," she stammered. Had he been the one who tried to run them off the road?

"Why are you talking about Alicia?" he demanded. He was built like a brick shithouse, as if he spent more time in the gym than he did at school. Those steroids were definitely working.

Trey growled at James. "Piss off."

James tugged his shirt collar and moved away, busying himself with the nearest customer he could find.

"Why are you talking to that freak about my girl-friend?" Trey spat.

Lenna stepped away and felt the aisle shelf press at her back. She raised her chin. "Don't you mean your ex-girlfriend?"

Trey slammed his fist against the shelf near her head, the metal crying in her ear at the impact. "Don't make me repeat my question," he said.

Lenna tried to steady her voice. "The school paper's doing a piece on Alicia, like an obituary talking about her life, and I thought you might want to give a quote or something."

Trey cocked his head. "And why the hell would you care? Alicia couldn't stand you."

Lenna's mouth went dry, her mind racing for something to say that wouldn't enrage him further.

Trey moved away and looked at her like she was dirt. "Get out of my sight."

Lenna didn't want to be around him for another second, but she couldn't leave without learning more. If he really did kill Alicia, she needed him to talk.

"Please," she said, stepping toward him now. "Just a few words are all I need for the article. Did you see her on Friday at all?"

Trey screwed his face like he'd eaten a bunch of Sour Patch Kids all at once. "Why is that important to your stupid article?"

Lenna continued. "When was the last time you saw her? Did you ask her to take you back? Did she say no again?"

His eyes bore through her. "Who have you been talking to? Do you know something?"

Lenna folded her arms. "About what?"

"About how she died," he said, his voice a growl. "What do you think you know?"

"Shouldn't I be asking you that question?"

He moved faster than she could react and seized

the top of her arm with his meaty hand, pressing so hard she thought it would break. "Tell me."

His grasp released as he stumbled back a few steps. "Hey, man, back off."

Damien stood next to her now, a shadow over his face as he stared down Trey.

"You shouldn't have done that," said the quarterback.

Damien stalked toward him, his arms open and antagonistic. "Why, what are you going to do about it?"

"Hey, hey," said Lenna, trying to get in between them. "Stop it."

The two boys squared off. Damien leaned on his toes, the leather of his boots showing the strain, like he was ready to pounce on the huge guy before him. Damien wasn't a beanpole by any means, but Trey had a lot of muscle on him.

A man in his fifties with thinning hair pushed his way between them before anything could happen. "I think it best if you two leave," he said to Lenna and Damien, his tone sharp but hushed. "Trey, I want a word with you in my office. Now." He strode off without a second look at any of them.

Trey watched who Lenna assumed to be his boss walk away before he turned back to them. "This isn't over," he promised and then stormed after the older man.

"Are you okay?" Damien asked, looking her over.

"Yeah," she said, a little shaken. She rubbed at her arm where Trey had grabbed her.

Damien put a hand over her arm, his touch light. "Did he hurt you?"

"Not really. He just scared me."

"Did you learn anything?" he asked, noticing his hand still on her arm and dropping it to his side.

"His reaction to my questions said more than his words," Lenna said. Trey seemed in a murderous mood. "Let's get out of here."

"Thrown out of class and a store in one afternoon," said Damien as they headed to the front. "You really know how to get a guy in trouble."

Lenna stopped as they passed the cash registers at the front of the garden center, zoning out as something caught her attention. The blood drained from her face.

"What is it?" asked Damien, like he expected Trey to come back.

She walked past the line of people and picked something out of the small display area along the checkout line.

It was a red rose, wrapped in golden foil.

Chapter 24

Lenna held onto the rose as Damien drove them back to Denwood.

"It's him," she said, trying not to clasp the rose too hard in case the thorns broke through the gold foil like they had with Alicia. "I know it."

"You need proof," said Damien, taking the exit back to town. "Something that can pin the douchebag to the murder and take him down. A rose isn't going to do that."

Lenna chucked the rose onto the dashboard. Adrenaline pumped through her system, her whole body tense now that she had found the killer. She felt sure of it. Why else would he act like that if he hadn't been the one who killed Alicia?

His last words replayed in her mind. *This isn't over.*

"I think we should go back to Alicia's house," said Lenna, formulating a plan. "There must be something there that can tell us what she was doing the night she died."

Before long, they found themselves outside the Santos house. Damien turned off the engine. "I'll leave the car unlocked. Beep the horn when you're out so I'll know when to split."

He got out of the car and walked to the front door, ringing the bell. A few moments later, Mrs. Santos answered the door. Lenna waited with crossed fingers as Damien talked his way inside, pretending as planned to act like another one of Alicia's friends from school.

When the front door closed, Lenna got out of the car, taking care when she shut the door. Keeping away from the big front window, she rushed up the porch and ran around the house until she reached the backyard. She peeked into the kitchen window to make sure the coast was clear.

The glass door was unlocked. She slid it open as silently as possible and slipped inside. Damien's voice sounded through the thick walls.

The kitchen was top of the line and had marble flooring, which didn't bode well for her heels. She took an experimental step forward and heard a loud click. Taking them off, she held the heels in one hand and padded across the kitchen.

Moving as fast as possible without making much noise, she crept down the foyer to the bottom of the staircase and traveled upstairs.

The wood creaked under her halfway up. Part of

her wanted to run the rest of the way, but she took each step one at a time, nice and slow. Once upstairs, she took a left to Alicia's room.

It hadn't changed much since her last visit in freshman year. The familiar pink wallpaper and ballerina poster stuck along Alicia's closet door made her heart pang. The glow-in-the-dark stars they'd stuck to her ceiling years before were still there, both of them having to jump up and down on Alicia's bed to reach.

Lenna had spent so much time here, Alicia's house like a second home. Now the bedroom felt hollow. A remnant of the past.

A floor-to-ceiling shelf stood along one wall filled with medals and trophies, most of them gold. Lenna ran a hand over the polished metal. There were a lot more since Lenna's last visit, where they used to dream about their futures. Alicia was going to be a star preforming on Broadway, and Lenna would be the big fashion designer who would make all her costumes.

They were dreams, sure, but Lenna never doubted that Alicia would make it. She was a terrific dancer and had been at the top of her game. Before, Alicia's shelf full of trophies were an indication of where she was headed in her life. Now, they were merely relics of a life taken far too soon.

Lenna ground her teeth. She would make sure Trey paid for what he had done if it was the last thing she ever did.

Leaving Alicia's wall of achievements, she searched the room for a laptop or tablet, anything she may have used to chat with her killer. A charger lay in the corner of the room next to a desk covered in Alicia's half-completed homework. On it sat a picture of her, Kayla, Ellie, and Zara, all of them smiling as they posed for the camera. Sadness gripped her chest, making it hard to breathe. Lenna used to be the one beside Alicia in all her photos.

Lenna bent down and looked at the charger. It was for a laptop, but it seemed to have been removed. Maybe the police had taken it.

She slumped on Alicia's bed. They were so close. There had to be something else. There had to be some way to find out where Alicia had been last Friday.

Lenna scooted over to the bedside cabinet and picked up a notebook. It was Alicia's diary, right next to her bed, out in the open for anyone to see. It didn't even have a lock on it.

What Lenna read didn't make sense.

She flicked to the last entry, the day before Alicia died, and read. Alicia summarized her day at school, mentioning what she'd learned in class and what homework she had, said she was excited for the weekend and spending time with Kayla.

She flipped back, skimming the pages, looking for Trey's name or anything that might indicate any plans she had for that fateful Friday night. All the entries she read felt the same, empty of the real Alicia.

The front of the book had the word diary on it, but this was far from that. This seemed more like Alicia's cover, like she knew her diary would be read. Nothing inside showed the real girl. It read generic and tame—two words Lenna would never use to describe a girl like Alicia.

Had she been lying to avoid getting grounded or was she trying to protect herself from something more?

"What the hell are you doing here?" said a voice behind her.

Mr. Santos stood at the door, blocking Lenna's only way out.

Chapter 25

Mr. Santos's face was like thunder, his eyes bloodshot like he hadn't stopped drinking since he had thrown her and Corey out the first time.

Lenna was trapped, a mouse in a lion's den. Would Mr. Santos hurt her? Had he hurt his own daughter? She eyed the fallen diary, Mr. Santos following her gaze.

"Have you been reading my daughter's diary?"

"I was just—" Lenna stuttered, calculating how fast she could reach the door and get the hell out of there. She slipped her feet into her heels.

"Just what? Sneaking into my house and reading my dead daughter's diary? How dare you!" he roared. "This is my daughter's room. You have no business being here!"

In a fit of rage, Mr. Santos bounded to the shelves

and swung his arm through a row of Alicia's trophies, sending them crashing to the ground in a clatter of metal and colored ribbons.

"I read that whole thing and not once did she mention you or your little friend," he said, chest heaving up and down. "What do you think you're doing? What are you looking for?"

Lenna didn't answer him. Anything she said would only make him angrier.

Mr. Santos studied her and his eyebrows knitted together. "Do you know something?"

"Lenna, are you okay?" interrupted Damien, panting at the foot of the door. He must've heard the crashing from downstairs.

"Who the hell are you?" shouted Mr. Santos, his attention on Damien now with his back to Lenna.

Lenna looked at the pile of broken trophies, lying like a heap of scrap metal. They glinted in the late afternoon sun that snuck in through the window. Amidst the wreckage were the diary and other casualties from the shelves. One thing caught her attention and she snatched it up, tucking the piece of thick paper into the waistband of her skirt before anyone saw her.

"Fred," said Mrs. Santos, reaching the door behind Damien. She watched her husband with wide eyes. "What's going on? Lenna? What are you doing here, dear?"

"Trespassing is what she's doing," spat Mr. Santos, turning his head to Damien. "And this one too, no doubt."

Mrs. Santos clutched the rosaries she hadn't parted with since Tuesday.

"Really, Mr. Santos, it's not what it looks like," began Lenna.

"I think everyone needs to calm down," said Damien, his attention never leaving Alicia's dad.

"Calm down?" Mr. Santos sent another row of his daughter's prized achievements to the floor.

Mrs. Santos gasped as they fell, piling onto the others. "Lenna, I think it best if you leave," she said, stepping away from the door with glistening eyes.

Lenna didn't need to be told twice. She crossed the room and grasped Damien by the arm, running down the stairs and out the front door without looking back.

They got into Damien's car, started the engine, and sped away as fast as they could.

"That escalated fast," said Damien, turning off their street. "Did you at least get any leads?"

"I found this." Lenna flattened out the paper she'd scooped up. The corner was missing, the very thing that caught her attention in the first place. She rummaged in her bag for a second and produced the evidence photo of the tiny piece of paper Mrs. Santos had given her on her first visit, the one that was in Alicia's jacket when she died.

Lenna placed the photo of the small piece next to the larger one, connecting them by the cut-off yellow circle. The circle was part of a logo at the top of a flyer for a new place that had opened in the next town.

A club named Echo.

amien dropped Lenna off at her house.

Her hearse was in the driveway and she found Corey sitting at the kitchen table when she went inside.

"Hey," she said, unable to get Trey and Mr. Santos out of her mind. Then there was Nichole.

Open workbooks lay in front of Corey, his messy handwriting scribbled over pages of homework. He'd been there a while. At least one of them was keeping up with school this week.

"I waited for you after school," he said, closing an AP biology textbook. "Figured I'd better bring your car here when you didn't show."

"You wouldn't believe the day I've had." Lenna plopped down on a chair and filled him in on everything.

Corey didn't interrupt once and sat in silence when she finished.

"You okay?" Lenna asked.

Corey bent his head down and stared at his entwined hands. "You and Damien, huh?"

"Yeah, he's not as weird as he seemed. It was a good thing he was there when Trey popped off." Lenna could still feel the grip of his fingers on her skin. Between that and the two bruises from Alicia, she was a missing tooth away from looking like a cage fighter.

"Why didn't you wait on me?" Corey asked, something like hurt behind his eyes.

Oh.

"I just wanted to get to Trey as soon as possible, and you were still in class," said Lenna, trying her best to brush it off.

Corey's brow creased above his glasses. "I'm sure Trey's shift started after school finished, since he's still a student. Sounds like you got there before he did."

Lenna got up from the table and turned on the coffee machine. "I didn't think."

"You thought long enough to take Damien with you," said Corey. "You didn't even know who he was until yesterday, besides being the dude who was creeping outside your house at night."

"He agreed to help find the killer," she said, busying herself with refilling the water.

"And I didn't? Am I no use to you now that Damien's here? I thought we were in this together." Corey gathered his homework in a haphazard pile.

"I didn't—" Lenna started, and stopped.

"What? Want me around in case I got in the way?"

Lenna turned and faced him. "Cor, it's not like that."

"Then what?" he asked, shoving the pile of books into his backpack and zipping it shut.

"We could have died last night," said Lenna, voice tight with emotion.

"I know," said Corey. "I was in the car with you. The killer came after us both, so I'm in this just as much as you are. I'm your best friend."

"Which is why I didn't want you to come with me

today," blurted Lenna. "I already have a lost friend downstairs in a drawer. I don't want to be responsible for you joining her. I got you involved and I shouldn't have. I dragged you into this and put you in danger. I couldn't live with myself if something happened to you."

Corey kicked his chair from under him and got up. "And you think I could live with myself knowing something terrible happened to you and I wasn't even there? We're supposed to be in this together. It's not your decision to leave me out."

"I just didn't want you to get hurt."

Corey hoisted his bag over his shoulder and looked at her. "Yeah, well, how did that work out?"

The basement door opened and her dad walked in, noting the tension in the air. "Is everything all right?"

"I was just leaving. Happy birthday, Mr. G." Corey tossed the spare key to Lenna's hearse on the counter and walked out without saying goodbye.

Lenna closed her eyes as her heart broke. How could she forget his birthday?

"Oh, Dad, I'm so sorry. I completely forgot it was today."

"That's okay," said her dad like it was nothing, but she could see she'd hurt him.

Lenna put a hand to her head. "No, it's not. I've been so wrapped up in everything with Alicia and it completely slipped my mind."

"I know, honey. It's fine, really," he assured her.

"I'll make it up to you," she promised.

Her dad forced a smile. "I better get back to work."

He closed the door, leaving Lenna feeling like the worst friend and daughter in the world.

―――――――――――――

Chapter 26

―――――――――――――

It was pitch-black when Lenna reached the park.

She drove through the gates and headed to the spot where Alicia died. Whispers lured her closer, leading her there with welcome, open arms. They were hungry.

Headlights spread over the grass field like a beacon, warning her to leave, to turn around and go home. But she couldn't.

Everything was so messed up. Lenna's life was crumbling around her, and she was still no closer to settling Alicia's unfinished business. The killer was still out there.

She must have missed something in Limbo, a vital clue. The deeper she delved into Alicia's death, the more complicated it got, not to mention dangerous.

She'd tried calling Corey, but he never picked up. Her dad stayed down in the basement, working on his birthday when he should be celebrating. The whole investigation was screwing everything. It needed to end.

Lenna stopped the car and got out, walking the rest of the way.

The park was deserted and bathed in darkness. Voices called to her among the howling wind that whipped her hair back from her face.

Come, they said.

Allowing the pull to take over her body, Lenna trudged to the scene of the crime. The hollowness of death kissed her forehead and she lost herself to it. She closed her eyes and reached out to the shadows.

Vertigo turned her world upside down and when she opened her eyes, she was in Limbo.

Screams that would shatter glass screeched all around her. Lenna walked forward, ignoring their pleas for help. She hadn't come for them. They were lost, but she could still save Alicia.

Lenna found her, lying on the grass like last time, consumed by the drugs that had ended her short life. Lenna's heart broke all over again as Alicia struggled to breathe, tears slipping down the side of her face.

Lightning came and Friday night's storm began. The last few minutes of Alicia's life played like a video on repeat.

Lenna searched around Alicia's body and the surrounding area on her hands and knees, desperate for another clue, anything that could tip the scale in her favor. The rose was there, blood red and gold, just like the one she'd found earlier in the garden center.

The headlights of the red car lit up the space, but still Lenna found nothing new.

The phantom of the killer approached and stood over Alicia just as before. Lenna got to her feet and came within inches of the killer. They were shrouded in shadow, indiscernible and as dark as oblivion.

With a last look at Alicia, they turned their back and headed for the car.

"You asshole!" screamed Lenna, running after them. "Who are you? Why did you do this?"

Lenna punched at the killer and her hand traveled right though them. She didn't stop, sending a tirade of blows that never landed.

The killer got in the car. Lenna checked through the windows, looking for anything that stood out. The glass was tinted by the darkness and her pained reflection stared back at her.

Were they alone? Was someone else in there? Was one driving while the other held Alicia down? Had they abducted her? Forced her into the car with them?

The car reversed and left as Alicia died in front of Lenna for the second time.

"No!" she cried.

Lenna sat with Alicia as the rain pelted down. After a while, Alicia's body began to fade. It grew translucent and blended into the darkness as a rotting corpse becomes one with the earth.

"Wait," said Lenna. "Come back."

Alicia dissipated into nothing as the replay of her demise fizzled out.

Lenna prepared herself for the sickening sensation to crash into her as she returned to the real world.

It never came.

"Go back," Lenna said, like she had any semblance of control in this place. "Take me back."

Hissing answered her from behind. Lenna glanced behind her, ice running down her spine. Spirits materialized from the shadows. Their long, distorted limbs reached out for her, jaws hinged back in eternal screams that bore into her soul.

Lenna ran, blind in the darkness. She tripped and landed facedown. Tongues spoke to her in unknown languages and tickled her ears with ill intention. Lenna rolled on to her back and hoisted herself up. A horde of spirits surrounded her, tearing each other to shreds to get near her. One of them leaped into the air and dived at her.

Lenna screamed. She clawed out at the shadows. Hands clamped over her wrists.

"Stop!" someone yelled.

Lenna opened her eyes, still screaming, struggling to break free.

Detective Gibbs yanked her arms. "I said stop!"

Lenna stopped fighting and stared in confusion at the detective. Nausea rushed through her and she threw up on the grass.

Detective Gibbs took a step back in disgust. "Is that blood?"

"I had tomato soup earlier," Lenna lied, her mouth

filled with the coppery taste of it. She leaned on her knees, unsure if she could stand up yet.

Gibbs clicked on a little flashlight, tilted Lenna's head up, and shone it in her eyes.

"Quit it," said Lenna. "What are you doing?"

Gibbs scanned her with a cop's X-ray vision. "Checking your pupils aren't dilated."

Lenna swatted the flashlight away. "I'm not on anything. I must have fainted or something."

Gibbs spoke police code into her radio. Someone responded at the other end. "What are you doing here?" she asked Lenna.

Lenna stretched her back, every part of her aching. "I could ask you the same thing," she retorted, spotting the detective's car down the path.

Gibbs scrutinized Lenna's every movement. "Killers are known for returning to the scene of the crime."

An eerie shiver crawled across Lenna's skin. "I thought the police and ME concluded Alicia's death was suicide?"

"They did."

The lights of a police car danced outside the gates and parked up behind Lenna's hearse. Gibbs left her and spoke to two uniformed officers. One of them got into the hearse and started the engine.

Gibbs came back, ignoring Lenna's protests over the cop in her car. "Come on, I'm taking you home."

Lenna stepped back. "I'll drive myself home."

"It wasn't a question."

etective Gibbs made Lenna wait in the car while she spoke with her dad.

They talked for five minutes, the detective doing most of the talking.

Gibbs came back and sat in the driver's seat. "Your father is waiting for you." She started to say something else, but Lenna got out and slammed the door.

Her dad met her at the door with a stern expression. It wasn't a look he wore often, especially not when it came to Lenna.

"Dad, I don't know what she said," began Lenna, but her dad raised a hand in silence.

He looked exhausted. "The police at my door bringing you home isn't what I expected as a birthday present."

Lenna didn't know what to say. How could she explain herself? What reason could she have for being out there? She couldn't tell him the truth. What if he didn't believe her? She had already gotten Corey involved, and she refused to put her dad in danger, even if it meant he was angry at her, like everyone else was.

She stared at her feet.

"Go to your room. I have a service first thing tomorrow morning, but I want you to come straight home after school. We're going to talk about this."

Chapter 27

Lenna woke to a shattering crash as shards of glass fell over her floor and bedsheets.

The wind whistled as it entered the hole in her window, the frame now decorated by jagged glass teeth. The curtains blew around like twin ghosts under the haunting glow of the waning moon.

Lenna kicked off her covers and darted across the room for her baseball bat. Her chest heaved as she waited in silence for someone, or something, to come through the smashed window.

Quick footsteps headed her way from the hall. Her mind leaped to Alicia's killer as the bedroom door swung open.

Lenna roared like a warrior and raised her bat to smash in the intruder's skull.

Her dad grabbed the top of the bat before Lenna knocked him out with it. Sleep was in his eyes, his long hair disheveled, but he was alert. Panicked, he scanned the area as he guarded in front of her.

"What happened?" he asked, crossing the room and looking out into the yard.

Lenna dropped her bat to the floor. A brick lay on her carpet with paper attached to it by a rubber band. Lenna skipped over pieces of glass in her bare feet and nudged the brick under her bed before her dad saw.

"I think it was the branches," she said, the old oak tree blowing in the wind next to her window.

"The storm is pretty bad," said her dad, looking back at her as he ran a hand through his hair. His posture relaxed. "I thought someone had broken in or something."

"Me too," she said, the tension still palpable between them.

She wished it had been the oak tree. Someone had done this. Someone had come to her house, stood on her lawn, and launched the brick through her window.

Sitting on her bed, she hugged herself from the cold she wasn't entirely sure came from the gaping hole in her window.

Her dad studied the mess with his hands on his hips.

"I'll get some boards from the basement to cover it up and call someone to fix it in the morning." He stepped over the glass shards that glinted up at them like diamonds. "Watch you don't cut your feet on the glass."

He left, and Lenna waited until she was sure he

was downstairs. She bent down and brought the brick out from under her bed with shaking hands. Taking off the rubber band, she opened the piece of paper. Visceral fear panged in the pit of her stomach as she read the message, written in a heavy, angry scrawl:

Stop digging or your dad will be burying you next!

<hr>

Chapter 28

Sleep evaded Lenna like Alicia's killer.

She tossed and turned on the living room couch, her bedroom abandoned until the window could be fixed.

Just when she thought things couldn't possibly get any worse, surprise, here's a death threat. The whole day had been a complete catastrophe from start to finish.

She was still nauseated from her time in Limbo, stomach sore like she'd eaten a bunch of needles. And it had all been for nothing. There weren't any clues she'd missed. That was her lot and it wasn't enough.

Why didn't she return to reality once Alicia died, like last time? Why did she get stuck? And what the hell was Gibbs doing out there alone in the park? The case was closed.

Lenna got up and went to the kitchen. She made hot chocolate with extra marshmallows, compensation for the crappy string of events the last twenty-four hours had brought. Heck, for the whole week.

Lenna slipped into her jacket and, steaming mug in hand, went down to the basement to see her old friend.

"Any news?" asked Alicia as soon as she walked in.

Lenna sat down and shivered. The heat from her mug died in the cold. "I've done a lot more digging, but none of it has paid off."

It was past midnight now. They had only three days left.

Lenna sipped her lukewarm hot chocolate and hissed as it traveled down her throat and reached her stomach. Irene was right; a nosebleed had been nothing. Her throat stung like she'd swallowed glass, and her mind hummed with the ring of voices somewhere far off in the distance.

Alicia moved closer and sat on a slab.

"Do you have a fake ID?" Lenna asked.

"No, why?"

"You had part of a flyer for a nightclub named Echo on you when you died." Lenna produced the part she'd found in Alicia's bedroom and laid it out in front of her. "Does it ring any bells?"

Alicia studied the flyer. "I've never heard of it."

Lenna huddled in her chair. She couldn't catch a break.

"Are you okay?" Alicia asked.

Lenna eyed Alicia. She was quieter this visit, more solemn. Her question seemed sincere.

"It's not the only thing I've found. Someone kindly

put this through my window with a brick attached a couple of hours ago." Lenna put the message beside the flyer. She told Alicia about the red car trying to run her and Corey off the road.

"I'm getting close. Or at least that's what they think." The killer was getting desperate.

In truth, Lenna had no idea who was behind it all. It was like she had pieces to a puzzle where nothing seemed to fit. She had her suspicions, yes, but nothing concrete, and without that, she might as well have nothing. The police weren't going to listen to her otherwise, especially after her run-in with Detective Gibbs in the park.

"Lenna."

Lenna broke out of her daze and looked at her ex-best friend. She inched her fingers close to Lenna's hand, careful not to touch her.

Alicia stared at their hands as she spoke, her hair covering most of her face. "I know things are messy with us and we've said and done a lot of things we can't take back, but thank you for doing this for me. I really mean that."

"Of course." Lenna blinked back guilt-ridden tears. "It's the least I can do."

Alicia looked at her, really looked at her, for the first time since she woke up dead. "I'm sorry for what I said. I shouldn't have expected you to know I was struggling back then when I used every bit of energy I had to hide it."

Lenna shook her head. "I should still have noticed

though. I knew you weren't yourself, but I thought it was because you were angry with me."

"I was," Alicia admitted with a sad smile. "Some of it was thanks to my strained mental health at the time but, if I'm honest, a lot of it wasn't. I could feel us drifting apart, and the more I saw it happening, the angrier I got. I shouldn't have been a bitch and taken it out on you the way I did. I was the one ignoring you for Trey and cheerleading, so of course you were going to find other friends. I should have accepted that and not let it affect us. It didn't need to split us apart."

Lenna simply stared for a moment, taking in Alicia's admission. She never expected to hear those words from her old friend. Hearing them now took her aback.

"Since we're being honest," Lenna said after a while, "I can't say that my intentions were always good when I used to rag on you about Trey. I was jealous of him for taking you away from me. I hated his guts for it. A part of me felt vindicated when I found out he was cheating on you."

It wasn't one of Lenna's best moments, but it was the truth. Even saying it out loud made her feel a bit better, like the weight of all the hurt from their friendship breakup seemed to release its hold. It was a conversation she'd longed to have, and it sucked it took until now to happen.

"Yeah, well, Trey's an asshole," said Alicia, rolling her eyes. "I think we can both agree on that one."

Yes, thought Lenna, *but is he also a killer?* "I guess we both messed things up," she said instead.

Alicia nudged closer to Lenna, careful not to touch her with her death flesh. "It all seems so stupid and petty now, doesn't it?"

Cold radiated from Alicia's presence, but her closeness was oddly comforting. "Death has a way of putting things into perspective," Lenna said.

Alicia let out a deep sigh, a puff of cold air escaping her mouth in a murky fog. "I can't believe I'm dead."

"Are you bored in here all day?" Lenna asked, thinking about it for the first time as she tried to move away from the touchy subject. She didn't want to sour the moment by dwelling on who had killed Alicia. They both deserved a little reprieve from that train of thought, even if only for a few minutes. "I can bring a TV down or something to pass the time. Or a book maybe? Though I don't know how you'd turn the pages."

"No thanks," Alicia said, leaning back and taking in the room. "I'm kinda enjoying the quiet. It's strange, I remember being so spooked out about this place when we were kids, but it's almost peaceful in a way."

"I always thought so," Lenna agreed. "Until you woke up, of course."

Alicia smiled, and for a second it almost felt like they were back to their old selves, sitting around and joking. Lenna hadn't realized how much she'd missed it until now.

"I heard you and your dad talking. I remember the

finger paint fiasco like it was yesterday." Alicia laughed, a real, life-filled laugh that resounded across the room. "Your dad was super mad, and we kept on wriggling away from him. I've never seen someone so flustered."

"I have," Lenna said, laughing too. "You seem to be forgetting about the time when we were ten and tried to sneak into the movies to watch some rated-R thing you just *had* to see."

Alicia gasped. "Oh my god, I totally forgot about that! Why did I try to make out we were eighteen?"

"I don't know," Lenna said, "but I blame our Dora the Explorer backpacks for giving us away."

"Yeah, thanks a lot, Dora. Good thing it was your dad the manager called. Mine would have killed me for arguing with the staff."

"'This is unacceptable,'" mimicked Lenna, recalling Alicia's exact words. "'I demand to speak with your manager, young man.'"

"My outraged white lady voice was on point."

"Poor Dad. I don't know why he put up with us."

Alicia shrugged. "We were harmless, really. I even think I remember him laughing a little with the manager."

"It is pretty hilarious thinking back on it," Lenna admitted, wiping tears of laughter from her face.

"Lenna," said Alicia, her eyes serious again. "Promise me you'll be careful. I don't want you to end up in the drawer next to mine."

Lenna shifted in her seat. She didn't want to make

any promises to Alicia she couldn't keep. "I'll try my best. Whoever did this to you seems dead set on keeping the truth buried."

The threat made on her life was very real, and if Lenna wasn't careful, she might very well be the killer's next victim.

Chapter 29

Lenna walked down the empty hallway, another pass in her hand to see a counselor, something that had become a handy get-out-of-class-free card. No one even questioned whether she'd actually gone yesterday.

She hadn't spoken to Corey since last night, and Damien was MIA.

Lenna took out her cell and called Brendan.

"Hi," he said, seeming surprised to hear from her.

Lenna walked up to the second floor. "Hi. I didn't think you'd answer. I was going to leave you a message." She thought he'd be in class.

"I'm in study hall, so no one really cares. Where are you?" he asked, people talking in the background.

"Oh, just walking around," she said, looking up and down the corridor to make sure that no hall monitors roamed near.

Gibbs was outside a classroom just down the hall,

speaking to Nichole Roach. Lenna ducked and hid behind a vending machine, peering around it to get a look at them. Why was the detective here, and what did she want with Nichole?

"Rebel," said Brendan.

"Yeah, so listen," she said, getting to the point of her call as she backtracked, taking the longer route to her destination. "I don't think I'm going to be able to go to the party tonight."

Not that Lenna would ever admit it, but part of her liked the idea of going to a party with Brendan.

"Why not?" he said, disappointed.

Oh, you know, thought Lenna, as she ran her hand over a row of lockers, *just a little matter of hunting down a murderer who's threatened my life before the soul of my ex-best friend gets sent to Limbo for the rest of eternity.*

"I forgot I told my dad I'd help him out with work," she said instead. "I can't get out of it."

"Oh, that's too bad," he replied.

"I'm sure the party will be great," she said, walking into the English department and trying to remember the room number. A party with a cute boy was so mundane and normal compared to the week she was having. Right now, normal sounded like heaven.

"I guess. To be honest, I was only going to go if you were coming. I'm not too big on parties."

"Me neither." Lenna stopped as she neared the right room, actually bummed she couldn't go to the party now. "Sorry I can't make it."

"What do you say about going on a date with me? You and me, the diner, tomorrow night? Unless you've changed your mind. It's totally fine if you have, I mean, I get it."

Lenna broke into a smile despite herself, glad he wasn't there to see it. Brendan was a far cry from his teammate Elliot, and practically the opposite of Trey. If those guys were the stereotypes, Brendan definitely broke the mold.

"I don't know if I can do tomorrow, but I might be able to squeeze you into my schedule," she teased. She had to catch a murderer first.

"You're a busy girl."

"Yeah, this week's been killer. I'll let you know about tomorrow."

"Promise?" he said.

"Yes," Lenna promised. "Besides, I'll be free the whole of next week."

Whatever happened, it would all be over one way or another by then. It didn't bear thinking about.

"Awesome," said Brendan. "My teacher's coming back so I'd better go. Text me about our date."

Lenna bit her lip, already thinking about what she should wear.

Ending the call, Lenna knocked on the classroom door and entered the English class where the stepsisters had a double period.

"Hi," she said to the teacher, an old woman waiting for retirement who seemed less interested than the students. "The principal wants to see Ellie and Zara Parsons in his office."

There was something about the girls she didn't like, aside from them being a pair of major bitches. It niggled at her, and talking to them might give her a new lead to follow. Time was running out and she was desperate.

The teacher peered over the romance novel she held close to her face. "They're not here. They went off to see one of the counselors," she said, checking her wristwatch, "about forty minutes ago now."

Lenna left the room, closing the door behind her without another word, and dashed down the hall. They'd be trying to get sent home again. She couldn't miss them. This was her last chance at seeing them in school before the weekend, and by then it could be too late.

Her heels clicked on the floor as she made her way to the stairway. Pushing herself against the heavy door, she reached the top of the stairs on the second floor, wishing she had worn her Doc Martens instead.

Taking hold of the handrail, she took the first step before someone reeled her back.

Gloved hands wrapped around her neck before she could react. They dug against her throat, crushing her windpipe.

Lenna clawed at the hands, trying to pry herself free, but they wouldn't budge. She panicked, her breathing labored. The more she struggled against them, the tighter they squeezed. She thrashed from side to side, trying anything she could to break free. She needed air. She needed to get away.

Using her heel, Lenna raised her leg and stomped down hard where she guessed her attacker's feet were. She missed on the first try, sending a stinging sensation up her right leg as she made impact with the ground.

Her second attempt found its mark, and the gloved hand released upon impact, giving her a moment to twist away from their grip.

She fell to her knees and sucked in air, her chest tight and lungs struggling. Her eyes watered as she panted. She needed to escape. To run.

Now.

Stumbling to her feet, Lenna lunged for the door to go back into the hallway, but an arm wrapped around her waist and dragged her back. How many attackers were there? Two? Three? Before she could get a look, a plastic bag went over her head.

She couldn't breathe. Lenna swung blindly for her attacker, kicked with her heels. She crashed into something hard. A wall. She grabbed for the plastic bag, heart pounding, lungs screaming. She scratched at the plastic at her mouth, tearing it open.

Free from the suffocating plastic, she gulped for air, like she'd reached the surface of the sea seconds before drowning, and pulled at the rest of the bag with frantic hands.

She tried to scream, but a hand covered her mouth, pressing down so hard her skin split and filled her mouth with warm blood.

Lenna stopped screaming, and as soon as the person relaxed their hand, she opened her mouth and bit down as hard as she could, tasting leather on her lips.

The attacker let go with a muffled grunt. Lenna reached behind her to pull the attacker's hair or poke an eye, anything that would buy her enough time to escape.

Her hand met some kind of plastic where the face should be. A mask.

Alicia's killer was carrying through with their warning. Whoever this was, whoever they were, they had come for Lenna.

The school bell rang, and the voices of students eager to get to their last class of the day filled the hallways.

"No!" she cried as she felt hands shove her forward, toward the top of the stairs. "No, please."

Lenna pushed back with all her weight, digging her heels in, but it was no use. She couldn't think, couldn't get away.

She tried to turn, to get a glimpse of who was attacking her, but before she could, they let go and pushed her with two hands in the back, sending her tripping forward over the top of the stairway and down the concrete steps below.

Chapter 30

Lenna lay at the bottom of the stairs.

Students spilled out of classrooms and her classmates spotted her from the top of the stairs. They ran down to help her.

"Oh my god, are you okay?" asked a girl as a crowd formed around Lenna. They all spoke at once and a worried yet excited buzz filled the air, the commotion of it all breaking up their boring day.

"What happened?"

"She's bleeding."

"It's that Lenna girl."

"Should I get the nurse?"

"No, I'm fine," said Lenna, sitting up. "I just slipped and fell." She tried not to gag as she swallowed the blood in her mouth, not wanting to draw more attention to herself by spitting it out. Her right arm ached and her shoes had slipped off during the fall.

She'd managed to protect her head on the way down, the rest of her body taking the worst of it.

"Hey," shouted someone at the back of the gathering mass, "get out of the way. Give her some room." Damien broke through the crowd and directed them to move back.

"Lenna, are you okay?" he asked, getting down on his knees. He hovered his hands above her, like he worried his touch would hurt.

"No," she said, keeping her voice low so only he could hear her.

"Come on," he said, getting her to her feet. Every part of her ached, and Damien pulled her up with ease despite her not helping. He put his arm around her waist and she leaned against him for support, her legs shaking. "I've got you."

People watched them as they left, whispering to each other.

Lenna didn't care. Gossip was the least of her worries. Someone wanted her dead, and they risked being caught to make it happen. If the bell hadn't rung when it did, they could have succeeded.

Damien took her into an empty classroom and closed the door. "Take a seat," he said, helping her sit on the teacher's desk.

"Are you hurt?" He looked her over with concerned eyes. He took her arm in his warm hands and she winced. Blood oozed from a cut on her elbow. "Yeah, we're going to need to clean that up."

Damien crossed the classroom and rummaged in the closet, coming back with a little first aid kit. He took out some gauze and brought it to her lips, gently padding the corner where blood had escaped from her mouth.

"Did you hit your head?" he asked, his voice low and deep.

"No," said Lenna, noticing how long his eyelashes were.

Damien put the gauze in the trash and turned his attention to her arm. He unwrapped a fresh square of cotton from its plastic and wet it with solution from a little bottle. "This will sting a little."

It did.

"What happened?" he asked while he worked.

Lenna swallowed a wave of emotion. "Someone attacked me. They threw me down the stairs."

The muscles along Damien's jaw tightened. "Did you get a look at them?"

"No, they came up right behind me." It all happened so fast. Lenna still felt her attacker's hands around her neck.

Once the cut was clean, Damien rubbed antibacterial cream on her wound with a light finger and placed a Band-Aid over it.

He leaned back and rested on a student desk across from her, his leg grazing her dangling foot. "I don't want to be *that* guy, but you shouldn't go anywhere alone right now. Take someone with you, call me, carry that bat of yours around too, and smack anyone who gets too close."

"They must think I'm close to discovering who they are," said Lenna, biting her nail.

"Maybe you are," said Damien. "Today was risky for them, out in the open like that."

"I'm not though. Aside from the rose, we've got nothing. I'm not even sure it was Trey anymore." Lenna gripped the desk. "I went into Limbo again last night to see if there was something I missed, but there was nothing else. All I did was get stuck. I couldn't get out."

Damien stood up. "You went into Limbo alone?"

"I can't take someone in with me," said Lenna.

Damien paced the floor. "No, but you need an anchor. Someone has to be with you at this end to bring you back."

Lenna groaned. They might have told her that. Then again, she hadn't stuck around for the finer details. "Detective Gibbs found me," she told him, frowning at the thought of her.

"Good," said Damien. "Getting stuck in Limbo is bad news."

"Noted." Lenna had no intention of ever returning to that place.

Damien sat back down. "What are we going to do now?"

Lenna had missed her chance with Ellie and Zara. They'd be long gone by now. Kayla still hadn't come back to school, and there was no chance of her learning anything else from Trey or Mr. and Mrs. Santos.

"I really don't know."

Lenna took a long, steaming-hot shower as soon as she got home. She let the warm water soothe her aches and pains, her tense muscles relenting somewhat in the heat.

Her attacker's hand left its mark on her neck, but her makeup would cover it. If only it could cover the memory of it all in her mind. It replayed in her head over and over again. She had come so close to dying.

When it came to the identity of the killer, she couldn't be further away. Her investigation had hit a brick wall, and she had no idea where to turn.

The door to the basement closed from the kitchen, signaling her dad was done for the day. Lenna wrapped herself in her robe, making sure the cuts and bruises she'd accumulated were covered and out of sight, and went down to face the inevitable.

"Hi, Dad," she said, sitting at the table, trepidation knotting her stomach.

"Hey." His temper from last night seemed to have fizzled out. He put a cup of tea in front of her and sat down with his own.

They were quiet for a moment, Lenna focusing on her cup instead of her dad.

"Are you going to tell me what's going on?" he said. "I know this is a tough time for you, but you've not been yourself. Why were you out there last night?"

What could she say to him without telling him the truth? There was no way she was getting him involved.

Not now. It was far too late, and much too dangerous, for that. "I don't know."

"Not good enough." Her dad waited for her answer.

"Alicia's gone and that was the last place she was alive." Lenna shut her mouth before she said any more. She looked anywhere but at her dad. It was like he could see right through her.

"Talk to me, Len," he said, his face softening.

Neither of them was good at this. They never had run-ins or issues like this. It was new territory and both stumbled through it.

"I'm feeling so overwhelmed," Lenna said, her lips betraying her. She wanted to cry in his arms and tell him everything, but if she let the tears fall, she wasn't sure they'd stop.

"I'm listening," said her dad, his presence soothing.

Her body felt like it was melting into the frame of the chair. She knew she shouldn't say anything, but she had nowhere else to go. Her dad was the person she ran to when things were bad, and Corey was still mad at her.

"Everything is screwed," she said eventually, looking down at her hands and picking at her matte-gray nail polish, which had begun to chip. "There's Alicia, and I've been off with you when I don't mean to. Even Corey's mad at me."

And someone almost killed her. Again.

If only she could curl up in her bed and sleep until this was all over. She'd wake up and realize it was just some seriously messed-up dream and everything was okay.

"I just feel like everything is crashing down on me, you know?" There was so much pressure on her right now, and it squashed her.

Her dad considered what she said before speaking. "You know, when people feel like that, it tends to be the things they can't control that stress them out. Alicia dying wasn't something in your control."

Her fate was, though.

"I've been trying hard to be strong, but nothing I do seems to work out right. I'm running out of time, and I don't know what to do."

"You have all the time in the world," said her dad, not understanding Lenna's meaning. She only had three days until Alicia's funeral, three days to save her. Three days to catch a killer before she became their next victim.

"What happened to Alicia was a horrible, horrible tragedy. That won't happen to you."

Her dad was way off, but Lenna couldn't help but talk. Everything had been building up inside her all week. The more she voiced her worries, the more the dark clouds clogging her mind began to depart.

"I'm scared," she admitted.

What if she failed? What if she couldn't catch the killer in time? How was she supposed to sleep at night knowing that Alicia was stuck in Limbo? What would that do to her?

Her whole life was up in the air, the rug swept out

from under her feet, and she had no idea how to get things back to normal, or if that was even possible anymore. Assuming the killer didn't get to her. She didn't want to die.

Her dad watched her, seeming pleased, which didn't make sense from where Lenna sat.

"That's very brave of you to admit," he said. He sat forward and took her hand. "People twice your age have a hard time admitting that. There's power in admitting you're afraid. Acknowledging it is the first step in controlling it, and it can be a powerful tool once you learn to recognize it for what it is. You can use it."

Lenna looked at him. He sounded like a self-help book, like he was speaking from experience.

"When I lost your mom, I was terrified. I felt like I could do anything with her beside me, but then she was torn away from us. I don't know how much you remember, but I was a mess. I didn't know how I was going to raise you alone. I feared that I would lose you too. I could've just given up, but I couldn't. I couldn't let you down. Instead, I used my fears to push me to make sure they never happened."

Lenna squeezed his hand.

"It's not easy, but once you grab hold of your fear, it can't control you. It takes time, but while you're working it out, do something you enjoy," said her dad. "Keep busy. It's a difficult time and you shouldn't be here all the time surrounded by death. Hang out with your friends, talk to them about how you feel. I'm sure a lot of them are feeling the same way. Surround yourself with the living instead of dwelling on a death you had no control over. Grieve together. You'd be surprised at how people open up at times like these."

Her dad's words sparked an idea in Lenna's head. She composed herself and said, "A bunch of people from school are having a memorial thing for Alicia tonight."

It wasn't a total lie. Nevertheless, taking advantage of her dad when he was being so supportive and understanding left a horrible taste in her mouth.

"You should go," he said. "And call Corey too. It's not like you two to fight."

Lenna got up from her seat and wrapped her arms around him. "I'm sorry, Dad."

He held her tight. "I just want you to be okay. And if you need to talk, I'm always here. Don't bottle things up."

Lenna would be okay.

As soon as she caught the killer.

Chapter 31

The party was the perfect place for Lenna to get information. If Brendan was going, that meant the rest of the football team would be there, too, and where the Denwood Demons went, the cheerleaders usually followed. No way would girls like Ellie and Zara miss out on a social event like that. They'd even mentioned a party last Monday in the bathroom.

Kayla might be there. Trey too.

Lenna opened her closet and chose a dress from its hanger just as the doorbell rang downstairs. She groaned and laid the dress on her bed and went down to answer the door.

The last person she expected to see was Detective Gibbs.

"What do you want?"

The detective walked in without an invitation, her hands resting on her hips.

Lenna kept the door open. She didn't have time for guests. "My dad's out collecting a body right now," she said, "but I can leave a message and get him to call you."

Detective Gibbs turned to her. "Actually, Ms. Gallows, I'm here to see you. I got a very interesting call from Mr. Santos today." The detective picked up a brochure for caskets from one of the coffee tables, flicking through the pages without really looking at any of them.

Lenna's heartbeat drummed in her ears, panic heavy in her gut. "You did?"

"Yes." Detective Gibbs put down the brochure, crossing her arms as she sat on one of the chairs. "He said he found you upstairs in his daughter's bedroom. That you snuck into his house and used some boy to distract his wife while you rummaged through his daughter's belongings."

Shit.

"Are his accusations false?" asked the detective when Lenna didn't respond.

"They're not false, so much as misunderstood," said Lenna, playing for time.

Detective Gibbs leaned back and put her feet on the polished table, her intention clear; she wasn't going anywhere. "What were you doing?"

"Nothing," Lenna replied, formulating a story in her head. Lenna sat on the seat next to the detective, keeping her posture open and her voice sad. "I just really missed Alicia, and I wanted to be around things that reminded me of her. It hasn't been easy this last week."

"That's funny, because Mr. Santos assures me you and his daughter weren't friends." The detective got up from the chair and glared down at Lenna. "In fact, he seems to remember you and Alicia having a big falling-out a while ago."

Damn it. Detective Gibbs didn't miss a beat.

"If you know something about Alicia's death that you're not telling me, I can arrest you for obstruction of justice," warned Gibbs, watching her like a hawk.

Lenna didn't take well to being threatened, especially by Gibbs, and especially when she was risking her life and doing the detective's job for her. Everything she had done was to help Alicia, and she sure as shit wasn't going to sit there and be threatened in her own house.

Lenna raised her chin. "Not that I do know anything, of course, but how would you know if I didn't tell you?"

The detective's body tensed as fire ignited behind her eyes. "All things come out in the end," she said.

Lenna sincerely hoped so.

"Well, Officer," said Lenna, knowing that calling her by a lower rank would piss her off, "unless you're here to arrest me or press charges, you can get yourself out of my house."

She pointed to the door, keeping her back straight.

Detective Gibbs walked right up to her, their noses almost touching. Lenna refused to move, refused to let Gibbs think she scared her. When she didn't back down, the detective gave up and sauntered to the door. She turned around before leaving.

"I'll be watching you."

Chapter 32

Lenna stopped outside Damien's house, still shaken from her run-in with Detective Gibbs. She kept glancing in the side mirror on her drive there, expecting Gibbs to be behind her. If the detective had spent as much time looking into Alicia's case as she did into bugging Lenna, then maybe Lenna wouldn't have had to sneak into Alicia's house in the first place.

Damien came out wearing a pair of jeans and a preppy shirt that looked about as foreign on him as a cheerleader outfit would on her.

"Nice shirt," Lenna said, raising an eyebrow at him as he got in the car.

"I figured it best to try and blend in," he said, looking pointedly at her. Maybe she should've gone with something a bit more preppy herself.

"How are you?" he asked, sarcasm gone.

"Don't ask," she said, driving out of the dirt road. Lenna brushed the attack to the back of her mind. She could freak out about it after this was over if she wanted, but right now she had her game face on.

"I caught up with Nichole after you left," said Damien as they headed back into town.

"And?"

"It wasn't her. She told me she was visiting her sick grandmother down in Florida during the weekend. She didn't get back until Sunday night."

"At least that's one person off our list." Nichole couldn't have killed Alicia if she was in another state.

"Where's this party at anyway?"

"Some senior's house." Thankfully Brendan had texted Lenna the address when she had originally agreed to go with him.

Lenna thought about calling Brendan to say she'd changed her mind, but if he decided not to go after she canceled, she didn't want him to change his plans. While she liked the whole flirting thing they had going on, she could do without the distraction.

"Where's Corey?" asked Damien as he played with the radio.

Lenna bit her lip. "He's not coming."

She took a left at the next road, down the street Brendan had told her. She didn't need to bother searching for the right house number. A horde of cars spilled out of one of the driveways and leaked onto the street in a long line. It looked like the whole school had been invited.

Lenna edged up to the curb and parked at the nearest empty space, careful to leave enough room in front of her so she could pull out later.

Damien frowned. "That's interesting."

In front of them was a red car, and coming out of it were Ellie and Zara.

Lenna held onto the steering wheel.

The stepsisters walked into the house without once looking back, their heads close together in deep conversation. Could it have been one of them she'd seen standing over Alicia's body? Had the other girl been there in the car? Were they the ones who'd attacked her?

They were supposed to be Alicia's friends, so getting her into their car last Friday would have been easy. Alicia may not have known what was happening until it was too late.

Lenna had never ruled the girls out of the mix, but she had admittedly put her focus on Trey and Mr. Santos. Seeing the stepsisters' car right in front of her flipped everything on its head.

"Does it look like the car you saw in Limbo?" asked Damien, taking off his seat belt.

Lenna tried to think back to what she'd seen, to the memories she would much rather forget. "I don't know. I mean, it could be the one."

They got out and walked to the house. Music blasted from the open door. A bunch of kids were hanging around outside with beer bottles and red Solo cups in hand, laughing and joking with each other in drunken tones.

Corey stood among them, dressed in a pair of black jeans and a T-shirt that read: "I SEE DUMB PEOPLE."

"Corey? What are you doing here?" asked Lenna.

Corey downed his drink and broke from the group. "Oh, I'm sorry. I didn't know you were in charge of everywhere I went." He didn't acknowledge Damien and looked around the front yard as if he wanted to be anywhere but standing talking to them.

"That's not what I meant." The tension from the day before lingered like a bad smell, and she didn't know how to fix it.

"Whatever. Enjoy the party," said Corey before walking off.

Lenna watched him go into the house. She wanted to go after him but knew this wasn't the time or place.

"What's up with him?" asked Damien.

"He's pissed at me because I left him out yesterday." Lenna sighed.

Damien went over to one of the coolers near the door and picked up a beer. He popped the cap and took a swig.

Lenna gave him a look. "Drinking on the job?"

Damien waved his arm around them. "Hey, all the cool kids are doing it."

"Just remember why we're here," she said and walked into the house, leaving him to mingle outside.

The house had an open layout, and every square

inch had been tediously thought out. The walls, pristine and white, made the house seem even bigger than it was, most of the furniture black and sparsely placed in a minimalist style.

She waved a hand in front of her nose, having walked past the stoners enough times at school to recognize pot smoke.

Dance music drummed through large speakers in the living area near a television screen that looked like it belonged in a theatre rather than a house. People danced in a large cluster in the dining room, the formal table pushed up next to the wall and covered in a mass of empty bottles and glasses.

Lenna went to the kitchen, a little overwhelmed. As someone whose attendance at social events tended to revolve around funerals, she wasn't used to parties. People ran around, shouting and screaming, laughter coming from all corners.

Occasionally someone noticed her and seemed confused, like they wondered if she was crashing or had gotten lost on the way home from school and stumbled into the mix.

Lenna edged into a corner near the counter and poured herself a cup of soda, which she guessed was only used as a mixer at these things. Everyone seemed pretty plastered already.

A bunch of guys in football shirts held a boy upside down over a silver keg, shouting "Chug, chug, chug!" as their willing victim tried to gulp down as much beer as possible. It escaped from the side of his mouth and ran down his face, his hair soaked with it.

"Hey, have you seen Ellie and Zara?" Lenna asked a girl in a cheer uniform.

The girl didn't seem interested, too busy giving the eye to one of the football players. She waved a hand to a door just off the kitchen without looking at Lenna. "Yeah, they went in there."

The door was open just enough for Lenna to catch a limited peek inside. She was about to go in when voices started.

Lenna pressed her ear against the door to try to hear above the loud music.

"I don't know," said someone inside.

"Know what?" snapped a husky voice. Lenna moved her head slightly and caught a glimpse of Ellie and Zara standing over a countertop in what seemed to be the laundry room.

"Look at what happened to Alicia," said Zara, her expression worried.

"That won't happen to you," said Ellie. "We're only taking a small amount. Just enough to have some fun."

Zara looked down at whatever was on the counter and then back to Ellie. "But—"

"But what, Zara?" She slapped a hand on the worktop. "Just shut up and take the K already. I need a drink."

Ellie turned with a huff and moved toward the door. Lenna made to move, but she was too slow. Ellie opened the door and regarded her with a stink face from head to toe and back again.

"Uh, hello," she said. "Can't you see we're busy here?"

"I was looking for a bathroom," Lenna lied.

"Yeah," agreed Ellie, "preferably one with a mirror. Did you even bother to look at what you threw on before coming here?"

Lenna looked down at her outfit, a long-sleeved lace dress and black tights. She wore it with an updo she'd learned from a YouTube tutorial and a pair of simple black shoes with silver on the heels. Simple, yet effective. Or so she thought.

She brushed off the girl's appraisal, not giving a shit what Ellie thought of her or what she wore.

"Who is it?" asked Zara from inside the room.

"That weird Lenore girl," Ellie called back, keeping the door half closed.

Lenna pushed past Ellie, pretending she was drunk so she could shove the girl extra hard.

"Watch it," whined Ellie.

"What are you doing?" Lenna asked. Zara held a rolled-up dollar bill in her hand that hovered over a line of white powder on the counter, the dusty remains of a second one next to it, which Ellie must've already snorted.

"Powdering our noses. What the hell does it look like?" spat Zara.

Ellie walked up to Lenna and got right in her face,

Zara pushing up behind her in an intimidating cheerleader sandwich.

Lenna tried to slip between them, but Ellie took a step to the side, blocking her from the way out.

Zara pushed her from behind, and her drink slipped out of her hands and fell to the floor, the brown liquid fizzing out around them.

"Who even invited you?" asked Ellie with narrow eyes.

Lenna was just about to sock Ellie in the face and make a run for it when someone spoke from the door.

"I did."

Brendan stepped forward and offered Lenna his hand. She took it gladly and stood next to him and the open door.

Brendan stared down at the drugs on the counter and regarded the two cheerleaders. "Nice. Real classy, ladies."

He walked out without as much as a second glance at them, taking Lenna with him. Lenna turned to see the girls' shocked and angry faces before the door slammed shut on them.

"What was that all about?" asked Brendan.

"Nothing to worry about," said Lenna, brushing off the subject. She stole a final look at the door. What would have happened if Brendan hadn't turned up?

She let go of his hand and walked over to the kitchen island. "Drink?" she asked.

Brendan stood close to her, their arms touching. "A beer, thanks."

Lenna handed him a cold one from a bucket of ice, her heart slowing to normal.

Brendan took the top off and drank a mouthful. "I thought you weren't coming," he said, his smile back now that they were away from the cheerleaders.

Lenna smiled back at him. "I changed my mind."

Chapter 33

Lenna sat with Brendan on one of the couches in the living area while everyone else around them made out to a slow song that vibrated over the room.

Brendan kept trying to get her into a conversation, but she couldn't concentrate. Not after what just happened with Ellie and Zara.

"I'm glad you decided to come tonight," said Brendan, leaning close to her.

A stumbling figure caught Lenna's attention, walking up the stairs to the second floor, relying on the railing for support. The girl's long blond hair and stunning figure gave her away, even from the back.

Lenna sprung up from the couch, keeping an eye glued to Kayla. "I gotta go to the bathroom real quick."

Lenna stopped herself from running as she followed Kayla. Dodging a couple who looked like they were eating each other's faces off, Lenna reached the top of the stairs to find the hall empty.

Damn it.

She opened the nearest door and instantly regretted it.

A couple in bed were doing a little more than the people on the stairs, although they seemed equally enthusiastic about it.

"This room's taken," said a girl's voice from beneath the sheets as the guy flung a pillow at Lenna.

"Sorry." Lenna snapped the door shut, her eyes wide as she tried to scratch the picture out of her mind before it settled into a memory.

She moved to the next door but knocked this time, just in case.

"Go away," called a voice inside.

"Kayla? Is that you?"

"Leave me alone."

Lenna opened the door and stuck her head inside. Kayla was there, hugging the toilet as she sprawled on the floor next to it, her head seeming too heavy to balance on her neck. The girl was wasted.

"Are you okay?" Lenna closed the door behind her.

"Why do you care?" Kayla drawled.

Lenna kneeled next to her. "Did something happen?"

"Yeah, my best friend killed herself, that's what happened."

Kayla coughed once and leaned her head over the toilet just in time to hurl. Lenna gagged at it splashing into the water. Give her a dead body any day, but the smell of vomit made her want to throw up right next to the girl.

She shuffled back as Kayla continued throwing up whatever she had been drinking. Her body convulsed with every retch, shaking all over.

When she finally stopped, she raised her head, wiping at her mouth with the back of her hand.

"Feel any better?" asked Lenna. She didn't look it.

Kayla answered her by throwing her head back into the toilet. Lenna pulled her hair away from her face.

Kayla started to cry, her sobs pitiful and weak after using up all her energy puking. She rested her sweaty forehead against the seat, strands of hair stuck to her face. Her lips moved lazily, her eyes half closed. "How could she do that to herself?"

"What did you say?" asked Lenna, tapping Kayla's face, trying to get her to snap out of it.

"How could she leave me?" she cried, tears streaming down her pretty face.

The tears came freely, Kayla far too drunk to care if Lenna witnessed it. The Kayla from the girls' bathroom on Monday wasn't there. Her coldhearted front may have worked for a while, but now the floodgates had opened, her walls completely broken and turned to rubble, leaving her with nothing but grief and pain.

"I loved her, you know," said Kayla, unable to move her head from the rim, her eyes opening but not seeing in front of her. They were so glazed, her pupils so dilated, that Lenna worried about her safety.

"I know you did." Lenna got up to pour Kayla some water, washing out and filling a red Solo cup that sat abandoned by her side.

"No," snapped Kayla, though it came out as more of a whine in her state. "I mean, I *loved* her, loved her."

"Oh," said Lenna. She placed the cup under Kayla's lips and tilted it until she opened her mouth. Kayla drank hungrily, finishing the entire cup in a few gulps. The cold water seemed to clear her head a bit.

"Did she know?" asked Lenna. "That you loved her, I mean?"

Kayla closed her eyes as more tears fell, her body trembling from complete and utter exhaustion. "I never told her," she said through her sobs. "I was too scared of what she'd say, what she'd think of me. Now, I'll never get the chance to tell her."

Lenna tucked Kayla's hair behind her ear and poured another cupful of cold water. "Do you know where Alicia went that night?" she asked when Kayla finished the cup. "Did she tell you where she was going or who she was planning to hang out with?"

"No," said Kayla, hiccupping. "She didn't even call to tell me to cover for her. She always did that." Kayla wiped away her tears, but more fell down her cheeks in their place.

"Except when she would go out with Trey," said Lenna, remembering what Alicia had told her.

Kayla spat into the toilet, her face in a growl. "Trey."

"Do you think Alicia could have gone out with him?"

"Who knows," she said. "Who knows what was going on in Alicia's head? I didn't. If I did, then maybe I could've helped her. If I had been a good enough friend, I would've noticed that something wasn't right. I should've known. I should've been there for her, but I wasn't. She didn't come to me, and now she's dead."

"Hey," said Lenna. "You did nothing wrong. Do you hear me? Nothing. This isn't your fault."

Kayla shook her head. She leaned forward and threw up the water, not even able to keep that down.

Kayla's guilt was destroying her. It made Lenna sick to her stomach at the thought of all Alicia's loved ones thinking the same way, that they were somehow to blame.

They deserved the truth.

Lenna lifted Kayla's head from the toilet seat and kept her steady, trying to get as much from her before she passed out into a drunken stupor.

"Do you know of anyone who would want to harm Alicia?" She had to get Kayla to talk. She might not be as willing sober, and they were running out of time.

"Why would anyone want to hurt her?" asked Kayla.

That right there was the million-dollar question, and Alicia was out of lifelines.

"Do you think it's possible Ellie and Zara could

have given Alicia the drugs?" Lenna pressed on, fighting a losing battle with Kayla's alcohol levels.

"No. I mean, they could have offered them to her, but she would never have taken them." Kayla let out another cry, shaking her head vigorously. "That's why I can't get my head around her doing that to herself."

"Do you know where Ellie and Zara were on Friday night?"

Kayla coughed like she was ready to throw up again, but nothing came up from her now-empty stomach. Her head lolled to the side as she began to doze off.

"Kayla—" Lenna snapped, the girl's eyes opening at her name. "Do you know where your friends were the night Alicia died?"

"They're not my friends," she moaned. "Not really."

"Kayla," someone called from out in the hall. "Kayla, where are you, girl?"

"In here," shouted Lenna. She got up from the floor and opened the door.

A sober-looking girl came in and eyed her drunken friend. Sam was her name, Lenna recalled, another cheerleader on Kayla's team.

"God, is she all right?" Sam bent down and rested a hand on Kayla's forehead.

"Yeah," said Lenna, helping Sam get Kayla to her unsteady feet. "She's just had too much to drink."

"I'll take her to my house and let her sleep it off,"

said Sam. "Her parents think she's staying over at my place anyway."

"Good idea," said Lenna.

Together they managed to get Kayla down the stairs and out into Sam's car. She sat in the passenger seat, sobbing into her hands as Lenna leaned over and put her seat belt on.

Lenna watched them leave, knowing one thing for certain: Kayla didn't kill Alicia.

Chapter 34

Lenna searched the party for Brendan. After roaming the house, and avoiding entering any closed doors without knocking first, she eventually gave up and went out to the backyard for some air.

The garden was meticulously landscaped with a large pool in the middle where a crowd of people were fooling around and diving in.

Lenna walked off to the edge of the yard, her arms wrapped around her waist.

Her mind needed a break, on the verge of shutting down, but she couldn't rest. The clock was ticking. Each second that passed moved Alicia closer and closer to Limbo.

Someone bumped into her, bringing her out of her troubled thoughts. She turned and came face-to-face with Ellie.

"Watch where you're going, bitch." She walked off

before Lenna could say anything, her heart thundering in her chest.

Lenna took a deep breath, the crisp air filling her lungs as she tried to push away the deep-seated unease.

Walking around the garden's edge, she saw Brendan alone, lying on one of the outdoor sofas, peering up at the stars.

"There you are," she said, sitting down as he made room for her. "I've been looking all over for you."

Brendan smiled, his eyes shiny in the moonlight. "Hey."

"Sorry I took so long. What are you doing?"

"Oh, nothing, just chilling." He pointed up to the sky, glass bottle in hand. "Checking out the stars."

The beer had taken effect and flushed his cheeks, making him cuter than usual. She nudged closer to him.

Steam rose from the heated pool and covered the yard in fog. The outdoor lights shone hazy because of it, creating a kind of warm glow over everything it touched.

"They're so pretty," she said, arching her head to get a good look at the twinkling balls of gas, staring down at them from trillions of miles away.

"They're not the only ones." Brendan ran a finger down her arm and rested his hand over hers. She didn't move it, enjoying just sitting there with him, away from the noise of the party.

"Where were you anyway?" he asked, rubbing his thumb over the top of her hand. His touch made her giddy and, in a moment of bravery, she took his hand, lacing her fingers with his.

"I got caught up with Kayla," she replied, hoping the girl was in bed sleeping by now. "She got far too wasted."

Brendan took another swig from his beer. "Yeah, I saw her throwing back some shots before you arrived."

"She's taking Alicia's death really hard."

"I get it, though," he said after a while, looking out into the yard.

"What do you mean?" asked Lenna.

Brendan finished his bottle. "That feeling of not wanting to be here anymore," he said, staring off. "Wanting to just end it." He picked at the edge of the bottle's label.

Lenna waited for him to continue, unsure what to say. It wasn't like they knew each other that well, and even if they did, she wasn't sure what the proper response was.

"I tried to kill myself once," Brendan explained.

"Why?" Lenna asked. "If you want to tell me, that is."

Brendan shrugged, his shoulders slumping. "Things just got to be too much, you know? I couldn't handle it."

Lenna didn't know. She'd never been to that place before, so hopeless that ending her life seemed like the only option. Not even when her mom died.

"My dad likes to get real 'hands on' with his so-called parenting, especially when he's drunk or high, which is always. I've lost count of how many times he beat the shit out of me and my older brothers and sisters. But they all grew up and left one screwed-up life for another, leaving me alone as his personal punching bag."

"Didn't your mom do anything to stop him?"

"She wouldn't dare stand up to him," Brendan said as he sat up, more sad than angry. "Things were okay while he was in jail, but when he got out, he was worse than ever."

Lenna watched him speak. It made her so appreciative of her dad and the upbringing she'd had. Not everyone had that luxury.

"One night, I just felt like going to sleep and never waking up again. I stole my dad's vodka and slammed the whole bottle before taking a razor to my wrists." He pulled back his sleeve, revealing a white line of healed skin along his wrist.

Lenna ran her hand over the scar, feeling the bump it made on his skin. Brendan shivered at her touch and met her eyes, his gaze vulnerable and open.

"Next thing I knew," he continued, "I woke up in the hospital. I just remember feeling annoyed it didn't work. Because once I was better ... I'd need to go back home, with him."

"I'm so sorry you went through that," she said, keeping her voice in check and free from pity. Brendan wouldn't want that.

"But I'm getting my ass out of that house as soon as I graduate. I managed to get a football scholarship for most of my tuition. Man, I worked my ass off for that. I'll still need to take out some loans, but it's enough to get me as far away from him as possible. It's my golden ticket out of here."

Alicia had similar hopes and dreams, to go to college and leave Denwood, only she could no longer make them happen. Lenna hoped Brendan would. He seemed determined enough at least.

"There's no way in hell I'm going to end up a deadbeat like him," he said, grasping the beer bottle so tightly, Lenna worried it might shatter.

"My whole family is the same. Good-for-nothing trash with more jail time than hours clocked at any kind of legit job. That's not going to be me, though. I'm going to prove them all wrong. I'm going to make something of myself."

He said the words, but the stress in his face showed his doubt. He stared at his lap.

"Sorry for venting. I shouldn't have." He raised the empty bottle in explanation. "Some date I turned out to be."

Lenna lifted his chin with her free hand, the other still laced with his. This close, she caught the lighter golden shades flecked in his brown eyes amid the warm light.

He had a little scar along the side of his right cheek, and his lower lip was a lot fuller than the top, giving him a kind of sad pout when he wasn't smiling. She ran a finger over them, soft to the touch compared to the light stubble that ran along his jaw.

If being around Alicia all week had taught Lenna anything, it was to live in the moment. There were no guarantees in life, and death came for everyone all too quickly. She wanted to lose herself, to feel connected with the living despite her link to the dead. She pretended she was a normal girl at a party with a guy she liked, even if only for a minute.

Lenna leaned forward and kissed him.

Chapter 35

Lenna pressed her lips against his. Brendan cupped her face with his strong hands and leaned into her with parted lips. She grabbed his shirt and pulled him closer, kissing deeper. Sparks flew between them and tingled all over her body.

Brendan brushed his tongue against her lips, and Lenna opened her mouth wider, letting him in. He tasted of beer and spearmint chewing gum, and she loved the way he explored her mouth, running his tongue over hers.

His hands traveled down from her face and stopped at her waist, holding her tightly as she leaned into him, losing herself.

Brendan bit her bottom lip and Lenna melted, a warm rush coursing through her body and heading south.

She wrapped her arms around him, brushing her fingers into his thick hair and holding on, every nerve in her body alight, enjoying his touch and the way he kissed her with such passion and need.

"Uh, hate to interrupt," said a voice from what seemed like a million miles away. Lenna ignored it and continued exploring Brendan's lips, panting heavily, too lost in each other to worry about breathing.

"Hello," said the voice, louder this time.

Lenna broke away from Brendan and turned her head to see who had so rudely interrupted them.

Damien stood in front of them with a blank face, Corey hanging from him with his head down.

Lenna crashed back to reality, like she had just been woken up from a lovely dream far too early in the morning.

"What's wrong with him?" she asked, untangling herself from Brendan and straightening her dress. Her cheeks burned under Damien's stare as she got up from the patio sofa, away from Brendan who sat with a stunned grin on his face.

"Someone can't hold their liquor," commented Damien in a bored tone as she approached Corey, raising his head to get a good look at him.

"Hey, Lenna," said Corey, just noticing her. He gave her a dopey smile, his glasses sitting lopsided on his nose.

She glared at Damien. "He's trashed."

"What?" Damien took a swig from a beer bottle in his free hand. "It's not my fault."

His blasé attitude grated on her. Or it might have

been because he had interrupted her blissful reprieve from her deadly situation.

"We need to get him home," she said. Or more correctly, back to her place so Corey's mom wouldn't freak out. It was a good thing his dad was mid-tour in the Middle East somewhere or else he'd be grounded until next year.

She walked over to Brendan, unable to help her lips curving at his amused face and starry eyes.

"Looks like you need to go," he said.

"Yeah," she replied, putting out her hand and lacing her fingers with his. The taste of his lips still lingered on hers. "I had fun, though."

"I did too."

Damien cleared his throat from behind her.

She sighed and unlaced her hand from Brendan's. "Good night."

"Good night, Lenna."

———

Corey had been hiccupping in the back seat of her hearse for the past five minutes, but he had gone quiet.

"Hey, Cor, you okay?" asked Lenna, hoping he didn't need to throw up. She tried to get a look at him in her rearview mirror, but it was too dark to see much more than his outline. The seat was positioned a little farther back than it would be in most cars, the pull-down kind along the interior side of the vehicle for someone to sit next to the coffin if they needed to.

"Hey man, you good?" asked Damien, turning himself in the front seat to get a better look at Corey. Damien was in a much better state than her best friend. Only subtle differences in the way he moved and carried himself gave him away. He seemed a little less forced than usual. Quieter too.

Corey hiccupped again in the back. "Fine," he replied after a moment.

"If you need to be sick, let me know, and I'll stop the car," Lenna told him, turning down the road surrounded by woods on the way to Damien's house. It was pitch-black outside, her headlights cutting through the darkness.

They drove in silence for a few minutes, the only noise coming from Corey and his hiccups.

"I'm sorry," he said after a while, leaning forward in his seat so his head popped out between her and Damien.

"Nothing to be sorry for, man," said Damien, reaching back and patting him on the shoulder. "You just got a little drunk, that's all."

"It's not that," Corey replied.

Lenna heard the change in her friend's voice. His head was down, hiding his face. "I'm useless," he said.

"You're not useless," Lenna replied, offended that anyone would say that about her best friend, even if it was Corey himself.

"Yes, I am. I'm a loser."

She put a hand at the side of his face, careful to keep the other securely on the steering wheel and her eyes on the winding road. "Corey, don't say that."

"It's true though," he continued. "You have this incredible gift that can really make a difference and help people, while all I can do is sit around and get in the way. I found out nothing tonight. All I did was get drunk."

Damien gave Lenna a questioning look. She never should have left Corey behind when they went to find Trey at work. He was right, it wasn't her choice.

"And you have this hot new guy," Corey said, pointing a thumb at Damien.

Where had he gotten that from? She had just been kissing Brendan. Surely he couldn't be that drunk?

Damien didn't react, or try to correct Corey. Thankfully, it was too dark for either of them to see Lenna's cheeks redden.

"What do I have?" her friend continued before she could say anything. "Asthma and panic attacks." He hung his head again. "I can't help you catch whoever killed Alicia. Who was I even kidding?"

He sat back in his chair.

Lenna bit the inside of her cheek. "Corey, I'm sorry." She refused to let all this effect their friendship. Over her dead body.

Corey answered her with a snore.

Damien peered into the back. "He's out."

Lenna took the turn onto the dirt road that led to Damien's house. "I messed up and hurt his feelings."

"He just had too much to drink."

She stopped the car and put it in park.

The old house looked extra creepy at night. The thing had crappy horror movie written all over it. If she didn't know better about where ghosts hung out, she would've guessed Damien's house was prime real estate for them. She shuddered at the thought of Irene sitting in there alone, speaking to herself in voices that didn't belong to her.

"I'll pick you up early tomorrow morning to go check out that club," she said to Damien. Echo could be their last hope of finding any evidence.

Damien opened the passenger door and got out, the cold wind creeping into the hearse with a whine. "Good night, Lenna."

Lenna watched him go.

It was almost midnight. They had two days left.

Chapter 36

Corey remained asleep in the back as Lenna drove out of the woods and into town. Her bed called to her.

A car drove up behind them, and her heart jumped. Was the killer back? Just before she hit the gas to get the hell away from there, the police lights flashed, signaling her to pull over.

She checked the time: eleven forty-five. Maybe it was just a random sobriety check. It was late on a Friday night after all.

Lenna pulled over and turned off her engine, waiting inside for the officer to approach. Corey slept through the police car's wail, snoring lightly behind her.

Detective Gibbs tapped the window.

"How can I help, Detective?" Lenna asked. Something was off.

"Please step out of the car," replied Gibbs, all business.

Lenna complied.

Gibbs held out her palm. "Give me your keys, and put your hands on the car."

"Is this really necessary?" Tonight had been long enough without some pointless run-in with the so-called "detective."

"Now," she ordered.

"Wow, calm down." Lenna smacked her keys down in Gibbs's hand.

"Hands on the car." Gibbs turned her around, kicking at the inside of her ankles to spread her legs.

"What the hell is going on?" demanded Lenna, boiling with rage. She had been thrown around enough.

"Is there anything in your possession that I should know about?" Gibbs said into her ear, so close behind her that Lenna got flashes of the attack by the stairs.

"What are you talking about?" Next thing Lenna knew, Gibbs was patting her down with her leather-gloved hands. She began at her legs and worked her way up, digging her hands into the pockets of Lenna's dress, rummaging around.

"Well, well, well," she said, "what do we have here?"

Gibbs shook the little bag filled with white powder in front of her face.

The detective shot her a smug, satisfied smirk. "I told you I'd be watching you."

Lenna and Corey sat in silence in Detective Gibbs's office.

The room had nothing personal in it aside from a dead plant in the corner of her unnaturally tidy desk. On it sat nothing but a perfectly aligned notepad and pen and a large bottle of hand sanitizer beside a dated computer. Boxes piled in a neat stack in the corner by the windows, unopened.

Gibbs called Lenna's dad and they were waiting for him to arrive. Luckily, the detective wasn't able to contact Corey's mom, who was working a nightshift at the hospital. At least one of them might get out of this okay. Besides, they didn't find any drugs on him.

The door was left open, and the hum of officers on nightshift floated through the room.

From what they'd heard so far, no one at the station had taken a shine to the new detective.

"Like I've got nothing better to do than write up some kids with a bag of Ket," said a female officer, refilling her mug full of black coffee so thick, it could pass as tar. "It's more trouble than it's worth. It's not like she cracked a drug den or anything."

"You heard her," said the guy next to her, adding three different packets of sugar to his own mug. "'She's the one in charge.' Better do what the boss says."

The female officer smacked the side of the coffee machine as it spluttered. "I better get overtime for this. My shift finished half an hour ago." The woman added cream to the cheap coffee and gave it a questionable sniff. "She needs to get laid."

"You can take one for the team with that one," said the male officer, jabbing the woman with his elbow.

Lenna's dad strode past the officers and into Gibbs's office. He took a deep breath before speaking. "Come on, you two." His voice was tight, posture rigid.

They got up without another word and followed behind him.

Gibbs passed them in the hall and called back as they reached the exit. "I advise you to get your daughter under control, Mr. Gallows. She's going down a slippery slope."

Her dad ignored Gibbs and left the station. He must have taken a cab there because they drove home in her hearse, none of them speaking. Lenna could feel her dad's anger bubbling in the air. She didn't know what to say.

When they got home, her dad sat down at the kitchen table and clasped his hands.

He cleared his throat and turned to her friend. "Corey, could you please go upstairs. I need a word alone with my daughter."

Corey gave her a sympathetic look and headed to the guest room, stumbling as he went, still drunk.

"Gibbs must have planted that on me," Lenna blurted. She couldn't believe it.

Her dad slammed his fist down on the table. "Don't you dare try to lie your way out of this, young lady.

Detective Gibbs received an anonymous phone call saying you were driving around town on drugs."

An anonymous tip.

"I can't believe it," continued her dad when she didn't reply. "Drugs? Really? After everything that's happened over the last week? Your friend dies from an overdose and you think it's a good idea to go out partying and take something that veterinarians give to goddamn horses?"

"But Dad—" she started.

"But nothing. You said you were going to a memorial. Do you realize how much trouble you're in? The detective is talking about pressing charges. A criminal record. My daughter. Good luck getting into college now. This could ruin your entire future. And then she tells me you broke into the Santoses' house yesterday. What has gotten into you?"

Lenna played with her hands. "I was only trying to—"

"Do you realize what that poor family is going through?"

Lenna didn't know what to say. She'd never seen her father this angry.

"This is not how your mother and I raised you."

Lenna looked up at him, tears stinging her eyes. He might as well have stabbed her in the heart. His anger was one thing, maybe she could have taken that, but his level of disappointment cut deeper than any knife could. It hurt like a physical wound.

Her bottom lip shook. "But I can explain."

Her dad got up from his chair and leaned against the counter with his back to her. "There's nothing to explain," he said, his voice tired and sharp. "Go to your room. I can't even look at you right now."

Lenna did as she was told and, for the first time since her mother's death, cried herself to sleep.

Chapter 37

Lenna took the stairs as soundlessly as she could to avoid waking her dad.

She shouldn't have bothered, because he sat right where he had last night, a mug of coffee between his hands. His shirt was wrinkled and bits of hair hung loose from his ponytail like he hadn't been to bed.

He looked her up and down, taking in her coat and shoes.

His voice was rough. "And where do you think you're going, young lady?"

She remained silent, trying to think of what to say to him, of how to convince him that she was still the daughter he knew, that she had been set up.

"What else are you keeping from me?" he asked before she could bring herself to say anything. He stared at her like she was a stranger to him. "What else don't I know?"

"What am I keeping from you?" she snapped. "You're one to talk."

"You watch your tone," he said, unable to hide his shock at her reply.

"Screw my tone," Lenna said, reaching boiling point and spilling over. "You won't even let me explain myself. You just believed that stupid detective over me, your own daughter."

"What do you expect me to do?" he said, matching her raised voice "You were caught with drugs, and you broke into someone's house and raided their dead daughter's bedroom. What am I supposed think of that?"

"Why didn't you tell me I had died, huh?" Lenna gritted her teeth as she watched him.

Her dad paled.

"Yeah, how am I supposed to feel like I can tell you anything when you keep something like that from me?"

Her dad blinked at her. "Who have you been talking to?"

She swiped the air with her hand. "That doesn't matter, and I'm done talking to you right now. I'm outta here."

"Don't you dare leave this house," her dad warned.

She turned and faced him, ignoring the tears that slipped down her cheeks. "Mom would've listened to me."

Grabbing her car keys from the counter, Lenna stormed out of the house and slammed the door behind her.

She had a murder to solve.

Lenna knocked on the old door for the second time, but Damien still didn't answer. She turned the rusting handle and found the door unlocked.

"Hello?" she called, opening the door and stepping inside. The floorboards groaned under her feet. "Damien?"

She entered the living room where, just a few days ago, she'd learned she had died, but no one was there. The room was cold and bare.

"He's upstairs," croaked a voice from behind her.

Lenna spun around to face Damien's grandmother. "Irene, you almost scared me to death."

Irene sniffed the air in front of her and regarded Lenna with a stern face. "You went back into Limbo. I can smell it on you." She stepped closer to her. "Do you hear them yet? The voices. Do they whisper things to you? Dark and terrible things? How are you sleeping?"

"Once I find Alicia's killer, I'm done," Lenna told her.

Irene let out a throaty laugh. "That's what I said too. Look how that turned out for me."

"I won't end up like you." Lenna couldn't—wouldn't—let that happen. Alicia would be the first and last dead person she'd help. There was just too much to risk, and standing in front of Irene was a stark reminder of that.

The old woman looked her dead in the eyes, like she could see into Lenna's soul. "For your sake, I hope you don't."

"I think I'll go see if Damien's ready." Lenna made her escape and headed up the rickety staircase without looking back.

She peeked inside the open door of the room to the left and saw boy clothes scattered around the floor. Damien wasn't there, but she decided to wait for him in his room instead of going back down to be freaked out by Irene.

His walls were covered with pieces of paper, large and small, all with sketches drawn on them in what looked like black charcoal. They were all hauntingly beautiful and dark, each different but clearly done by the same hand.

Trees with weeping faces in the trunks were pinned up next to rough sketches of the human form in motion. Shadows and smoke danced on black paper, the detail minute and showing figures within the swirls.

A floorboard creaked behind her.

Damien stood at the threshold of his bedroom, wearing nothing but a towel and a surprised expression. Water ran down his torso, his hair damp and wavy.

"Sorry, I didn't know you were naked," she blurted, turning around to face the wall. "Showering," she corrected, wanting to slap herself. "I mean showering."

"Uh, hey," he replied. She heard him walk over to the side of the room and open a drawer.

"I'll just wait for you in my car," she said, wondering how she could get out of the room without making things more awkward.

"No big deal. Just give me a sec, and I'll be ready."

She heard some moving around but didn't dare look. Not that she didn't like what she saw.

"All clear," Damien said after a moment.

Lenna hesitantly turned to find him in a pair of jeans, his towel hanging around his neck and down over his naked torso as he rummaged through his drawers for a shirt. She tried not to let her eyes linger, not to notice the line of hair that ran from his belly button down beyond the waist of his jeans. A tattoo lay over his chest above his heart, words in a language she couldn't read.

She cleared her throat and averted her eyes to the pictures on the walls. "You drew all these?" she asked, trying to change the subject and intrigued about them at the same time.

"Yeah." He threw a black T-shirt over his head.

"They're beautiful." Lenna hovered her hand over a picture of an old man sitting on a park bench, feeding birds. "You're really good."

Damien scratched the back of his head. "They're okay. Nothing special."

Either he was blind or extremely modest.

Lenna walked over to a desk by the window littered with stacks of paper and pieces of charcoal. An empty coffee cup sat on top of a stack of paperbacks in the corner, the spines broken in a thousand places, as if he'd read them over and over.

She scanned them, running a finger down the stack, noting classics like Oscar Wilde and the complete works of Poe. "You like Stevenson?" she asked, noting the well-read copy of *The Strange Case of Dr. Jekyll and Mr. Hyde.*

Damien crossed the room and collected the pieces of paper on the desk before she could see what he had drawn, shoving them in another drawer. "He's good," he said. "You read his stuff?"

"Yeah," said Lenna, eyeing the drawer. "I did an essay on him last year. I kinda prefer fantasy books to classics though," she admitted.

Damien sat on his bed and put on his boots, tying the laces. "Fantasy's cool. They're good to escape into."

Lenna noted the bookshelf by his bed, overstuffed with books wedged in wherever they would fit. A deliberate space had been left on the second shelf down, leaving enough room to fit a small framed photo of a woman in her mid- to late thirties.

"Who's this?" she asked.

"My mom," he replied. "I don't see her much." He held his face in a bland expression, blinking a bit too much as he rubbed his hand over his mouth.

Lenna gazed back down at the picture, seeing the resemblance right away. He had his mother's eyes, a light steel blue that reminded her of the sky just before it rained.

"That girl left him at my door years ago," came Irene's craggy voice from the entrance of Damien's room, shaking her head as she looked in. "Only calls when she needs money for bail."

The atmosphere changed as soon as Irene spoke. Lenna put the photo back in its place, unsure of what to say. She got the feeling they didn't talk about Damien's mother much.

Damien got up from his bed and grabbed the jacket hanging over his desk chair. He walked right past Irene without acknowledgement. "Come on, Lenna. We should get going."

Chapter 38

Lenna parked across the street from the club. It was a large three-story building at the corner of two connecting streets in the busy town center, surrounded by bars and restaurants that come tonight would all be bustling with activity. A large sign above the main doors displayed the same logo from the flyer Lenna found in Alicia's room.

Echo.

Her list of suspects was shrinking, but Lenna had nothing concrete on any of them yet. Alicia's funeral was tomorrow and this was their last lead.

"It looks closed," said Damien.

They got out of the hearse and crossed the street to the front entrance. The door was locked.

"Shit." Lenna kicked an empty soda can lying on the street with the toe of her shoe.

Damien peered through the glass door with his hands at his eyes. "Nobody's home."

"Hello!" Lenna hammered on the door with her fist, but no one answered. She turned away from the club and plopped down on the edge of the sidewalk.

The dumb crime shows on TV made it look so easy. They had the mystery solved within the hour, and that was including time for commercials. Real life, as it turned out, was a lot harder. She never assumed any of this would be easy, but she didn't think it would be this hard.

"It's over," she said. They were out of leads and out of time.

"We can come back later," said Damien above her.

"We're not getting in there at night." Neither of them passed for twenty-one. They wouldn't even get beyond security.

"We can still do this."

Lenna gave Damien the side-eye. "When did you become so optimistic?"

"Someone has to be." He offered her his hand.

She took it, and Damien helped her up from her seat of self-pity.

A clinking sound came from somewhere. "Did you hear that?" said Lenna, putting her arm out to stop Damien from crossing back over to the hearse.

"Hear what?"

"There it is again." Lenna followed the noise around the corner of the building into a dank alley at the back. A girl in her twenties was putting bags of trash into a large recycling bin, the bottles inside clinking against each other as she heaved them in. A fire exit to Echo stood near the trash cans, held open by a chair.

The girl tossed in her final bag and leaned against the wall, taking out a pack of cigarettes from her jeans pocket.

"Hey," called Lenna. She ran down the alley, ignoring the acrid smell of trash and avoiding questionable puddles. Damien followed behind her.

"Do you work here?" Lenna asked the girl.

"I'm on my break," she said, sparking up her cigarette and blowing a puff of smoke toward them. Her long blond hair was tied up away from her face, which still wore last night's makeup.

Lenna spotted the girl's name embroidered on the Echo shirt she wore. "Marie, were you working last Friday night?"

Marie tapped her phone screen. "Why?"

Lenna took out a picture of Alicia from last year's yearbook and held it out over the phone. "I need to know if my friend was here last Friday. Do you recognize her?"

Marie swiped the photo away with her hand. "It was opening night. Do you know how many people were here?"

"Please," said Lenna. She was desperate.

Marie glanced up from her phone. "Is she okay?"

"No. Something bad happened to her."

Marie took the picture from Lenna's hand and gave it a once-over. "I was working the bar on the second floor that night. I think I saw her."

"You did?" Lenna's pulse raced. "Was she with anyone?"

Marie snubbed her cigarette out against the wall and shivered in the cold air. "Yeah, she was with some guy. I remember them because he tried to say I short-changed him." She handed the picture back to Lenna.

Alicia had been there, and whoever she was with hadn't come forward to the police. Marie might have been the last person to see Alicia alive.

"What did the guy look like?" asked Damien.

"He was a big guy," she replied, gesturing with her arms. "White, athletic, brown hair, tall. Kinda hot too, if he hadn't been such an asshole."

Trey.

The description fit him to a tee, especially the part about being an asshole.

A surge of energy burst inside her. Trey. Her gut told her it was him all along, and now they had him.

"Were they with anyone else?" asked Damien.

"Just the two of them," said Marie, checking the time on her watch. "I think they were on a date or something."

"What time did they leave? Can you remember?" Lenna would need all the information she could get if she was going to go to the police with this.

"Must have been around midnight. Your girl had a little too much to drink."

Alicia wasn't drunk. She was drugged.

Trey had drugged her in the club and taken her away.

It was him.

This was just the break they needed. An eyewitness. Someone who could place Trey with Alicia the night she died. Lenna tilted her head to the sky in relief.

A camera hung above the fire exit door, positioned to capture the length of the alley. "Does the club have CCTV?" asked Lenna.

Marie nodded.

"Inside and out?" Lenna checked.

"Yeah, the footage is all stored on our computer."

Lenna's teeth chattered from the adrenaline that rushed through her body. This was it.

Trey killed Alicia. He murdered his ex-girlfriend and now they had the evidence to prove it.

Chapter 39

Lenna dropped off Damien and promised to keep him updated, before returning straight home and calling Gibbs.

The detective wasn't at the station, but the officer manning the desk promised an insistent Lenna he'd pass on her message for Gibbs to meet her at her place tonight as soon as she got back to work. It was time she told the police everything she'd learned, minus the weird and unexplainable stuff, of course.

With nothing else to do but wait, Lenna entered the storage room for the dead to speak with Alicia for what could be the last time. She wasn't there.

"Alicia," called Lenna.

Was she gone? Had she moved on now that her unfinished business was dealt with? Just like that? Lenna didn't even get to see her off.

She crossed the room to the refrigerated unit and

placed her palm on Alicia's drawer. There was so much she had wanted to say. Now she'd never get the chance. At least she could do that one last thing for her old friend. Alicia wouldn't face an eternity in Limbo, and now she could rest in peace.

Lenna pulled out the drawer, preparing to say one last goodbye. She removed the white sheet from Alicia's face and—

"Hey, Lenna."

Lenna yelped and stepped back.

Alicia's ghost sat up from her body. "What's the matter?"

"You scared the shit out of me," said Lenna, holding onto her chest. "I thought you'd moved on."

Alicia got up from her drawer. "Why would you think I had moved on?" Fear painted her dead face as thick as the special makeup Lenna used on their clients. "You said the crazy old woman told you I had until my funeral?"

"You're not going to Limbo," Lenna told her. "I got him."

"Him?" said Alicia, her voice shaking. She stood deadly still next to her own body.

There was no sugarcoating what Lenna had to tell Alicia, so she just ripped the Band-Aid off and got straight to the point. "Trey killed you."

"Trey."

Alicia broke down, bursting into tears.

Any sense of pride or accomplishment Lenna had

on the way downstairs had up and left the building at hearing Alicia lose it like that, having to watch yet being unable to even comfort her and tell her everything was going to be okay. It was over, but things weren't okay. Alicia was still dead. Her ex-boyfriend killed her.

She cried for a long time and Lenna sat by her side. Once she calmed down, Lenna told Alicia everything.

"What now?" Alicia asked in a detached monotone.

"I called the detective who was working your case. She's coming over tonight and I'm telling her everything."

Lenna could have told the guy at the station about Trey over the phone, but a prideful part of Lenna wanted to be the one to tell Gibbs the truth. To watch the detective's reaction when she realized she'd wasted so much time on Lenna, who was actually out there doing the real police work. Gibbs had made things bad between Lenna and her dad, too, and she wasn't about to make it easy on the detective who had done nothing but hold Lenna back in her quest for the truth.

But the truth was a bitter pill to swallow. While Lenna had discovered what really happened before it was too late, nothing she could discover or do could change things. Alicia's life had still been taken from her.

"They'll arrest Trey and have the evidence to prove he was the one who—" Lenna cleared her throat, holding back emotion and the urge to hug Alicia. "After that, I guess we wait until your funeral and you'll move on."

"To where?" asked Alicia. The question was so innocent, so simple.

Lenna busied herself with straightening out the white sheet that covered Alicia's dead body. "I don't know."

Lenna had spent so much time focusing on making sure Alicia didn't end up in Limbo that she never considered what the alternative was. Until a few days ago, she didn't know an afterlife even existed. Perhaps that was one mystery she would never solve. At least not until she passed on herself.

Lenna gave her a smile that she hoped was at least somewhat reassuring. "Wherever you go on to, it has to be better than Limbo, believe me."

"'To die will be an awfully big adventure,'" said Alicia, quoting one of her favorite books from when they were little.

Lenna closed the drawer. "The biggest."

"At least I'll never have to worry about getting wrinkles," said Alicia. They laughed, but their hearts weren't in it. They fell silent.

"Thank you, Lenna."

Lenna wiped her eyes. "You're welcome."

Alicia stared down at her lap. "I'm sorry for, well, everything."

"And I'm sorry too," said Lenna, sitting up next to her on the slab. "I'm glad we were able to talk, or yell, about it and get it all out before it was too late for us."

"Me too. It was our unfinished business." Alicia held up her open hand and Lenna followed suit, hovering them next to each other as close as they could.

At least it was one thing that could end right. At least through all the mess and tragedy, one good thing came out of it. They were able to resolve their issues and finally lay them to rest.

Lenna knocked on the guest room door.

"Come in," said Corey.

His black hair was damp from the shower, and he had changed out of his clothes from last night and into his "I HEART SPOCK" T-shirt. "Morning," he said, flopping down onto the bed and lying on his back.

Lenna laughed. "You mean afternoon."

He held his hand to his head and groaned. "I feel like death."

"Coffee makes everything right," she said, waving a strong, steaming cup in front of him.

"I don't think I can move," said Corey, but he managed to sit up and take the cup from her, his face almost as pale as the clients down in the basement.

Lenna plopped herself next to him. He smelled like lemon soap and toothpaste. "I'm sorry for leaving you out."

Corey gulped his coffee. "I'm the one who should be apologizing," he said, setting his cup on the bedside table and resting his chin on her head. "You've had so much on your plate and I was being a jerk."

Lenna jabbed him. "You're not a jerk, so quit saying it. And you were right; I shouldn't have kept you out of the investigation. I was freaked out over us being attacked the night before and the thought of you getting hurt was too much to handle. I got scared and made the wrong call."

Corey inched to the edge of the bed. "I would've probably said the wrong thing to Trey and gotten in the way as usual."

"I said enough of the wrong thing to him for the both of us," said Lenna. A couple of minutes with her and Trey had been ready to tear the whole place down. "And you're never in the way."

"I was last night. I should have been trying to get a lead on the case but instead I got wasted."

Lenna moved to sit next to him. "Stop being down on yourself. So you got a little drunk."

"A lot drunk," said Corey.

Lenna nudged him. "The point is, I need you. You're the Hermione to my Harry. The Watson to my Sherlock. The Spock to my Captain Kurt."

Corey smirked. "Kirk."

"Whatever. You know what I mean. We're a team, and I couldn't have done any of it without you. Heck, if you hadn't been so great with Mrs. Santos, we would never have known about Echo."

"What about Echo?" he asked.

"I just got back." Lenna smiled. "Cor, we got him. Someone who works at the bar saw Alicia there that night with Trey and they have it on camera. I'm speaking to Detective Gibbs tonight. She'll arrest his ass, and all of this will be over."

"Really?" Corey wrapped his arms around her in a hug. "This is great, Len. You did it."

"We did it," she corrected. "So, are we good?"

"Always," said Corey into her ear.

Lenna exhaled a deep breath and relaxed. As long as things were okay between them, she could deal with anything.

"Did you tell Alicia?" Corey asked.

"Yeah, I'm giving her some time to process it all."

Lenna's cell buzzed in her pocket. A text message.

Corey leaned back. "Was that your phone, or are you just excited to see me?"

She laughed and took out her phone. It was Brendan, asking if they were on for their date later.

Corey read the message beside her. She began texting an excuse when he snatched it out of her hands.

"What do you think you're doing?" he asked.

"Canceling," she said, trying to get it back.

"Why?" said Corey, raising his hand to the ceiling so she couldn't reach it. "It's not like you have a murder to solve anymore."

Lenna gave up trying to get the cell. Their height difference was totally unfair. "I should really stay here and wait for Detective Gibbs," she said. "Besides, I'm pretty sure I'm grounded."

"What time is she coming?"

"Around eight. The guy I spoke to at the station said she'd be out all day."

That would hopefully give Marie and her boss time to comb through the CCTV footage and have it ready for Gibbs. The sooner she and the rest of the cops picked up Trey, the safer everyone would be and the more relaxed Lenna would feel.

"Then move the date forward a little and be back by tonight." Corey snatched a pillow off the bed and chucked it at her. "I'll stay here, and if Gibbs comes earlier than expected, I'll call and let you know. After everything you've done, the least you deserve is a fun date with a cute guy."

Lenna held onto the pillow. "I don't know." Canceling on Brendan a second time in one week would suck, especially because she wanted to see him. She bit her lip, reliving the kiss they'd shared. "If it were any other time, I'd totally go, but—"

"But nothing," Corey interrupted. "Don't make me drag your ass there."

Lenna checked the time on the alarm clock by the bed. Gibbs wouldn't be here for hours yet, giving her nothing to do but sit around and wait.

Plus, things with her dad were up in the air and she really needed to hash it out with him. She wasn't looking forward to it, and he would be back home soon. His unwillingness to listen to her still hurt, not to mention the fact she'd have to find a way to explain everything with Alicia. Going out with Brendan would delay their conversation.

"Fine," said Lenna with her hand out. "Give me my phone so I can say yes and see if Brendan can go out earlier."

Corey tossed the cell back to her. "I already did."

Chapter 40

Lenna wore her black dungaree dress with a white shirt underneath, which she tied at the top with a cute little bow tie she found online. She put her hair in a simple updo and picked out a pair of her favorite heels to finish off the look.

She spritzed a cloud of perfume in front of her and walked through it. "Do you think this is okay?"

Corey stood behind her and looked in the mirror. "Perfect."

A car horn beeped outside.

"Sounds like your date's here," said Corey. "Have fun."

Lenna went over to her newly fixed window and saw Brendan standing next to his car, smiling up at her.

"You look beautiful," said Brendan as she stepped outside. He walked over to the passenger side of his car and opened the door for her.

"Are you pretending you're a gentleman or something?" she teased as she got in, appreciating the way his blue polo shirt stretched across his broad shoulders.

"Trying to be," he replied. He hopped in on his side, and they drove to Greasy Joe's, a little diner that served the best junk food in town. It opened way back in the sixties and still had most of its original décor, giving it an old-time feel. The seats were covered in cracked red leather, and the floor was adorned with black and white tiling like a chessboard.

They walked in and a waiter sat them in a booth near the back.

"What can I get you kids?" he asked with a smile.

Lenna mused over the menu. Everything sounded good. "I'd like a bacon double patty with a side of chili-cheese fries, please." She handed the menu to the waiter and looked at Brendan, who nodded his approval.

"That sounds delicious." Brendan turned to the waiter. "I'll have the same, thanks."

"And to drink?"

"Two Cokes, please," replied Brendan.

"Coming right up." The waiter jotted down their order and hurried off to another table.

Brendan leaned forward, bridging the space the table made between them.

"I'm kinda surprised you came tonight after everything I told you at the party." He fiddled with his fingers and looked down. "I, uh, didn't mean to do that."

"I won't tell anyone," Lenna assured him, and his

body relaxed into his seat. "If you ever need to talk, or even just vent, I'm here." It couldn't be easy for him with everything going on at home.

Brendan reached out and took her hand. It was a little sweaty, but she didn't care. She was nervous too. A giddy tingling danced in her stomach as he rubbed the top of her hand. "You're a great girl, Lenna." He gave her one of those dimpled smiles she liked so much. "And a good kisser too."

Lenna lowered her gaze to his mouth, the memory of his kiss fresh on her lips. "Sorry I had to leave early," she said.

Brendan laughed. "Your friend was so wasted. He must've had a killer hangover."

"Oh yeah, he suffered for it today." The waiter came with their drinks and scooted off to someone calling for their bill. Lenna took a sip of her Coke. "Did you stay long after I left?"

"It wasn't as fun without you there," he said, playing with his napkin. "I bounced pretty soon after you guys did."

The waiter returned with their food. The smell of the crispy bacon and melted cheese made Lenna's mouth water.

Brendan dug in. "Man, the burgers here are awesome."

"They're the best. I've been coming here since I was a little girl." Her mom used to bring her on the weekends, and they'd drink milkshakes and have dessert for dinner. She missed those little mother-daughter dates.

"What are your plans for the rest of the weekend?" asked Brendan, popping fries into his mouth.

"Sleeping till noon, mostly," she replied between bites of burger. It would be nice to have a normal Sunday, hanging out and not having to worry about dead girls or murderers. "I might go to the movies later."

"Have you seen the trailer for that new horror movie? The one with the creepy summer camp?" Brendan made a spooky noise and waved his fingers like a ghost does in cartoons.

"You mean *Camp Blackwater*?" said Lenna, sitting forward. "I've been dying to see it. It looks so good."

"You maybe wanna see it together sometime?" asked Brendan.

Trying to secure a second date before the first one is even over? He must be enjoying himself as much as she was. "Sure," said Lenna.

"I can't tomorrow though. I have practice."

"Football practice on a Sunday?"

"Yeah, we have a big game coming up next week and Coach is working us hard," said Brendan, finishing off his burger. "He wants me to fill in as quarterback since Trey's been skipping school lately. Did you manage to get a hold of him?"

"Huh?" said Lenna, a jolt of panic stabbing her at the mention of his name. "Oh, right." Brendan didn't know yet. Most people didn't. "There's something I need to tell you."

"Oh yeah?" he said, not following and trying to flirt.

Lenna took a deep breath. "Trey killed Alicia. The police are going to arrest him."

Brendan did a double take. "I thought the police said she killed herself?"

Lenna lowered her voice so they wouldn't be overheard. "It looked like it, but there's evidence that proves otherwise." She wiped her hands on her dress under the table, her anxiety rising at the thought of what happened to Alicia that night.

Brendan leaned on his elbows. "What kind of evidence?"

"The kind that will put him away for a very long time."

"Wow," said Brendan, sitting back in his seat. "I can't believe he would do that. How do you know all this?"

She didn't need to tell him, but Brendan had trusted her with his own story. "I'm sort of the one who discovered the evidence."

Brendan looked behind him and turned back. "Is that why you were really looking for him?" he whispered.

"I knew something wasn't right about it all."

"That's crazy." Brendan's eyes moved around the place as her news settled in, his mind visibly doing overtime.

"I know he was your friend," she said.

"Not really. Aside from being on the team, I didn't really hang out with him or anything. Still, talk about messed up." Brendan ran a hand over his jaw.

"I'm meeting with the police after our date. That's why I asked to move it forward."

"You haven't spoken to them yet?"

"The detective working the case isn't on shift until later tonight. Anyway, let's not talk about that scumbag anymore." She had done enough of that already. "We're supposed to be on a date."

"You're right," agreed Brendan. He reached across the table and took her hand again. "Enough about him."

Lenna checked the time on her phone. They still had over an hour before Gibbs was due to arrive at her place, which allowed time for dessert. She scanned the menu. "Wanna share a sundae?"

"Only if it's double chocolate," said Brendan.

"You read my mind." Lenna got up from the booth. "I'll be back in a minute."

Lenna got up from her seat and weaved through the tables to the ladies' room. It had grown dark outside, the fall weather slowly changing to early winter. The bathroom only had two stalls and no one else was there, allowing her to talk freely. She walked into the one nearest the wall and locked the door.

Taking out her cell, she hit her speed dial and called Corey. "Hey, any updates?" she asked as soon as he picked up his phone.

"Uh, aren't you supposed to be on a date?"

"Yeah, but I wanted to check on things. Any sign of Gibbs?" She sat down on the toilet.

"Nope, not yet. Guess she's going to be on time though, because the guy from the station called to make sure someone was home."

"Oh god, did my dad answer?"

"No, they called before he got home. He's here now though."

"Good." Lenna had a lot of explaining to do, and her dad deserved answers for her weird behavior. The police calling or arriving unannounced on their doorstep might have been enough to send him over the edge.

"My mom called, wanting me home for dinner," Corey said. "I'm going to head over. Call me when you're home and let me know what Gibbs said."

"Thanks for waiting for me, Cor. I'll call you as soon as the detective leaves."

"Wait, are you peeing while you're talking to me?" interrupted Corey.

"I'm not going to lie, it's a possibility."

"Gross." Corey laughed. "How's it going?"

"Really good. He's funny, and there haven't been any of those awkward silences."

"Silence? With you there?" teased Corey.

Lenna did some maneuvering while holding her cell to her ear and left the cubicle. "I hate to love you and leave you, but I have a hot guy waiting for me who I need to get back to."

"Wash your hands on the way out," said Corey by way of a goodbye.

Lenna giggled and put her cell away. After washing her hands and fixing her hair, she went back out to her date. Her head ached a little, a dull pounding behind her eyes. Probably from lack of sleep, or the stress of the past week. Either way, she refused to let it interrupt her reprieve of normalcy. She'd be back to reality soon enough as it was.

"I got you another soda," Brendan said as she sat down.

"Thanks." She took a large drink, her throat dry from the burger and fries, and eyed the sundae that had arrived while she was away. She picked up her spoon.

"You can have the cherry," said Brendan, scooting it over to her side of the mound of whipped cream.

"Thanks," she said, scooping it up and eating it.

Brendan laughed. "You've got a bit of cream right there."

"Where?" she asked, putting her hand over her chin in case she missed her mouth.

He leaned over the table and touched the tip of her nose, wiping off a dollop of whipped cream, and put it in his mouth. Lenna licked her lips as she watched him, and they shared a look, a weird gaze that said they wanted to kiss without having to say it.

Lenna leaned in and parted her mouth, meeting him halfway. They locked their lips and kissed, soft little ones at first before they got deeper and more sensual.

They forgot about everyone else in the diner, too wrapped up in themselves and the moment, hidden away in their booth at the back. Brendan moaned as she bit his lip, like he had done the night before. She ran her hand along his jawline and up to the back of his head where she grabbed his hair, pulling him closer.

A wave of dizziness came over her out of nowhere, and not the good kind. She let go of Brendan and put her hand over her forehead, which had started to tingle with a dull pain. It was like she had just come off a carnival ride after staying on for too long.

"Are you okay?" asked Brendan.

"I'm not feeling so good." Sweat trickled down her neck as she tried to latch on to a thought. They seemed to slip from her mind like running water.

Lenna got up from the booth to go to the bathroom and wash her face. The room was hotter than it had been five minutes ago. A few steps forward, and her legs buckled from under her and she fell. Her palms came out just in time to stop her from hitting her head on the tiled floor.

Brendan was by her in a second, lifting her to her feet and wrapping her arm over him for support. "Come on, I'll take you home."

He left some money on the table and helped her out of the diner. She couldn't concentrate long enough to see the other diners watch her as they passed, but she heard them ask if she was okay.

"Thanks, Brendan," she slurred. "I'm so sorry about this. I don't know what happened."

The temperature changed, cooling her as they crossed the parking lot and headed to his car. Her mind cleared a little as the wind hit her face.

"Maybe it was the food," said Brendan.

"Yeah, maybe," she said as he helped her into his red car.

Chapter 41

Lenna rolled down the window to let the fresh air brush past her face as Brendan drove out of the parking lot. She held a palm over her damp forehead, trying to collect her thoughts into one coherent stream.

A sudden inclination to laugh for no reason came over her. Her head bobbed back and forth on her neck, but she had no control over it. Her entire body was running on overdrive and heating up far too fast. She needed water, her mouth parched, even though she'd had two Cokes.

Thank god Brendan was there. She just needed to sleep it off, whatever it was. Residual side effects from entering Limbo the second time, maybe?

Lenna tugged at where her seat belt crossed over her chest and pulled it away from her neck where her pulse beat so hard, she could feel it move under her skin. Her hands searched for the button at her side to free her of the belt.

A firm hand moved hers away from it. "You need to keep that on," said Brendan.

A blurred figure was all she saw of him before her eyes rolled to the back of her head.

No.

She couldn't sleep. Not now. Brendan was here.

Lenna caught a glimpse of her house out the window before it rushed past her.

"Hey, you missed my turn," she told him.

Brendan's eyes didn't leave the road as he sped farther away from the house. "Did I?"

"Yeah, my house is down that way." She began to laugh, a light and childish giggle that sounded wrong. It didn't belong to her, but she couldn't help it. The giddiness hung around her, combining with the cloudiness of her thoughts and the dull pain in her head.

"Oh," replied Brendan.

Something buzzed against her leg and she ran her fingers toward it, into her dress pocket. Her hands wrapped around her cell phone just as it stopped buzzing. Taking it out, she held it in front of her face, squinting at the screen to get a good look, Brendan's missed turn forgotten.

The caller left a voicemail. Lenna held the cell to her ear to listen to it and Gibbs's voice echoed in her ear.

"Lenna, this is Detective Gibbs. I got your message. I have something to look into first and will be over a little later tonight than requested. This had better be good."

Lenna tapped the screen of her cell to call Gibbs back, but it slipped from her loose, clumsy fingers and fell down into the side of her seat, landing behind her on the floor of the back seat.

Turning around as best she could, Lenna blindly searched for the cell. She pulled her hand back and took with it some fabric instead of her phone. From what she could make out, it was a shirt in an ugly forest-green color.

Lenna frowned. She recognized it.

It looked just like the one Trey had on when she and Damien found him at the garden center. Lenna ran her thumb over the embroidered logo at the chest. It wasn't *like* Trey's shirt, it was the exact same.

"Why do you have Trey's work sweater in your car?" she asked.

Brendan glanced at the sweater. "That's not Trey's. It's mine."

"You work at the garden center too?"

"Of course. How else would I have gotten those shifts of Trey's you asked for?"

"Were you working last Friday?"

Lenna had checked Trey's schedule when Brendan first sent it to her. Trey didn't work Fridays. The barmaid at Echo said she saw him with Alicia. She described him perfectly. Tall, an athletic build, and good-looking with brown hair. It had to be him. But something was off. Something wrong.

The cogs in her mind began to churn, slower than normal, but working all the same. A deep sense of panic welled inside her.

"No," Brendan said. "I had Trey cover my shift on Friday."

Glancing outside as they drove farther away from her house, she caught sight of the car's hood.

It was red.

Flashes of what she saw in Limbo came to the forefront of her mind, of how confused and out of it Alicia looked, the liquid ecstasy mixing with the alcohol in her system until it became too much for her body to take.

The pieces to a puzzle Lenna thought she had already solved began to split apart and rearranged into a new picture, one she never saw coming.

Biting down on the inside of her cheek to keep from screaming, she searched for her cell, trying not to make any sudden movements. Her fingers brushed against it and she plucked it from the ground.

Brendan saw her and reached for the phone. Lenna dug her nails into his meaty hands, but he proved too strong for her. He took her cell and tossed it out the open window.

"You won't be needing that."

Chapter 42

Lenna leaned as far away from Brendan as she could. From Alicia's killer.

"It was you."

Brendan stared back at her in silence, his eyes dangerous.

How could she have been so blind? It all made sense, all the hints and clues pointing to him, adding up in her head like an equation so simple, even her awful math skills could work out the answer. She had been wrong, too focused on Alicia's ex to see what was right in front of her all this time.

The drugs Brendan must have slipped into her Coke were still working, but Lenna's high dropped with her realization. His description matched Trey's. Marie saw Brendan in Echo with Alicia that night, not Trey. Brendan is the one they would see on the CCTV footage at the club. He was the one who killed Alicia. The one who caused all of this.

"Let me go," she said, yanking at her belt. She was trapped in the moving car, the same red car she had seen in Limbo, only now she could see it clearly, see *him* for what he really was. A killer. A murderer.

Brendan shook his head. "I can't do that."

"Yes, you can." Lenna's voice quivered. Her whole body was sluggish and limp, but she couldn't afford to fall under the spell of the ecstasy that ran through her veins. She needed to stay awake and alert. She was in a car with a killer.

Her door clicked, locking her in, as Brendan pressed a button on his dash.

"Why did you need to go snooping around?" Brendan spat. "Everyone else was happy to believe Alicia killed herself, even the cops. Why couldn't you?"

Lenna raised her chin and looked him dead in the eye. "Why did you kill her?"

"I didn't mean to," he snapped.

Didn't mean to. Lenna's hand itched to slap him.

"You dumped her in the park and left her there to die alone in the rain," she said through gritted teeth.

Brendan glowered. "How do you know?"

If only she could take him into Limbo so he could see what he had done, so he could watch Alicia die like she had. She'd leave him there with the savage spirits to tear away at him. "How could anyone do that to someone? You left her!"

Brendan slammed his fists against the steering wheel. "I told you, I didn't mean to, all right?"

Lenna shot out a laugh full of venom. "Didn't mean to? She's dead."

"It wasn't my fault," said Brendan, his words like a mantra he spoke to himself over and over, like maybe someday he could convince himself it wasn't a lie.

"You drugged her," said Lenna. "You drugged me."

The ecstasy made her head pound. Alicia had died from the same thing coursing through Lenna's veins, lethally mixing with the alcohol in her system. Was she going to die too? Was Brendan driving around, waiting for it to kill her before dumping her like a piece of trash?

"You tried to run me off the road." He was the one who broke her window with the warning. "You tried to suffocate me and threw me down the stairs."

"I was trying to scare you off. You knew too much. Were asking too many questions," said Brendan, his knuckles bone white as he grasped the wheel. "I knew something was up when you were looking around for Trey. Writing for the school newspaper, my ass. I never bought that crock of shit for a second. I made sure to keep you close."

His words stung, jagged like thorns from a rose. He'd never liked her. He was using her, making sure she didn't get too close to the truth.

"You planted drugs on me last night too. It wasn't Ellie or Detective Gibbs," she slurred. "It was you." He must have done it when she was kissing him. Oh my god, she'd kissed him. Bile rose in her throat.

"What evidence did you find? What did you dig up on me?" Brendan demanded.

Lenna sneered. "Enough. More than enough to tie you to everything."

"Where is it? What is it? If you hand over what you've found, then this can all stop."

Lenna didn't believe him. Not for a second. Not when he'd drugged her just like he'd done Alicia. Not when he'd already tried to kill her. Brendan may want to believe he was just trying to scare her off investigating, but she could have died both time times he'd attacked her.

"Tell me what happened," Lenna ordered instead, keeping him talking.

Brendan regarded her for a moment, free from the mask he wore at the diner. That Brendan was a lie, a disguise used to trick her.

It was like night and day. His easy smile was gone, even that part of him as much a lie as everything else. He wasn't interested in her. He'd planned all this. To find out how much she knew.

A terrified chill slithered down Lenna's spine. She'd told him about the evidence. As good as held up a giant sign that read she was the one who caught him.

"The police know everything," she said.

"No, they don't. You told me you hadn't met with them yet."

"I lied. I've already handed over everything."

"Nice try, Lenna, but you're going to need to do better than that. Now, tell me what you know and where this evidence of yours is and I'll let you go. After you promise to keep quiet."

He didn't know the CCTV would already tie him to the murder. That Corey, Damien, and Marie from Echo all knew about it. At least that was one thing she hadn't idiotically told him.

But even sitting there, drugged and confused, Lenna could see Brendan had no intention to let her go. In his eyes, it didn't matter if she knew the truth because she wouldn't get to tell anyone else. He had her now. He'd tried to kill her twice, and he wouldn't fail this time.

"Tell me what happened first," Lenna demanded. "Then I'll tell you everything."

"I didn't give her much," he said, painfully casual. Like it was normal. Like he'd done it before. "Just enough to loosen her up a bit."

"Loosen her up?" Lenna's voice shook with anger.

"Trey always bragged about how good Alicia was in the sack. When she dumped him, I figured I'd step in, so I asked her out."

Lenna closed her eyes. Alicia never slept with Trey. Why did stupid boys feel the need to lie about girls like that? She tugged her skirt down closer to her knees, acutely aware of how vulnerable she was trapped in his car with him. "And Alicia said yes?" she asked.

"I think it was more to get back at Trey, but I didn't care," he said, like they were talking about next week's football game. "I just wanted to get laid."

"Let me guess, she wasn't up for that, was she?" Lenna fought back her rage. Ecstasy made people impulsive, and she had to play this carefully. Her life depended on it.

"None of this would've happened if she had just played along. I even got her a stupid rose from work and everything."

Lenna chided herself for missing the link. It hadn't occurred to her to wonder how Brendan had gotten a hold of Trey's shifts. She had been too focused on Trey and everyone else on her suspect list. Now that mistake could cost her her life.

"She got a kick out of it when I told her Trey was covering for me that night," he continued, having the nerve to laugh.

Brendan never referred to Alicia by her name, like she had been an object to him and not a human being. Night had well and truly fallen outside, the streets dark with shadow. Bitter wind blew into the open window, but she kept it open. She needed it to stay focused and present despite the drug's effects.

"You took Alicia to Echo," Lenna said, keeping him talking. "Thought you'd get her drunk?"

Brendan scowled. "Even then she wouldn't go back to my car with me."

"So, what," snapped Lenna, "you thought you'd drug her? Rape her?"

Brendan stuck a finger in her face. "I wouldn't rape her. She wanted it."

Lenna pressed her foot down hard against the floor,

slamming phantom brakes. "You're a monster," she said. "You were going to rape her after you drugged her. But things didn't work out for you, did they? You gave her too much ecstasy."

"It wasn't much. I've taken more than that and been fine," he yelled. "I didn't know it would kill her."

Lenna swiped away her falling tears and raised her voice to match his, not backing down. She could yell just as loudly as he could. "Yeah, well, tell that to her dead body. To her friends. To her parents who loved her."

"Shut up!"

Lenna pressed on. She didn't care. Anger won the battle with her self-control. "Why didn't you take her to the hospital?" Alicia could have lived. None of this had to happen.

"So they could arrest my ass?" Brendan shook his head. "I don't think so. I couldn't risk that."

"So you just dumped her in the park?" Lenna saw it all over again in her head, a sight she'd never be able to forget. It would stay with her for as long as she lived, which might not be that long now.

Brendan turned to her and the car jarred to the right with him. "She was OD'ing. Why should both our lives be wasted because of a mistake?"

"It wasn't a mistake. You slipped her those drugs when you knew she'd been drinking. She overdosed because of you. You killed her. You were going to rape her, and you killed her."

"Shut up!" Brendan made to grab her, but Lenna

fought him off. The car almost hit the sidewalk and Brendan had to grapple the wheel to straighten back up.

"You're a monster," she said.

Brendan sneered at her with scathing disdain. "You think you have it all figured out, don't you? You don't know what it's like for me."

Lenna was over listening to him trying to justify killing Alicia. She pulled out the big guns. "Is this the part where you whine about your crappy childhood? Daddy doesn't love me, he beats me up, and all that other bullshit? Well, that doesn't excuse you for what you've done."

Brendan took a sharp turn down another street and the wheels screeched in protest. "I have worked too goddamn hard to get the hell out of Denwood and away from *him*. Away from them all. I am not going to let a stupid girl get in the way of that. I can't. I won't end up like the rest of my brothers and sisters. I won't become a waste of space like my mom and dad. I'm going to make something of myself."

When Lenna first heard this little speech of his, she'd felt sorry for him. She kissed him and wished he could achieve his dreams of escape. His troubled, horrible past and present meant nothing to her now. Not when he had stolen Alicia's future.

"You think you can sweep all of this under a rug and go on with the rest of your life? Get a grip, asshole. Alicia doesn't get to go to college. She doesn't get to move on with her life, so why the hell should you?

You're a monster and you deserve to be locked up for what you did."

"I'm not a monster!" screamed Brendan, the vein in his neck bulging. "I've lived and suffered with a monster my whole life. My life has been nothing but a nightmare."

Lenna reached out and turned the rearview mirror to face him. "Look in the mirror," she said. "You're just like him."

Brendan tore his eyes away from his reflection, unable to look at himself. "I will never be like him."

"No, you won't. You're worse," said Lenna. She leaned forward and spoke with as much authority as she could muster. "Now, stop the car and let me go."

"No," said Brendan with a growl.

"Yes," she said and reached for the keys in the ignition. "Just let me out of the goddamn car!"

"No." Brendan roared and slapped her across the face with the back of his hand. "Not until you tell me what you know."

Lenna's head snapped back and hit the edge of the window frame. The GHB coursing through her numbed her body and she barely registered the pain. Wiping at the edge of her mouth with her finger, she looked down and saw red, the same color as the rose Brendan had given Alicia just hours before he left her to die.

Brendan couldn't let her go. Not if he wanted the future he'd worked so hard to get. A future he had covered up a murder for. He would never let Lenna go. He had already killed once, and he would do it again.

He might not intend to let Lenna go, but that didn't mean she was going to sit around and wait to see what he had planned for her. She refused to make it easy for him. She refused to die at his hands and let him get away with all he had done.

Lenna lunged over Brendan and yanked the wheel, turning it hard to the right with all her weight, sending them off the road and straight into a streetlight.

Chapter 43

Lenna stirred in her seat, her body aching like someone had kicked fifty shades of shit out of her. Her forehead was sticky and slick with blood. At least she'd had her seat belt on when they crashed.

The streetlight bent over them in a crooked hunch, damaged from the impact of Brendan's red car. Alicia's killer lay unconscious, his top half hanging over the steering wheel.

Unraveling herself from her seat belt, she pulled the handle of her door and tried to exit.

"Damn it," she said, hitting the door with her fist when it wouldn't open. The impact of the crash had bent the door out of shape, jamming it shut. Smoke danced from under the hood to the music of the horn blaring. The windshield had cracked, splintering into a spiderweb of glass shards. The airbags hadn't released, but in this case, Lenna couldn't argue. Brendan was out of it, thanks to that little mishap.

Thankfully, her passenger side window was open. Hissing at the pain, she lifted herself up and out of the car. She stumbled to the sidewalk and up to the front door of the nearest house.

The lights were off. She banged on the door, but no one answered.

Looking down the street, the next house lay across the road and past the car. Lenna headed for the house when Brendan cursed from inside.

For a second she stood dead in the middle of the street, unsure of what to do, frozen by fear. Could she make it past the car and to the next house before he got out? Could she risk it? What if no one was there?

Looking around, Lenna gathered her bearings. Her house was five blocks away. She headed for home in the opposite direction of the car. She could do this.

Taking off her heels, she took a deep breath and bolted down the street. Brendan screamed at her as he staggered out of the car.

"Bitch!"

Not once did she turn around to see if he followed her. That would only slow her down and add fire to her blazing panic. Instead, she counted her footsteps, ignoring the throbbing in her bleeding head and the stabs in her bare feet whenever she ran over a stone.

An eternity passed, but she made it to her house. Lenna cut through the yard as fast as she could and bounded through the front door.

"Dad!"

No answer.

"Corey! Detective Gibbs!"

Forcing herself to move again, she went to the kitchen. Her heart sank as she saw the little note on the table. Her dad had been called out to pick up a body.

Gibbs hadn't arrived yet either. Corey had said he was heading home for dinner.

No one was home.

Trying not to freak out, Lenna picked up the house phone and dialed 911. Leaning against the wall, she closed her eyes and waited for the operator to answer at the other end.

The phone died in her hands just before the electricity went out.

Chapter 44

Lenna ran to the kitchen door and turned the lock before sprinting down the hall and doing the same to the front. She looked outside from the window by the door, watching for him.

She could make a run for it, try to reach Corey's house or some other safe haven, but she didn't know where Brendan was. He could be out there waiting for her to do just that, ready to pounce. If he caught her, she was dead. He wouldn't let her get away from him again. He'd kill her quick and be done with it. No way was he letting her out of this alive given what she knew.

Brendan had cut the electricity, leaving her with no way to contact anyone, in complete and utter darkness, and trapped inside her house.

Waiting for her eyes to adjust, she took long, deep breaths, trying to calm her thundering heart. Cautious not to make a sound, she crept back to the kitchen and pulled out the drawer nearest the sink where her dad kept his cooking knives. Careful not to cut herself, she rummaged through until she found the biggest, sharpest one and held it tight.

Moving over to the kitchen door, she got on her tiptoes and looked out the little glass window into the driveway. She had to do something. Waiting inside only made her a sitting duck.

Holding the lock with her free hand and her knife in the other, she counted down from three before trying to make a run for it. Brendan moved toward the door at the other side when she reached two.

Her eyes widened as their gazes met. She took a step away from the door and looked around, trying to think through her panic and drug-induced haze. Brendan rammed the door, his muffled taunts coming through with each bang of his strong, muscled body. The door wouldn't hold long.

Lenna headed for the front door. A crashing boomed behind her as the lock broke and the back door slammed against the wall, succumbing to Brendan's sheer brute force. He was too close for her to make for the front entrance. He'd catch her by the time she got out into the lawn.

Taking a right, she ran through her house, careful not to bump into anything or make a noise. Her bare feet were soundless on the carpeted floor as she crossed the service room and hid behind the partition which covered the elevator doors that lead down to the basement.

Brendan's footsteps resounded over the empty house, louder in the darkness, getting closer and closer.

"I know you're here," he said. From what she could make out, he was by the front door, blocking her exit. She considered leaving through the window, but it would make too much noise.

She had to think. If this were a horror movie, then she should be heading upstairs right now, making things easy on the killer by effectively leading herself to a dead end or a fatal fall from her bedroom window. But Lenna wasn't one of those bimbos from the eighties with their big perms and death wishes. She intended to live.

Brendan called out to her as he moved around the main floor. He overturned furniture, knocking over anything he passed. A vase smashed across the floor. "Come out, come out, wherever you are."

His voice made her shiver. She bit down on her lip, letting her resolve steady her for what she must do. It was a long shot, but it just might work.

Moving slow and as quietly as she could, she walked over and opened the door to the industrial elevator they used to transport the bodies in their caskets from the basement to the first floor. Thank god the elevator was wired to the basement's emergency power grid.

Getting ready to run in and shut the doors, she snuck out behind the partition and ran to the window across the room. She opened it, making as much noise as she could to catch Brendan's attention before running back and into the elevator.

Footsteps ran to the window and she pressed the button to descend to the basement.

The doors opened, and she found herself alone in the dark. There was no light coming in from the street down here. Everything was darker than it had been upstairs, almost black.

Straining her ears for any sign of Brendan's presence, she crossed the basement and slinked up the staircase that led to the kitchen. Lenna stood by the door, knife at the ready. All she had to do was run out of the broken back door before he had time to reach her from the other end of the house. Her car keys would be in the bowl on the counter where she always kept them.

Something crashed against the door from the other side and Lenna stepped back in shock, almost tripping down the stairs. Brendan roared in anger, throwing dishes and smashing chairs against the kitchen walls.

She couldn't get out. Not that way. Not now.

He had blocked her path without knowing it.

Getting back up in the elevator would cause too much attention. He'd be listening for any hint of where she was hiding, her trick with the window a failure. He knew she was still in the house.

With no other option, she backtracked down the stairs. If he caught her down there, that would be it. She would be just another dead body, one of hundreds the walls had seen over the years.

Being stuck in the basement gave her very few options, all of which involved hiding. She hated the idea, but there was nothing else to do. She had to if she wanted to live.

Tiptoeing along, she entered the storage room and closed the door. The generator had kicked in and the refrigerated unit hummed at the back wall. The emergency lights above her were a dull blue and created sinister shadows all around her.

"Lenna?" Alicia stepped out from a dark corner. "What's going on?"

"Trey didn't kill you," she whispered, looking around the room for a good place to hide. "It was Brendan."

Alicia gasped. "Brendan?"

The time for explanations could wait. Right now, she had to hide. "Yes, and he's here. He knows I know it was him, and he's trying to kill me."

"What are you doing? Call the police," said Alicia, moving around her in circles like her life was on the line too.

"I tried, but he cut the power from outside."

Alicia's face dropped, and she looked past Lenna toward the door. "Did you hear that?" she asked.

Lenna strained her ears, standing still on the spot. The kitchen door to the basement just closed. "Shit."

"Hide!" screamed Alicia, in full panic mode.

Brendan's footsteps travelled down to them like a drum counting the beats until he reached her, until she ended up like Alicia.

With no time to reconsider, Lenna pulled out an empty unit drawer on the second row up from the floor and jumped on it. She lay down flat on her back and pulled herself inside until it fully closed.

Her breathing was too loud to her ears in the tight, enclosed space. She couldn't see a thing. All she could do was listen to Brendan's footsteps get closer and closer to her as he reached the bottom of the stairs. She clutched her knife close to her body.

"Lenna, he's here," called Alicia from outside the unit.

She heard Brendan walk into the room, oblivious to the ghost of his first victim standing there with him, forced to watch on but unable to do anything.

"It was you," Alicia said outside to her killer. "I remember now."

Lying down didn't seem to agree with Lenna. Dizziness clogged her mind and her chest heaved, panting as she struggled to breathe. Her head lolled to the side, her grip on the knife loosening as the sound of Brendan's footsteps grew nearer.

"You son of a bitch," cried Alicia, hysterical now as it all came back to her.

The atmosphere in the room grew colder as Alicia wailed and swore at her murderer. Lenna couldn't tell if it was the girl's presence that caused it or if it was her own body going into shock. She didn't want to die the same way as Alicia, alone and scared. She didn't want to die at all.

Metal rattled against metal to Lenna's left and

Brendan swore in disgust as he discovered one of their clients in another drawer.

Lenna's instincts screamed at her to bolt, to jump out and run away, but she couldn't. All she could do was hope he wouldn't try all the drawers.

Another earth-shattering rattle sounded directly above her and she tried not to squeal, covering her mouth with her free hand. He slammed the drawer back into its place with such force, it shook the entire unit, making everything around her vibrate.

"Lenna, watch out!" called Alicia.

Brendan pulled open the drawer, and Lenna screamed as he reached down for her with his bare hands.

Chapter 45

Brendan seized Lenna by the hair and dragged her out of the drawer with one easy pull. Lenna screamed as locks of her hair ripped from their roots and she tried to wriggle free from him.

Remembering her knife, Lenna blindly aimed it in his direction. Brendan yelled but didn't let go of her, his arm trickling warm blood where she grazed his skin.

She went to aim again, but he smashed his fist across her jaw and knocked the knife away with his other hand.

Alicia screamed in the background, clawing at Brendan, but her punches and kicks traveled right through him. Brendan ignored the haunting cold, too focused on Lenna. He put all his weight on her to stop her from moving or getting away from him. Sweat beaded on his forehead.

His hands wrapped around her neck, but Lenna couldn't muster the strength to fight him off.

"What evidence did you find? Tell me or I'll kill you."

Lenna dug her nails into Brendan's flesh and dragged them down as hard as she could until blood ran from the broken skin at the tops of his hands. Still, he continued to press down on her throat, stopping the air from reaching her lungs and crushing her windpipe so hard, she thought her neck might snap.

Her lungs burned, crying out for air that wouldn't come. He pinned her in place and no matter how hard she tried to kick or squirm away to freedom, she couldn't so much as budge.

"You should've stayed out of this, you little bitch. Now I'm going to have to find a way to cover up this whole mess."

Lenna's chest convulsed and black dots danced before her eyes.

She'd never contemplated how she would die. It seemed funny now as she lay there suffocating under Brendan's death grip. You would think the daughter of a mortician would have at least given some thought as to how she might die one day. Lenna never would have guessed this was how she'd go.

Would her spirit pass on and move to the other side as soon as her heart stopped? She didn't want to end up in Limbo for all eternity. Would she be like Alicia with her unfinished business? Either way, she'd soon find out.

At least she'd solved Alicia's murder. Surely the police would catch Brendan when they got hold of the

CCTV footage from the club. If he ran off before then, she and Alicia might both end up spending a whole bunch of time together in that dark, shadowy void.

A tear slid down the side of her face at the thought of leaving her dad. He'd be all alone.

Lenna's mom was on the other side. They could wait for him together.

Her time was almost up. She could feel it coming.

She would die, again. Only this time, there would be no coming back. This death was final.

Lenna closed her eyes and let the moment come.

A sense of release washed over her, almost like she could breathe again, only it was sluggish and painful. Clearly, death wasn't going to be easy. She didn't know why she thought otherwise; it wasn't like life was easy either.

She opened her eyes, unsure of what she would see. Maybe her body as her spirit left it and floated up into the sky, or a bright light she needed to walk toward.

She saw neither of those things.

Instead, Lenna looked up to see Corey standing over Brendan's limp body, a shovel in his hands. Her eyes rolled into the back of her head, and Lenna fell into darkness.

____

Chapter 46

____

Beep. Beep. Beep.

"I think she's awake."

Lenna felt like death. If this was heaven, then it sure as hell had been overhyped. Her entire body ached, especially her throat, like someone had strangled her with their bare hands.

Oh wait. They had.

It all came back, flooding her with a tsunami of memories replaying everything that happened since she'd discovered Alicia dead and awake down in her basement. Limbo. The red rose. Alicia dying. The red car. Echo. The diner. *Him.*

Brendan.

"Her hand just moved."

"Lenna, can you hear me?" said a new voice.

Someone touched her hand. "Len?"

Lenna opened her eyes in narrow slits, squinting at the fluorescent lights above her. Standing by her bed was her best friend, in this life and the afterlife. "Hey, Cor."

Her lips shook when she saw her dad, and it took all she had not to bawl like a baby. "Dad."

Her dad squeezed her hand and a single tear ran down his handsome face. "I'll get the nurse."

Corey brought a glass of tepid water to her lips, careful not to spill any down her hospital gown. Not that it could've possibly made her look any more hideous. She emptied the glass in three deep gulps.

The beeping continued in the background, thanks to the heart monitor attached to her chest. Beside it was an IV stand with a half-full bag of clear liquid, its tube leading to the needle taped into her hand.

Flowers and cards surrounded her, placed wherever they could fit on the windowsill, on top of the set of drawers in the corner, and on her table at the bottom of her bed. A "get well soon" balloon floated in the corner next to a stuffed bear sitting on a chair beside the door.

"What's with all the cards and stuff?" she asked Corey, who stood silent next to her.

He cleared his throat. "They're from everyone wishing you well. Everyone knows what happened."

"Wow, news really does travel fast in Denwood," she said.

Stories would be spreading faster than butter on warm toast, each with their own minor embellishments, or complete rewrites, as the truth trickled down the line, becoming more fiction than fact. Ironically, they'd never believe the full story if they were told. Still, it was nice people had gone out of their way for her.

"How long have I been here?" she asked. Corey's eyes were bloodshot with dark circles under them, his clothes creased and appearing slept in.

"It's Sunday afternoon."

"I've been asleep for a whole day?" She sat up at the news, far too fast, sending her into a dizzy spell. Bad idea.

Corey pushed her back down on her bed with a gentle hand and tucked the covers under her chin. "Well, if you count almost being in a coma as sleeping, then yes."

Her eyes were heavy, but she had been out of it long enough. "What happened after I passed out?"

"They had to pump your stomach when they got you here."

Lenna ran a hand over her stomach, her insides sore. "From the way I feel, I don't doubt it."

A rogue spring dug into her back from the mattress, but she didn't complain. It beat the hell out of lying in a coffin.

Corey wrung his fists around the metal guard at the side of her bed. "That bastard almost killed you."

"He didn't, though." Lenna rested her hand on his arm. "Thanks to you."

"It was nothing."

Lenna slapped his arm lightly. "You saved my life," she stressed. "I'd be dead if it weren't for you."

He scratched the back of his neck. "Maybe I'm not so useless after all."

"See, I told you so." Lenna smiled, and it sent pain across the side of her face where Brendan had smacked her, twice.

Corey took a deep breath. "Maybe next time I'll just take your word for it," he said. "I don't think I can go through all that again."

"You got him good, though. That must have left a mark." It probably took some teeth with it too.

"He deserves a lot more than that," said Corey.

"What happened to him?"

Corey dragged a chair beside her bed and sat down in a tired flop. "The police came and took him away. Detective Gibbs was there. She was really worried about you."

"There's a shocker," said Lenna.

Corey leaned his arms on her bed. "I don't think she's that bad. Just really intense about her job."

Lenna sighed. "I guess our job is done."

They did it. For real this time. Brendan had been arrested; everyone would know the truth behind Alicia's death. Alicia could move on, and so could they. Her unfinished business was over. They were all safe.

"Yeah, I guess," said Corey. "Damien was here earlier, by the way."

That caught her off guard. "He was?"

Corey nodded. "Yeah, he stayed overnight. Refused to leave. Your dad sent him home to get some sleep when it looked like you wouldn't be waking up anytime soon."

Lenna didn't think she'd ever wake up again—alive, at least. She had a lot to be thankful for.

"I think he might have a thing for you." Corey wiggled his eyebrows.

Lenna laughed and pain erupted in her throat. That drip she was wired to better have some morphine or something in it.

"Considering my last choice proved to be a lying, murdering scumbag who almost choked me to death, I think I'll lay off the dating scene for a while."

"That's probably a good idea."

"He is kinda cute though," she mused, thinking of Damien's walls of drawings and stacks of books by his bed, the way his face took on a whole new light when he let out a laugh or an unguarded smile.

"Obviously," said Corey. "Besides, I hear the whole brooding, tortured soul thing is in again."

"Thank you," said Lenna.

Corey frowned at her tangent. "Huh?"

"For saving me. Thank you."

Corey got up from his seat, careful not to put any of his weight on her, and hugged her close. "You had me so worried."

Lenna closed her eyes and breathed in his familiar scent. "I was worried myself."

The door to her room opened, and her dad walked in with a burly-looking nurse.

"Okay, kiddo, time to go," the nurse said to Corey, walking over to the monitors.

"But she just woke up," protested Corey.

"She needs her rest." The nurse gave him a stern look that said she wasn't to be messed with. Lenna liked her instantly.

Corey leaned in and kissed Lenna's forehead. "I'll be back first thing tomorrow," he promised before getting up and leaving.

Her dad walked to the side of her bed and sat down at the edge, looking her over with worried eyes. "I'll drop him off and be right back. Do you want me to pick you up anything?"

"I'm good," she said, trying to act as perky as she could for him.

He cupped her face, fighting his emotions. "You remind me so much of your mother."

He kissed her on the head too, and moved toward the door.

"Hey, Dad," she called. "How did Alicia's funeral go?"

"It's been postponed until tomorrow. Joe needed to re-examine her, given what we know now."

"I want to go."

"Honey, you need to stay here until you're back in good health."

"Please," she interrupted. "It's important." She had to see this through to the end. Alicia deserved that much.

Her dad caved. "I'll speak to your doctor and see what he says."

"Thanks," she said.

"Get some rest, honey. I love you."

"I love you too."

Lenna closed her eyes and fell into a deep, dreamless sleep, feeling peaceful and safe for the first time in over a week.

Chapter 47

Lenna woke with a start to find a face hovering over her.

She screamed and tried to get up from her bed, her heart frantic, but the person pushed her back down with an easy hand.

"Hey, hey," said Detective Gibbs in a hushed tone. "It's okay."

Lenna blinked at her as the beeping monitor slowed down. "What are you doing here, scaring me like that?" She thought it was Brendan.

"I heard you had woken up."

"You here to arrest me for something else I didn't do?" she snapped.

Gibbs didn't reply. Lenna pushed herself up in her bed, pushing the little button at the side of the frame to raise her into a sitting position.

"I'm guessing by now you got my drug test back," Lenna continued, still angry with the detective about that. "It was him, you know. Brendan. He was your anonymous caller. He slipped the drugs on me before I left the party. You were talking to the killer on the phone while I was out trying to catch him."

Lenna grimaced. She'd kissed Brendan that night, enjoyed it too. Just the thought of it made her want to brush her teeth a hundred times. Talk about bad taste in boys.

The detective let out a heavy sigh and sat down in the chair next to the bed. Lenna had told her dad to go home and come back in the morning. He was exhausted, and he had Alicia's funeral to prepare for after all. Her tough-nut nurse helped usher him out when he'd tried to stay.

"I guess I deserve that," said Gibbs. "And no, I'm not here to arrest you." She leaned her elbows on her knees, her face tired.

"Then why are you here? It's the middle of the night."

Gibbs looked around the room, her body language uncomfortable. "I wanted to check that you were okay," she said, "and to thank you."

Lenna was taken aback, speechless for once in her life. Of all the things the detective could have said, "thank you" was the last thing Lenna would have ever guessed.

"If it weren't for you, that boy would still be out there," said Gibbs. "Who knows what he might have done next."

"I was lucky my friend was there to save me," she said, picturing Corey with the shovel in his hand.

Gibbs brought her fist to her mouth. "If I had done better, worked the case more, then it all could have been avoided." She turned back to Lenna. "For that, I'm sorry."

Lenna's anger deflated. Despite being a thorn in her side the last week, the woman was only doing her job. "It's not your fault," she said. "Most cops wouldn't have given it a second thought after the cause of death came out. You did."

"Regardless, I'm sorry. I could've handled things better, which includes how I dealt with you." Gibbs looked away. "I'm not the best when it comes to people."

"No shit," said Lenna with a smirk. People may not be her strong suit, but she could see now that the detective meant well. "What will happen with Brendan?"

"I spoke to the judge earlier," she said, back to business. "Brendan turns eighteen in a couple of months and will be tried as an adult. He's going away for a long time."

"Good," said Lenna. Karma was a bitch.

"Anyway," said Gibbs, getting to her feet. "I'll let you get back to sleep."

"Don't you need me to give a statement?" asked Lenna.

"Corey filled me in on most of it while you were sleeping." Gibbs hovered at the door, her hand on the handle. "I can get your side of the story from you later.

Say goodbye to your friend first, and stop by the station when you're ready."

Lenna sat at the kitchen table with her dad, a mug of coffee held in each of their hands, her bag full of stuff from the hospital sitting unpacked at the bottom of the stairs.

The doctor cleared her to go to the funeral and said she could stay home if she stopped by every day that week so they could check on her. She changed into her old faithful dress, all ready to go. There was something she had been itching to know that couldn't wait until after Alicia's funeral.

"Dad, how did I die?"

His head shot up from his morning paper. "How did you die?" he repeated, stalling.

"Why didn't you tell me?"

He tugged at his shirt collar and took a deep drink from his mug. "Your mother and I never really spoke about it once it was over. As much as I'm around death, it's another thing entirely when it happens to your own child."

Lenna wrapped her hands around her mug, letting the warmth absorb into her palms. "What happened?"

Her dad started talking, a far-off look in his eyes, as if he were reliving the moment. A moment that, for her, changed everything.

"When you were born, you came out silent, no

crying at all. At first I didn't understand what was happening, I was just so overwhelmed at how beautiful you were, and that you had arrived, but the doctors pushed me out of the way as they tried to get you breathing again."

He focused on his mug. "You came back around pretty quick, but you'd died. For a moment, the happiest day of my life turned into my worst nightmare. Your mother and I were so scared we had lost you. It wasn't something we liked to think about, never mind tell you about it."

"I understand," she said, after a moment, unable to stay mad. Besides, he had taken her escapades over the last week pretty well, and she didn't want to push her luck.

"Len," said her dad, meeting her eyes. "I'm so sorry for not listening to you."

She reached out and gave his hand a little squeeze.

"Your mother would be very proud of you," he said. "I know I am."

They'd be okay. Always had been, and always would be.

It was all over, but Lenna still had one final job to do.

Lenna peered down at the dead body and examined her work.

"How do I look?" asked Alicia, staring over Lenna to see her own body.

She put the lid on the tube of lip gloss and placed it back in her makeup bag. "You look ready."

The casket would be closed during the funeral, so no one would get to see Lenna's handiwork, but she did it for Alicia. After everything she'd been through, she deserved a little pampering before her final send-off. She washed and curled her hair into long, gorgeous waves and dressed her in the white gown her mom had given them.

"I guess this is it," said Alicia, jittery with nerves.

"It is," said Lenna, taking her hands. Her touch no longer caused Lenna any pain or horrible bruising like before, the cold gone. It was like the weight of having her unfinished business resolved took it all away from her.

"You know," said Alicia, smiling, "I never thought I would say this, but I wish we had still been friends before all of this happened."

"Me too." It was funny how much could change in a week.

"Thank you," said Alicia, embracing Lenna. "For everything."

"You're welcome," said Lenna, the moment bittersweet. She broke their hug and led her friend toward the top of the casket. "It's time."

Alicia took a deep breath she didn't need.

"This is scary," Alicia said, turning back to Lenna.

Lenna rubbed her arm. "You can do this."

Alicia closed her eyes and when she opened them again, she was the calm and confident girl she'd always been. "Okay. Bye, Lenna. Maybe I'll see you again one day."

"I hope so," she replied. "Goodbye, Alicia."

Alicia hovered high into the air, above where her body lay in its casket. A glow cast from her ghost, bright and beautiful, as she descended to meet her physical self. She merged into her corporeal form and they became one. A final, content sigh left her lips and she was gone, ready for her next adventure.

Chapter 48

The rain took a day off, giving Alicia a beautiful fall morning in the cemetery.

The service had been nice and personal, for a Catholic funeral. Her friends and family spoke of her and how full of life she had been. It was always a sad affair when someone had been taken so young, even more so given the circumstances of her death.

Kayla and Trey were there, but Lenna stayed away and gave them space to say their goodbyes. She hoped Trey forgave her for believing he was the killer. Ellie and Zara were there, too, among a large crowd of students from Denwood High.

Lenna stood off from the rest of the mourners, watching from the top of the hill in the town cemetery as Alicia's casket was laid into the ground. Leaves danced in the wind in shades of amber and gold, the air cool and crisp as the sun shone down on them all.

She held Corey's hand. Her hero.

His breath made little clouds in front of him. Winter would be here before they knew it.

"I don't know about you," said Lenna, leaning into him, "but after this, I could sure go for a horror movie marathon with, like, a gallon of ice cream."

Corey leaned his head back and moaned. "That sounds like heaven."

Someone cleared their throat behind them, and they turned to find Mr. Santos standing alone, his face hollow and grief stricken.

Corey gave her a look, checking to see if she would be all right alone with him. Lenna gave him a nod, and headed down towards the rest of the mourners.

Mr. Santos had shaved since she last saw him, and his eyes were no longer bloodshot from too much beer. She didn't really know what to say to him, thinking of their last meeting and how it had gone, but he spoke first.

"I don't know how you did it," he said, his voice tight, "but thank you for catching the monster who took my baby away from us." He stood with his back straight, trying to stay together.

Something changed inside Lenna with his words. It had been stirring since she watched Alicia move on, the feeling that she was doing what she was supposed to do.

"I'm sorry for your loss, Mr. Santos," she said. "Alicia was a great girl." She let the poor man go back to his wife and headed over to her hearse.

Damien watched her from an old willow tree near the gates.

She walked up to him, putting her hands into her jacket pockets, out of the cold. "Hey."

"Hi," said Damien. He was dressed in a shirt and tie under his leather jacket, his hair slicked back.

"You're not following me around again, are you?"

He gave her a rare, unguarded smile. It suited him. "You must be feeling better if you're making jokes."

Rows of headstones surrounded them, engraved with the names of the dead and their dates of death. "Can't complain." She was alive.

"You did good," he said, standing by her side as the cemetery began to empty of mourners.

"I couldn't have done it without you."

"I'm sure you would've pulled something off."

"Will you and Irene move back home now that this is all over?" she asked, trying not to sound too interested.

Damien stared off at the view of Denwood before them. "I don't know. I kinda like it here."

"Wow," she said. "Your old town must have sucked."

"It'll only get tougher from here," said Damien.

"I know." Watching Alicia move on earlier had changed everything for her. Irene had warned her that it would, that once she started helping the dead, she wouldn't be able to stop. But she couldn't walk away now, not if there were others who needed her help. Not when she could make a difference.

"I've got your back," Damien said, like it was nothing.

"Thanks," Lenna said, relieved she wasn't in this alone. She had Corey, her dad, and now Damien too. "I have a feeling I'm going to need as much help as I can get."

Lenna didn't ask for her abilities, nor would she have taken them if offered to her. Yet, she could do something not many others could. She could be the voice for those who could no longer speak. She could bring justice to those who would otherwise get away with their crimes. She could make sure that no one who crossed her path would suffer the nightmare of an eternity in Limbo.

There was power in that, and Lenna intended to use it.

Thank you for reading DEAD AWAKE! If you enjoyed the book, I would greatly appreciate it if you could consider adding a review on your online bookstore of choice.

Reviews make a huge difference to the success or failure of a book, especially for newer writers like myself. The more reviews a book has, the more people are likely to take a shot on picking it up. The review need only be a line or two, and it really would make the world of difference for me if you could spare the three minutes it takes to leave one.

With all my thanks,

Jack McSporran

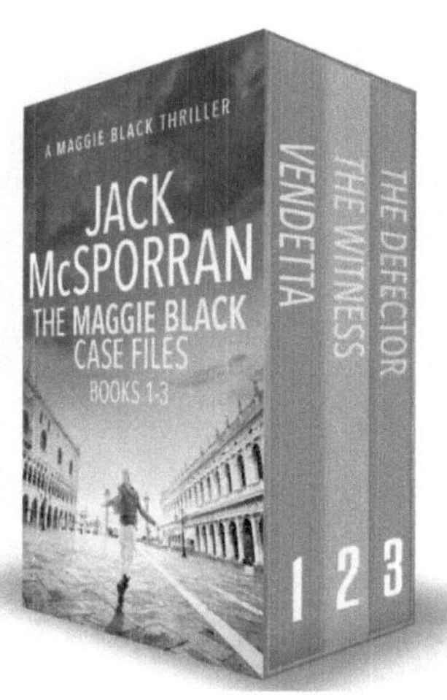

Have *you* met secret agent Maggie Black?

She's deadly, beautiful, and the first person the British government calls when things go wrong. Now, for the first time, read all three books in this collated collection and discover the bestselling thriller series that's exploded onto the scene. If you like adrenaline fuelled action, shocking twists, and heart-pounding thrill rides across the globe, these are the books for you!

Visit http://books2read.com/u/3JoMPA to delve into the Maggie Black thriller series today!

www.ingramcontent.com/pod-product-compliance
Lightning Source LLC
Chambersburg PA
CBHW061046190726
48286CB00006B/1633